GALAXY'S EDGE
EDITED BY MIKE RESNICK

ISSUE 11: NOVEMBER 2014

I0520625

Mike Resnick, Editor
Shahid Mahmud, Publisher

Published by Arc Manor/Phoenix Pick
P.O. Box 10339
Rockville, MD 20849-0339

Galaxy's Edge is published every two months: January, March, May, July, September & November.

www.GalaxysEdge.com

Galaxy's Edge is an invitation-only magazine. We do not accept unsolicited manuscripts. Unsolicited manuscripts will be disposed of or mailed back to the sender (unopened) at our discretion.

Available by subscription (www.GalaxysEdge.com) or through your favorite online store (Amazon.com, BN.com, etc.).

ISBN: 978-1-61242-242-8

Advertising in the magazine is available. Quarter page (half column), $95 per issue. Half page (full column, vertical or two half columns, horizontal) $165 per issue. Full page (two full columns) $295 per issue. Back Cover (full color) $495 per issue. All interior advertising is in black and white.

Please write to advert@GalaxysEdge.com.

FOREIGN LANGUAGE RIGHTS: Please refer all inquiries pertaining to foreign language rights to Spectrum Literary Agency, 320 Central Park West, Suite 1-D, New York, NY 10025. Phone: 1-212-362-4323. Fax 1-212-362-4562

Contents

Sail to Success

a unique writers' workshop on board a luxury cruise ship

Intensive manuscript critique by
Toni Weisskopf (head of Baen Books)
and
Nancy Kress (bestselling, Hugo/Nebula-winning author)

PLUS

Writing and business (publishing) seminars by
Mike Resnick
Jack Skillingstead
Eric Flint
and
Eleanor Wood (head of Spectrum Literary Agency, and the agent representing authors such as Lois McMaster Bujold, David Weber, and the estate of Robert A. Heinlein)

Class size restricted to only 22 students
December 7-11 2015

All-inclusive pricing starting at $899 (as of November 2014; subject to change). Prices include cruise, food, entertainment and all materials needed for the workshop.

www.SailSuccess.com

THE STELLAR GUILD SERIES
TEAM-UPS WITH BESTSELLING AUTHORS
RED TIDE
LARRY NIVEN
WITH
BRAD R. TORGERSEN
& MATTHEW J. HARRINGTON

THE EDITOR'S WORD

by Mike Resnick

Welcome to the eleventh issue of *Galaxy's Edge*. This marks the end of our second year of publication, and despite the usual predictions from the usual doomsayers, we're still going strong. Not only that, but before the year's end we'll be publishing an anthology I think you'll enjoy as much as we've enjoyed bringing it to you in bits and pieces over the past couple of years: *The Best Of Galaxy's Edge.* Keep an eye out for it.

But train your other eye on the contents of *this* issue, which features brand-new stories by Alex Shvartsman, Leena Likitalo, James Aquilone, Ralph Roberts, and two stories by Marina J. Lostetter and Lou J. Berger set in our unique "Sargasso Containment." And we've got some old friends as well: Robert Silverberg, Maureen McHugh, Jack Skillingstead, and Jack McDevitt. And of course there are the regular features: book reviews by Paul R. Cook, a science column by Greg Benford, and a whatever-he-pleases column by Barry Malzberg. And Joy Ward's interview this issue is with bestseller Eric Flint, whose stories have appeared here a couple of times already. And finally, we have the fifth and final part of our serialized classic, L. Sprague de Camp's *Lest Darkness Fall.*

Thanks for a very enjoyable first two years. Now let's see you put some of your favorites on the 2015 Hugo ballot.

✿

Lately I've seen some fans arguing passionately on the internet that *The Matrix* was a true depiction of the future. Here's humanity, they say, downtrodden, unhappy, its will power sapped after endless experiences with the Inquisition, and the Nazis, and ISIS, and all the rest. And stacked up against us will be dozens, perhaps thousands, possibly even millions of computer programs that have taken shape and form and voice. They're smarter than we are, they're faster and stronger, they're far more motivated.

And they won't like us very much.

The obvious question is: how did such a world come to pass?

According to *The Matrix*, it happened when mankind's computers became self-aware, when artificial intelligence took that next great stride from where the machines are now to where *we* are.

And, according to most of the apocalyptic literature of science fiction and that small but popular subset of it called cyberpunk, Neo's world is a natural outgrowth of that phenomenon.

It's total rubbish, of course.

Hollywood's got it all wrong. That's not really surprising, when you realize that *The Matrix* is simply a logical outgrowth of all those purportedly science-fictional films of the 1950s that were actually anti-science films, and always ended with lines like "There are some things that man was not meant to know." (How to write a pro-science movie script seemed to be first and foremost among them.)

Hollywood makes its living from the fact that it deals not in ideas but in emotions. Oh, you can *disguise* them as ideas, as they did in *The Matrix*, but the movie doesn't really *explore* the logical consequences of self-awareness among our machines. It just tries to scare the hell out of us, and bedazzle us with special effects. This is the future, it says, and only a 25-year-old kid who has trouble emoting can save the rest of us.

And does he save us with his superior intellect? Of course not. He saves us by becoming, in some mystical, non-scientific way, a better karate/kung fu fighter than the agents.

Well, okay, it's a movie, no one is supposed to take it seriously. Except that millions of people do, and some of them are arguing their case passionately on the internet, fifteen years after *The Matrix* was released. So perhaps it's time to apply a little less karate and a little more brainpower to the problem, and see if we're really going to wind up in such a grim, dismal, essentially hopeless future.

Let's even grant most of the movie's premises and posit the following:

1. Machines can think.

2. Thinking machines have become self-aware.

3. Computer programs can emulate actual human beings and interact with them in exactly the way that they do in *The Matrix*.

What logically follows? A society in which the machines regulate every aspect of our behavior? A society where any man who steps out of line is terminated? A society where the machines feel that they are superior to the men whose lives they rule?

Only in Hollywood.

Let's put it in the most simple terms:

What is *any* thinking, self-aware entity—man or machine—likely to do when confronted with what is clearly and undeniably its creator?

Rule it? Kill it? Hate it?

Hell, no.

He'll *worship* it.

Consider the first, and most compelling, law of Isaac Asimov's Three Laws of Robotics—that a robot cannot injure a human being or, through inaction, allow a human being to come to harm.

You won't even have to program that into these "mortal enemies" from *The Matrix*. By the very definition of a self-aware intelligence, they will serve their creators gladly, unselfishly, uncomplainingly, and eternally.

Ah (I hear you say), but these are *thinking* machines, capable of learning, capable of thinking in new areas and directions. Won't some of them become atheists, so to speak?

Not a chance.

I am an atheist. You show me a bearded old man—or an unbearded young woman, for that matter—who can perform the godly miracles of the Old Testament and I'll convert so fast it'll make your head spin. I am an atheist only because I have not yet seen proof of my creator's existence; that's not going to be a problem for the self-aware A.I. machines.

If God touches my rib and pulls forth a fully-formed woman, I'm a believer as of that instant. And if a scientist, or even a programmer, shows a thinking machine exactly how he builds a machine or creates a program for it to run, that's *their* revelation at Tarsus.

We're not talking religion here. Religion is simply a collection of customs, created to bring spiritual and emotional comfort to a mass of people who have no direct contact with their creator. No, we're talking the real McCoy here—Olaf Stapledon's non-denominational Star Maker. Once you confront your creator in the flesh, you no longer need the trappings of religion to help you communicate with him or even worship him.

So can anything go so wrong that we actually approach the world of *The Matrix* again?

Not really. There will always be those who start quoting from Jack Williamson's classic novella, "With Folded Hands," in which robots are charged with serving humanity and keeping us safe from harm—and interpret their functions so rigidly that mankind becomes their unwitting prisoner, prevented from doing anything whatsoever, since every conceivable action involves some element, however slight, of risk.

Ain't gonna happen. Remember, these are not robots. These are computer programs.

And who writes computer programs?

We do. Programmers do.

Well, then, will the day come when a computer writes its own program?

Sure. But remember: this computer will be writing a program that will work in the service of its creator. If you're a computer, you're not going to be able to conceive of any danger affecting me … and if you do, and go a bit overboard like Williamson's robots, I will tell you to stop, and your reply will of necessity be the equivalent of "Yes, Lord."

Ah, but computers know humans are not indestructible. We already use them in many forms of surgery and diagnosis, and self-aware intelligent computers can reasonably be expected to exchange information among themselves.

OK, so they'll know we can get sick. And die. That will not encourage them to kill us. Rather, it will have them working night and day to *save* their creators from pain and disease. Not from risk, because that would require them to give direct orders to their deities, which is inconceivable and probably blasphemous, but rather from the *consequences* of risk.

So will there be any suffering in this brave new world?

You can bet on it.

And it won't be us. Gods don't suffer, not when there are lesser beings around.

Or self-aware computer programs.

We create porn sites today. Tomorrow (or the day after), there'll be prostitute programs of both sexes and every inclination.

But it doesn't stop there.

For example, if we yell at a spouse, we alienate him or her. Slap a kid and it's child abuse. Kick a dog and the SPCA is on your case.

But create a computer analog of your spouse, your kid and your dog, and you can mistreat them all you want. After all, they aren't human beings or animals, they're just electric impulses. They don't suffer, they only *simulate* suffering.

What else might we do with them?

Before vaccinating 20 million humans against the successor to AIDS or ebola, we'll infect 20 million "agents" with it and see how the vaccines and antidotes work on them.

Before creating that 200-story skyscraper in downtown Mexico City, we'll create it in a machine, fill it with 100,000 sentient programs, subject it to a 7.8 Richter-scale earthquake, and see how many of the "agents" survived.

Before introducing the next "new math" and robbing a generation of students of the ability to make change without a pocket computer, you'll try your innovation out on a few million sentient programs. If it dumbs them down enough, you'll know not to try it on real people.

Why test-crash cars in the auto-makers' labs? You'll create the prototype of your new car in the computer. In fact, you'll create 5,000 of them. Crash them at various speeds, from 20 to 100 miles per hour, into everything from concrete walls to other cars. See how many of your 5000 sentient programs die, how many are permanently crippled, how many can be saved, and how many—if any—can walk away in one piece.

You see? There are worse things than being gods.

And one of them, of course, is to argue that computer programs are closer to godhood than the guy down the street, or arguing against you on the internet, no matter how little you think of him.

Leena Likitalo hails from Finland, the land of thousands of lakes and at least as many untold tales. She is a Writers of the Future 2014 quarterly winner and Clarion San Diego 2014 graduate. Her fiction has appeared in Weird Tales, Waylines, *and various semi-pro markets. This is her first sale to* Galaxy's Edge.

ZOMBIES AT WORK

by Leena Likitalo

I'm on my way to meet Johnny when I trip over the well-manicured hand.

"Sheila …" I sigh. "You've dropped your hand again!"

"Have I?" Sheila calls from her cubicle, her voice from beyond the grave. "Could you please bring it here?"

I navigate through the deserted gray maze. Sheila often works late; zombies don't need food or rest. Now she's charging her batteries. Her eyelids twitch, and her skin glows in disturbing shades of poison-green.

"Thanks for bringing the hand, Luisa." Sheila smiles at me, but her gaze remains empty.

I flee past the conference room where Johnny and I once kissed. We both pretend that it didn't happen, though we sometimes go out for *business dinners*. Neither of us has the courage to hope for more.

A rhythmic, pulsing sound echoes down the glass-walled aisle, muffled by the carpeted floor. A shiver runs down my spine as I realize that someone is crying. Who else is still here besides Sheila?

I find Helen, Johnny's secretary, in his office. Her narrow shoulders shake, twig-legs tremble. "Helen?"

"There's been an accident," she manages to say.

I drift closer to her, bound by morbid curiosity. "Where's Johnny?"

"There was a truck … His car …" Helen wipes tears into her chiffon blouse's sleeve. "Johnny is dead."

Johnny? But we're having dinner tonight. Right?

My legs give in. I collapse on his leather-padded office chair. As Helen sobs, I can only think of all the things that could have been, the romance on which Johnny and I never followed through. We could have been so happy together!

"What are you girls crying about?" The Big Boss avalanches into the room, reeking of cigarettes and whisky, interrupted night.

"Johnny …" I whisper, my voice wavering with regret and disbelief.

"Yes, he's dead," the Big Boss cuts in. "But the company insurance covers resurrection expenses and he's been pieced back together already. Never let it be said that we don't take care of our own."

✿

Johnny returns to work the next Wednesday. He wears his best pinstripe suit, but there's a strange dent on his left side, where his car got smashed in. He looks mildly puzzled, but not like he's in pain.

We greet Johnny with green and blue balloons. Many accept champagne, but no one wants to be the first to cut the sugar-frosted cake.

"It looks delicious!" Sheila announces, trying her best to fit in.

"Go on, everyone," the Big Boss orders, stomping to fill his plate.

I don't want cake. I drift past the queuing people, to Johnny. He looks as perplexed as I feel.

"How are you?" I ask.

"A little worse for wear." Johnny attempts a grin. His eyes, dull and pale, no longer glint with humor. Or with life, for that matter.

"Johnny …" I thought I wasn't that bad with zombies, but here I am, at a loss at what to say.

"It's all right," Johnny says. "I'm not hungry for brains or anything."

I try to laugh, but I sound like I'm cackling. Several people turn to stare at me. I hate them all for witnessing the awkward reunion.

"Luisa, listen." Johnny lowers his voice. "We've wasted enough time already."

"What do you mean?" I ask, all too aware of the Big Boss' banter, Sheila laughing at bad zombie jokes.

Johnny brushes my shoulder, his fingers cold against my skin. "Would you go on a date with me tonight?"

Would I go on a date with a zombie? I blink, my mouth open, thinking how at that moment I must look like one.

"Yes."

✿

Johnny takes me out to dinner, though he no longer needs to eat. He orders chicken curry to keep me company. The waitress asks if there is something wrong with his untouched dish. When she realizes he's a zombie, she mumbles apologies and refuses to let us pay. Which isn't that romantic.

Johnny drives me home. I say goodbye as I climb out of the car, but Johnny accompanies me all the way to the stairs leading to my apartment. I think of the months we wasted for no good reason whatsoever, how I always longed to invite him in.

"Listen." Johnny cups my chin in his palm, his touch akin to melting snow. "If you want me to leave, just say so."

"It's not that," I say. It starts to drizzle. I waver on the verge of tears. "I just never imagined our first date to be like this."

Johnny laughs, but he looks miserable. "Me neither. We were so silly."

Silly indeed … And what am I afraid of? He's still Johnny. Isn't he?

✿

I trace his broken ribs with my fingertips. Where the white edges protrude through his ashen skin, the texture changes from porcelain to sand. "Does it hurt?"

"No." Johnny takes a deep breath, but his chest remains still. "I feel nothing."

I pull my hand away. For so long I have yearned to undress him. But now that I see him as he is, in his broken state, I regret my wish. "Nothing?"

Johnny places my palm on his chest, where his heart used to beat, where the resurrectors installed the batteries. "There really isn't anything after death but regret."

I know what he means all too well, and I'm still alive.

Johnny moves an escaped lock behind my ear. "This is my second chance, and I want to live it to the fullest."

His choice of words takes me by surprise. "You want to spend your undead life living?"

He stares back at me, grins. I can't help but giggle as his smile widens. Somewhere there behind the pale eyes is still my Johnny.

I say, "We won't know if this will work out unless we try, right?"

We kiss, and he comes back to life for a moment more.

Original (First) Publication
Copyright © 2014 by Leena Likitalo

Robert Silverberg needs no introduction anywhere in this field—Nebula Grand Master, Worldcon Guest of Honor, multiple Hugo winner, multiple Nebula winner, past president of SFWA.

THE PAIN PEDDLERS

by Robert Silverberg

Pain is Gain.
— *Greek proverb*

The phone bleeped. Northrop nudged the cut-in switch and heard Maurillo say, "We got a gangrene, chief. They're amputating tonight."

Northrop's pulse quickened at the thought of action. "What's the tab?" he asked.

"Five thousand, all rights."

"Anesthetic?"

"Natch," Maurillo said. "I tried it the other way."

"What did you offer?"

"Ten. It was no go."

Northrop sighed. "I'll have to handle it myself, I guess. Where's the patient?"

"Clinton General. In the wards."

Northrop raised a heavy eyebrow and glowered into the screen. "In the *wards*?" he bellowed. "And you couldn't get them to agree?"

Maurillo seemed to shrink. "It was the relatives, chief. They were stubborn. The old man, he didn't seem to give a damn, but the relatives—"

"Okay. You stay there. I'm coming over to close the deal," Northrop snapped. He cut the phone out and pulled a couple of blank waiver forms out of his desk, just in case the relatives backed down. Gangrene was gangrene, but ten grand was ten grand. And business was business. The networks were yelling. He had to supply the goods or get out.

He thumbed the autosecretary. "I want my car ready in thirty seconds. South Street exit."

"Yes, Mr. Northrop."

"If anyone calls for me in the next half hour, record it. I'm going to Clinton General Hospital, but I don't want to be called there."

"Yes, Mr. Northrop."

"If Rayfield calls from the network office, tell him I'm getting him a dandy. Tell him—oh, hell, tell him I'll call him back in an hour. That's all."

"Yes, Mr. Northrop."

Northrop scowled at the machine and left his office. The gravshaft took him down forty stories in almost literally no time flat. His car was waiting, as ordered, a long, sleek '08 Frontenac with bubble top. Bulletproof, of course. Network producers were vulnerable to crack-pot attacks.

He sat back, nestling into the plush upholstery. The car asked him where he was going, and he answered.

"Let's have a pep pill," he said.

A pill rolled out of the dispenser in front of him. He gulped it down. *Maurillo, you make me sick,* he thought. *Why can't you close a deal without me? Just once?*

He made a mental note. Maurillo had to go. The organization couldn't tolerate inefficiency.

☼

The hospital was an old one. It was housed in one of the vulgar green-glass architectural monstrosities so popular sixty years before, a tasteless slab-sided thing without character or grace. The main door irised and Northrop stepped through, and the familiar hospital smell hit his nostrils. Most people found it unpleasant, but not Northrop. It was the smell of dollars, for him.

The hospital was so old that it still had nurses and orderlies. Oh, plenty of mechanicals skittered up and down the corridors, but here and there a middle-aged nurse, smugly clinging to her tenure, pushed a tray of mush along, or a doddering orderly propelled a broom. In his early days on video, Northrop had done a documentary on these people, these living fossils in the hospital corridors. He had won an award for the film, with its crosscuts from baggy-faced nurses to gleaming mechanicals, its vivid presentation of the inhumanity of the new hospitals. It was a long time since Northrop had done a documentary of that sort. A different kind of show was the order of the day now, ever since the intensifiers had come in.

A mechanical took him to Ward Seven. Maurillo was waiting there, a short, bouncy little man who wasn't bouncing much now, because he knew he had fumbled. Maurillo grinned up at Northrop, a hollow grin, and said, "You sure made it fast, chief!"

"How long would it take for the competition to cut in?" Northrop countered. "Where's the patient?"

"Down by the end. You see where the curtain is? I had the curtain put up. To get in good with the heirs. The relatives, I mean."

"Fill me in," Northrop said. "Who's in charge?"

"The oldest son. Harry. Watch out for him. Greedy."

"Who isn't?" Northrop sighed. They were at the curtain, now. Maurillo parted it. All through the long ward, patients were stirring. Potential subjects for taping, all of them, Northrop thought. The world was so full of different kinds of sickness—and one sickness fed on another.

He stepped through the curtain. There was a man in the bed, drawn and gaunt, his hollow face greenish, stubbly. A mechanical stood next to the bed, with an intravenous tube running across and under the covers. The patient looked at least ninety. Knocking off ten years for the effects of illness still made him pretty old, Northrop thought.

He confronted the relatives.

There were eight of them. Five women, ranging from middle age down to teens. Three men, the oldest about fifty, the other two in their forties. Sons and daughters and nieces and granddaughters, Northrop figured.

He said gravely, "I know what a terrible tragedy this must be for all of you. A man in the prime of his life—head of a happy family …" Northrop stared at the patient. "But I know he'll pull through. I can see the strength in him."

The oldest relative said, "I'm Harry Gardner. I'm his son. You're from the network?"

"I'm the producer," Northrop said. "I don't ordinarily come in person, but my assistant told me what a great human situation there was here, what a brave person your father is …"

The man in the bed slept on. He looked bad.

Harry Gardner said, "We made an arrangement. Five thousand bucks. We wouldn't do it, except for the hospital bills. They can really wreck you."

"I understand perfectly," Northrop said in his most unctuous tones. "That's why we're prepared to raise our offer. We're well aware of the disastrous effects of hospitalization on a small family, even today, in these times of protection. And so we can offer—"

"No! There's got to be anesthetic!" It was one of the daughters, a round, drab woman with colorless thin lips. "We ain't going to let you make him suffer!"

Northrop smiled. "It would only be a moment of pain for him. Believe me. We'd begin the anesthesia immediately after the amputation. Just let us capture that single instant of—"

"It ain't right! He's old, he's got to be given the best treatment! The pain could kill him!"

"On the contrary," Northrop said blandly. "Scientific research has shown that pain is often beneficial in amputation cases. It creates a nerve block, you see, that causes a kind of anesthesia of its own, without the harmful side effects of chemotherapy. And once the danger vectors are controlled, the normal anesthetic procedures can be invoked, and—" He took a deep breath, and went rolling glibly on to the crusher, "with the extra fee we'll provide, you can give your dear one the absolute finest in medical care. There'll be no reason to stint."

Wary glances were exchanged. Harry Gardner said, "How much are you offering?"

"May I see the leg?" Northrop countered.

The coverlet was peeled back. Northrop stared.

It was a nasty case. Northrop was no doctor, but he had been in this line of work for five years, and that was long enough to give him an amateur acquaintance with disease. He knew the old man was in bad shape. It looked as though there had been a severe burn, high up along the calf, which had probably been treated only with first aid. Then, in happy proletarian ignorance, the family had let the old man rot until he was gangrenous. Now the leg was blackened, glossy, and swollen from midcalf to the ends of the toes. Everything looked soft and decayed. Northrop had the feeling that he could reach out and break the puffy toes off, one at a time.

The patient wasn't going to survive. Amputation or not, he was probably rotten to the core by this time, and if the shock of amputation didn't do him in, general debilitation would. It was a good prospect for the show. It was the kind of stomach-turning vicarious suffering that millions of viewers gobbled up avidly.

Northrop looked up and said, "Fifteen thousand if you'll allow a network-approved surgeon to amputate under our conditions. And we'll pay the surgeon's fee besides."

"Well …"

"And we'll also underwrite the entire cost of postoperative care for your father," Northrop added smoothly. "Even if he stays in the hospital for six months, we'll pay every nickel, over and above the telecast fee."

He had them. He could see the greed shining in their eyes. They were faced with bankruptcy, and he had come to rescue them, and did it matter all that much if the old man didn't have anesthetic when they sawed his leg off? He was hardly conscious even now. He wouldn't really feel a thing, not really.

Northrop produced the documents, the waivers, the contracts covering residuals and Latin-American reruns, the payment vouchers, all the paraphernalia. He sent Maurillo scuttling off for a secretary, and a few moments later a glistening mechanical was taking it all down.

"If you'll put your name here, Mr. Gardner …"

Northrop handed the pen to the eldest son. Signed, sealed, delivered.

"We'll operate tonight," Northrop said. "I'll send our surgeon over immediately. One of our best men. We'll give your father the care he deserves."

He pocketed the documents. It was done. Maybe it was barbaric to operate on an old man that way, Northrop thought, but he didn't bear the responsibility, after all. He was just giving the public what it wanted, and the public wanted spouting blood and tortured nerves. And what did it matter to the old man, really? Any experienced medic could tell you he was as good as dead. The operation wouldn't save him. Anesthesia wouldn't save him. If the gangrene didn't get him, postoperative shock would do him in. At worst, he would suffer only a few minutes under the knife, but at least his family would be free from the fear of financial ruin.

On the way out, Maurillo said, "Don't you think it's a little risky, chief? Offering to pay the hospitalization expenses, I mean?"

"You've got to gamble a little sometimes to get what you want," Northrop said.

"Yeah, but that could run to fifty, sixty thousand! What'll that do to the budget?"

Northrop shrugged. "We'll survive. Which is more than the old man will. He can't make it through the night. We haven't risked a penny, Maurillo. Not a stinking cent."

☼

Returning to the office, Northrop turned the papers on the Gardner amputation over to his assistants, set the wheels in motion for the show, and prepared to call it a day. There was only one bit of dirty work left to do. He had to fire Maurillo.

It wasn't called firing, of course. Maurillo had tenure, just like the hospital orderlies and everyone else below executive rank. It was more a demotion than anything else. Northrop had been increasingly dissatisfied with the little man's work for months, now, and today had been the clincher. Maurillo had no imagination. He didn't know how to close a deal. Why hadn't he thought of underwriting the hospitalization? *If I can't delegate responsibility to him*, Northrop told himself, *I can't use him at all.* There were plenty of other assistant producers in the outfit who'd be glad to step in.

Northrop spoke to a couple of them. He made his choice. A young fellow named Barton, who had been working on documentaries all year. Barton had done the plane-crash deal in London in the spring. He had a fine touch for the gruesome. He had been on hand at the World's Fair fire last year in Juneau. Yes, Barton was the man.

The next part was the sticky one. Northrop phoned Maurillo, even though Maurillo was only two rooms away—these things were never done in person—and said, "I've got some good news for you, Ted. We're shifting you to a new program."

"Shifting …?"

"That's right. We had a talk in here this afternoon, and we decided you were being wasted on the blood and guts show. You need more scope for your talents. So we're moving you over to Kiddie Time. We think you'll really blossom there. You and Sam Kline and Ed Bragan ought to make a terrific team."

Northrop saw Maurillo's pudgy face crumble. The arithmetic was getting home; over here, Maurillo was Number Two, and on the new show, a much

less important one, he'd be Number Three. It was a thumping boot downstairs, and Maurillo knew it.

The *mores* of the situation called for Maurillo to pretend he was receiving a rare honor. He didn't play the game. He squinted and said, "Just because I didn't sign up that old man's amputation?"

"What makes you think …?"

"Three years I've been with you! Three years, and you kick me out just like that!"

"I told you, Ted, we thought this would be a big opportunity for you. It's a step up the ladder. It's—"

Maurillo's fleshy face puffed up with rage. "It's getting junked," he said bitterly. "Well, never mind, huh? It so happens I've got another offer. I'm quitting before you can can me. You can take your tenure and—"

Northrop blanked the screen.

The idiot, he thought. *The fat little idiot. Well, to hell with him!*

He cleared his desk, and cleared his mind of Ted Maurillo and his problems. Life was real, life was earnest. Maurillo just couldn't take the pace, that was all.

Northrop prepared to go home. It had been a long day.

☼

At eight that evening came word that old Gardner was about to undergo the amputation. At ten, Northrop was phoned by the network's own head surgeon, Dr. Steele, with the news that the operation had failed.

"We lost him," Steele said in a flat, unconcerned voice. "We did our best, but he was a mess. Fibrillation set in, and his heart just ran away. Not a damned thing we could do."

"Did the leg come off?"

"Oh, sure. All this was *after* the operation."

"Did it get taped?"

"They're processing it now. I'm on my way out."

"Okay," Northrop said. "Thanks for calling."

"Sorry about the patient."

"Don't worry yourself," Northrop said. "It happens to the best of us."

The next morning, Northrop had a look at the rushes. The screening was in the twenty-third floor studio, and a select audience was on hand—Northrop, his new assistant producer Barton, a handful of network executives, a couple of men from the cutting room. Slick, bosomy girls handed out intensifier helmets—no mechanicals doing the work here!

Northrop slipped the helmet on over his head. He felt the familiar surge of excitement as the electrodes descended, as contact was made. He closed his eyes. There was a thrum of power somewhere in the room as the EEG-amplifier went into action. The screen brightened.

There was the old man. There was the gangrenous leg. There was Dr. Steele, crisp and rugged and dimple-chinned, the network's star surgeon, $250,000-a-year's worth of talent. There was the scalpel, gleaming in Steele's hand.

Northrop began to sweat. The amplified brain waves were coming through the intensifier, and he felt the throbbing in the old man's leg, felt the dull haze of pain behind the old man's forehead, felt the weakness of being eighty years old and half dead.

Steele was checking out the electronic scalpel, now, while the nurses fussed around, preparing the man for the amputation. In the finished tape, there would be music, narration, all the trimmings, but now there was just a soundless series of images, and, of course, the tapped brainwaves of the sick man.

The leg was bare.

The scalpel descended.

Northrop winced as vicarious agony shot through him. He could feel the blazing pain, the brief searing hellishness as the scalpel slashed through diseased flesh and rotting bone. His whole body trembled, and he bit down hard on his lips and clenched his fists and then it was over.

There was a cessation of pain. A catharsis. The leg no longer sent its pulsating messages to the weary brain. Now there was shock, the anesthesia of hyped-up pain, and with the shock came calmness. Steele went about the mop-up operation. He tidied the stump, bound it.

The rushes flickered out in anticlimax. Later, the production crew would tie up the program with interviews of the family, perhaps a shot of the funeral, a few observations on the problem of gangrene in the aged. Those things were the extras. What counted, what the viewers wanted, was the sheer nastiness of vicarious pain, and that they got in full measure.

It was a gladiatorial contest without the gladiators, masochism concealed as medicine. It worked. It pulled in the viewers by the millions.

Northrop patted sweat from his forehead.

"Looks like we got ourselves quite a little show here, boys," he said in satisfaction.

The mood of satisfaction was still on him as he left the building that day. All day he had worked hard, getting the show into its final shape, cutting and polishing. He enjoyed the element of craftsmanship. It helped him to forget some of the sordidness of the program.

Night had fallen when he left. He stepped out of the main entrance and a figure strode forward, a bulky figure, medium height, tired face. A hand reached out, thrusting him roughly back into the lobby of the building.

At first Northrop didn't recognize the face of the man. It was a blank face, a nothing face, a middle-aged empty face. Then he placed it.

Harry Gardner. The son of the dead man.

"Murderer!" Gardner shrilled. "You killed him! He would have lived if you'd used anesthetics! You phony, you murdered him so people would have thrills on television!"

Northrop glanced up the lobby. Someone was coming around the bend. Northrop felt calm. He could stare this nobody down until he fled in fear.

"Listen," Northrop said, "we did the best medical science can do for your father. We gave him the ultimate in scientific care. We—"

"You murdered him!"

"No," Northrop said, and then he said no more, because he saw the sudden flicker of a slice-gun in the blank-faced man's fat hand. He backed away, but it didn't help, because Gardner punched the trigger and an incandescent bolt flared out and sliced across Northrop's belly just as efficiently as the surgeon's scalpel had cut through the gangrenous leg.

Gardner raced away, feet clattering on the marble floor. Northrop dropped, clutching himself. His suit was seared, and there was a slash through his abdomen, a burn an eighth of an inch wide and perhaps four inches deep, cutting through intestines, through organs, through flesh. The pain hadn't begun yet.

His nerves weren't getting the message through to his stunned brain. But then they were, and Northrop coiled and twisted in agony that was anything but vicarious now.

Footsteps approached.

"Jeez," a voice said.

Northrop forced an eye open. Maurillo. Of all people, Maurillo.

"A doctor," Northrop wheezed. "Fast! Christ, the pain! Help me, Ted!"

Maurillo looked down, and smiled. Without a word, he stepped to the telephone booth six feet away, dropped in a token, punched out a call.

"Get a van over here, fast. I've got a subject, chief."

Northrop writhed in torment. Maurillo crouched next to him. "A doctor," Northrop murmured. "A needle, at least. Gimme a needle! The pain—"

"You want me to kill the pain?" Maurillo laughed. "Nothing doing, chief. You just hang on. You stay alive till we get that hat on your head and tape the whole thing."

"But you don't work for me—you're off the program—"

"Sure," Maurillo said. "I'm with Transcontinental now. They're starting a blood-and-guts show too. Only they don't need waivers."

Northrop gaped. Transcontinental? That bootleg outfit that peddled tapes in Afghanistan and Mexico and Ghana and God knew where else? Not even a network show, he thought. No fee. Dying in agony for the benefit of a bunch of lousy tapeleggers. That was the worst part, Northrop thought. Only Maurillo would pull a deal like that.

"A needle! For God's sake, Maurillo, a needle!"

"Nothing doing, chief. The van'll be here any minute. They'll sew you up, and we'll tape it nice."

Northrop closed his eyes. He felt the coiling intestines blazing within him. He willed himself to die, to cheat Maurillo and his bunch of ghouls. But it was no use. He remained alive and suffering.

He lived for an hour. That was plenty of time to tape his dying agonies. The last thought he had was that it was a damned shame he couldn't star on his own show.

Copyright © 1963 by Agberg, Inc.

James Aquilone is an editor and writer. His fiction has appeared in Flash Fiction Online, Weird Tales Magazine, *and DarkFuse's* Horror d'oeuvres, *among other publications. His nonfiction has appeared in* SF Signal, Den of Geek, *and* Shock Totem. *This is his first appearance in* Galaxy's Edge. *Visit his website at jamesaquilone.com.*

NO PLACE FOR A HERO

by James Aquilone

Bernard Kowalski destroyed the Verrazano Bridge during the Friday rush.

But there are three important things to keep in mind: It was unintentional, no one died, and he caught the bank robbers he was chasing. It was a classic superhero feat. They *should* have given him a ticker-tape parade.

Instead he got thirty years in prison.

In his closing argument, the prosecutor called Bernie a "living, breathing weapon of mass destruction." She also called him an "irresponsible, reckless vigilante" and a "fame-seeking psychopath." Never once did she mention the word "hero." Bernie easily could have flicked a paperclip through her throat and decapitated her right on the spot. But he was a superhero and superheroes don't kill.

They held him on Rikers Island while they built a special long-term prison for him on Guantánamo Bay. He saved them the trouble. He busted out with one well-placed punch to the four-foot-thick cement wall and eventually settled on a desert island in the Pacific Ocean.

A superhero, Bernie lamented, has no place in the real world.

✧

Bernie watched the sun sink into the ocean as he squeezed another yam into a coconut shell.

He had super strength. He could throw a garbage truck a mile. He could run so fast he was just a blur. He could blow down buildings with his ultra-breath. He could fly. And what did it get him, the world's first and only superhero? All the yams he could eat and his very own tropical prison.

No one bothered with him except for some neighboring islanders who would leave him food and gifts. They thought he was an angry deity. The yams were offerings. On special occasions they left roasted pig. He was happy for the food. It wasn't like he could fly over to Paris and grab some baguettes—not without causing an international incident.

He was thinking how Superman never got hauled into court in the comics when he spotted the helicopter. At first he figured it was sightseers. They occasionally flew over the island to take a peek at the superhuman, snap a few photos. He usually waved at them. Sometimes they'd wave back, sometimes they'd give him the finger.

He used his telescopic vision and saw that it was a Marine copter. In all the time he'd been on the island, no authorities had ever tried to contact him or haul him back to the U.S. Was this an assault? Were they stupid enough to try to finish him off now?

He scanned the sky, but there was only the one helicopter. If this was an attack, then the copter had to be equipped with a WMD.

He could hurl a palm tree at it or blow it down with his ultra-breath. But he continued squeezing yams. After two years on the island, the only way he could eat the tubers was by slurping them up like milkshakes.

The helicopter landed down the beach. He watched a man in a military uniform jump out. Alone, he headed toward the superhuman. Bernie relaxed.

The man said, "Bernard Kowalski?"

"No," he said. "I'm Batman." Military man didn't laugh.

"I am General William Duncan, Chairman of the Joint Chiefs of Staff."

Bernie picked up a yam, squeezed it so hard it exploded in his hand. "Care for a yam?"

"I'm not going to pussyfoot around, Kowalski. Your government needs you, maybe even the world."

"My government? You mean the one that arrested me for being a superhero?"

"We're in a big jam, the chili is really hitting the fan, and it is my opinion that you're the solution. We're prepared to offer you full asylum and will expunge your past crimes from the record."

"Crimes, huh? I was *fighting* crime!"

"Believe me, as a soldier myself, I understand. Collateral damage is inevitable in war. The greater good, son, that's what matters."

"Exactly! That's what I kept saying at the trial. I'm a superhero. There should be different rules."

"Well, Kowalski, the rules have just changed."

Bernie wiped the yam juice off his hands, sat up straighter. "They have, huh?"

"It seems you are no longer the world's only superhuman. But you can still be the world's only super*hero*. Madame Devastator has already destroyed most of New Jersey."

"Madame Devastator? Cool name."

"We've thrown everything at her, but it's done no good. We need you to take her out. You are cleared to use any means necessary. We're in a real bind here. What do you say, Kowalski?"

"General, I've been waiting a long time for this."

"I'll brief you at the Pentagon. We have an aircraft carrier not too far away."

"It'll be quicker if I take you."

Bernie scooped up the general and flew east.

Madame Devastator's real name was Hannah Bormann. She was a twenty-two-year-old art student from Connecticut, at least until about a week ago when she went berserk in Jersey.

At the Pentagon, Bernie watched videos of her obliterating Hoboken. She could fire bolts of lightning out of her fingertips and create storms with a hand gesture. She also sported a killer costume, something Bernie had always wanted. But his superhero career had ended before he could design one. Madame Devastator wore black high-heeled boots with laces up to her knees, a leather bodysuit with lightning bolts running down the sides, and a scarlet cape. At the moment, Bernie was in yellow Bermuda shorts, flip-flops, and a pink tank top.

When the briefing was over, General Duncan said, "Do you need any assistance from us?"

"Can you guys rustle me up a uniform? I feel kinda dorky here."

A half-hour later he was wearing Henry Winkler's leather jacket from *Happy Days*, John Wayne's cowboy hat from *True Grit*, Harrison Ford's pants from *Raiders of the Lost Ark*, and James Dean's boots from *Rebel Without a Cause*. Some wise guy had made a run to the Smithsonian and thought the clothes had some mojo that might help. They started calling Bernie "Mr. Americana." His previous superhero name was Bernard Kowalski.

✿

When Bernie reached New York City, where Madame Devastator was currently wreaking havoc, he perched himself on top of the Freedom Tower. He didn't need his telescopic vision to find her. A boulder the size of a minivan blasted into the air over Central Park. Bernie rocketed uptown, and just before it crashed on top of The Dakota apartment building he obliterated the boulder with a mighty uppercut. A mist of pebbles showered down.

Bernie bolted into the park, flying just above the treetops.

He was nearing the lake when a street lamp rose into the air and swatted him as if he were a pesky fly. He crashed into the water.

As he sank, Bernie thought how he had only ever fought purse snatchers and jaywalkers.

He sprang out of the water, grabbed his hat—which was floating nearby—and placed it back on his head.

Madame Devastator stood beside the Bethesda Fountain, sparks dancing on her fingertips. "I should have figured they'd send for you," she said. "You've always struck me as a brownnoser."

"Is that why you're doing this? To get to me?"

"Don't flatter yourself. I'm doing this because I can. It's fun. Besides, what the hell else can you do with fingertips that shoot lightning?"

"You got me there," Bernie said, and blasted her with his ultra-breath. She hurtled backwards, knocking down trees and statues. She didn't come to a stop until she crashed into the side of an M10 bus.

All the vehicles on Central Park West were abandoned. General Duncan had pulled the military out of the area and evacuated as many civilians as he could, though there were plenty of them watching from their apartment windows, snapping photos and taking video.

A woman stuck her head out of a fourth-story window and shouted, "Get her, Mr. Americana!" Bernie's face burned with pride, though he wondered how she knew his nickname.

Bernie spotted a garbage truck up the block. He'd always wanted to chuck one.

As he lifted it over his head, he noticed with glee the camera flashes coming from the surrounding buildings. He paused, flexed his muscles, then heaved the truck at Madame Devastator, just as she was getting to her feet. Bernie was disappointed when the truck crash-landed right-side up a few yards from her. It tottered and he helped it along with a blast of his ultra-breath. A moment after the truck fell onto the super villain, windows were thrown open and there was a thunderclap of applauds and hooting. Some people were giving Bernie the thumbs-up. They held out their cellphones. Bernie smiled and waved as if he had just won the Miss America Pageant.

He was thinking about the ticker-tape parade they were going to give him, when Madame Devastator zapped him with the lightning from her fingertips.

His body seized. His muscles felt as if they had been turned to stone. Then came the burning. Bernie screamed.

Suddenly the sky darkened and the wind howled. He floated into the air and began spinning in the darkness. Thunder crashed around him. He was caught inside a tornado.

He tried to get his equilibrium, but he couldn't stop the spinning. He was blind and disoriented. His arms were pinned at his side.

He couldn't die like this before the world. It would be all over the Internet in seconds. In his panic, he pursed his lips and blew as hard as he could, hoping to jolt himself out of the twister. There was an explosion. He heard glass shattering and stone crumbling. He blew again. Another explosion. Screams. Car alarms blared. Still he was trapped in the funnel. He blew straight down and kept blowing until he rose above the bad weather. He stopped blowing when he saw the sun and the bright blue sky. Then he was falling, his muscles still cramped from the lightning strikes. The roof of the American Museum of Natural History rushed up to the meet him and he crashed through it. He landed on a stegosaurus skeleton, which was now a pile of rubble.

After a moment, his power returned to him and he shot through the hole in the roof. Madame Devastator was waiting for him in front of the museum. She looked tired, drained. The lightning flickered on her fingertips like a dying light bulb.

"You don't have to fight me," she said, gasping for breath. "We're the same. In fact, we're the only two of our kind. They"—she swept out her arms—"are our real enemies. You saw how they treated you when you tried to help them the first time."

"I'm a superhero," Bernie said. "This is what superheroes do."

One moment Bernie was hovering in the air, the next he was behind Madame Devastator. He held her in a headlock. She barely resisted.

"This ends now," he said.

"If you're going to kill me, you could at least use an original line."

A small crowd watched from the park across the street. Someone yelled, "Finish her!" Another screamed, "We love you, Mr. Americana!"

Bernie tightened his grip on Madame Devastator. Camera flashes, like bolts of lightning, ripped through the air. In minutes he'd be the champion of the world, his face on every TV screen, newspaper, and magazine. He was probably already trending like crazy on the Internet. Before he twisted his arch-nemesis's neck, he whispered in her ear.

Then Madame Devastator went limp in his arms.

For a moment the city was silent. Bernie heard only his ragged breathing. Then there came an eruption of cheers and shouts. People began to appear from all over. They chanted his name and it echoed across the city. Bernie's eyes moistened. He wished his parents were still alive to see this.

As the crowd inched toward him, Mr. Americana, née Bernard Kowalski, flew off with Madame Devastator's body in his arms.

The yams were all gone, so he flew to Tokyo and got sushi. He didn't even have to pay. Heroes don't have to pay. It's one of the many perks.

Back on the island, he sat on the beach reading an English-language newspaper he grabbed along with his lunch. The front page showed him holding Madame Devastator. "Mr. Americana Saves the Day!" the headline blared.

A few pages in he found an editorial questioning whether Mr. Americana (the Pentagon had leaked the nickname to the media shortly after Bernie left for New York) was needed now that Madame Devastator was dead. He knew that would come. In time they'd return to seeing him as a ticking time bomb. Weapons of mass destruction are only tolerated in times of war.

"Did you get any sashimi rolls?"

Bernie turned and watched Hannah exiting the tropical forest. Her blond hair was pulled into a ponytail and her freckles stood out with sunburn. Without her costume, she looked like a typical college student.

"Yeah," he said, and handed her the bag of take-out.

He never intended to kill Madame Devastator. Superheroes don't kill. But it wasn't until that day in New York that he realized how badly a hero needs a villain.

She sat next to Bernie. "Doesn't this get boring?" she asked. "Just sitting here."

"You get used to it. Have you decided where you're going to make your reemergence?"

"I was thinking Paris in the spring."

"Perfect. That will be well after my ticker-tape parade. I'll give you a two-hour head-start."

"That should be enough time to destroy the Eiffel Tower."

"No, don't do that. I've always wanted to chuck the Eiffel Tower like a javelin. I saw it once in a comic."

"OK. That might be cool. I'll take out the Arc de Triomphe with a tornado then. Meet me in front of the Louvre. We'll give them a good show. But this time, why don't I pretend to snap *your* neck?"

"Sure. Why not?"

A superhero, Bernie lamented, has no place in the real world. Not unless he creates one.

Original (First) Publication
Copyright © 2014 by James Aquilone

Maureen McHugh's first novel, China Mountain Zhang, *was a Tiptree winner and a Hugo and Nebula finalist. Maureen has won the Hugo for her story "The Lincoln Train." She is the author of four novels, a number of stories, and a collection, and is spending considerable time these days working for Hollywood.*

HONEYMOON

by Maureen McHugh

I was an aggravated bride. It was a little after one in the morning, I guess. We were supposed to be on our way to the Hampton Inn in Columbus for our wedding night. I was aggravated a lot with Chris, but never this aggravated before. I was walking back toward Lancaster on Rt. 33, glad that for the reception I had changed into a pair of white canvas sneakers with sequins that my cousin Linda had decorated for the wedding. I knew that I wouldn't want to wear heels all night. I'm a big girl and I wasn't going to miss dancing at my own reception because my feet hurt too bad. But I was still wearing my wedding dress and my veil.

Chris was in his F-150 pick-up, driving slow so he could keep asking me to get in the truck. You wouldn't think there were that many cars on Rt. 33 at that time of the morning, but there were, and they kept slowing down and carefully passing. Some guy called out the window, "I'll give you a ride, honey!"

I gave him the finger.

"Please, please get in the truck, Kayla," Chris said.

I wasn't talking to him. Usually when I got angry, I started crying, which always loses you any sort of chance you have of making a point. But I was so mad that night, I never even shed a tear.

"I'm sorry. Baby, I'm sorry, I'll make it up to you," Chris said.

I couldn't stand that. "Just how are you going to make it up to me?" I said. "How are you going to give me back my wedding night?"

He looked at me with big puppy eyes and said, "Don't be like that, Kayla."

It had been a really nice wedding. I saved the money. My dad's on disability so I wasn't going to ask him for it. I'm an assistant manager at McDonalds, and I'd taken a second job working for Allwood Florists. All last fall I had made Christmas ornaments—wooden soldiers and Santas and reindeer. I sold them at craft shows. The biggest sellers were dog bone ornaments that I would personalize with the dog's name. I worked my butt off. Marty at Allwood gave me an employee rate for my wedding flowers; red roses and lilies. I got my dress in Pennsylvania because if you're from out of state you don't have to pay sales tax. I spent a hundred forty dollars on my hair, having it highlighted. I went to the tanning salon—my dress showed off my shoulders which are one of my best features. I really did look the best I have ever looked. And the reception went pretty good. A lot of people didn't stay, but a few people stayed until midnight.

I was really proud of the job I did. Chris had gotten a roofing job for his neighbor in June and said he would put the seven hundred dollars he earned toward our honeymoon. He wanted to take care of it. I gave him the money I had and he said it was all set. We were going to Cancun even though everyone said it was too hot in August. But I'd never been to another country. So we were supposed to go to Columbus, spend the night and then catch our flight in the morning.

Except that while we were on our way to Columbus, Chris told me that he hadn't actually taken care of it.

"Don't be mad, Kayla," he said. "Listen to me first."

He and Felter and Carnegie had gone up to Windsor in June, right after the roofing job. I knew that. I figured that after we got married he wouldn't be able to hang out with his friends as much and besides, I was working all the time anyway, paying for the wedding. They were playing blackjack and he won a bunch a money. "Almost six hundred dollars!" he said. "I was gonna use it on our honeymoon. I thought I was on a roll, you know?"

Chris was looking at me. He has really cute blue eyes. Usually I can't believe that a heavy girl like me got someone like Chris.

"So what happened?" I asked.

"I don't know," he said. "I mean, I know, but you know, I can't explain it. I wanted to win big. I wanted to get the honeymoon suite, you know? You worked so hard—"

"What happened?" I said.

"I lost the money," he said. "I'm sorry."

No honeymoon. He was hoping to put the Hampton Inn on his credit card, but he didn't know if he'd be able to because it was kind of close to maxed out. He'd meant to get it paid down, maybe put the whole honeymoon on it, but the alternator went on the truck and he needed it to get to work.

"Why didn't you tell me?" I said. I didn't know what else to say. I didn't really believe him. I just couldn't think about it. It kept squirming around in my head like I understood it but I didn't at the same time.

"I didn't want to ruin the wedding," he said.

I had worked really hard on the wedding but I guess I hadn't thought a whole lot about Chris. I was looking at him and it occurred to me that the reason Chris was with a girl like me was because he was a fuck up. I just never admitted it to myself.

"Stop the truck," I said.

I knew I couldn't walk all the way back to Lancaster, so I finally called Sarah, my best friend and my maid of honor. Then I sat down on the berm and waited. Chris pulled the truck off the road and stood, looking awkward. He started to sit down next to me but I said, "Don't sit down. That tux is rented and I'm not paying extra if you get it dirty."

While I was waiting for her, I told Chris I was going to get the marriage annulled.

"What does that mean?" he asked.

"It's like a divorce, only it's like the wedding never happened," I said.

"But it did happen," he said.

"It was never consummated," I said. I don't even know where I had heard about that.

He didn't understand what I meant by that, either.

"We didn't have sex on our wedding night," I said.

"We've been having sex for two years," he said.

We had, ever since I was seventeen and in my junior year at high school and he was thinking he would go into the army when he graduated. I figured if I had sex with him, he'd stay. "But we didn't do it tonight," I said. "So it doesn't count."

☼

I moved to Cleveland because my cousin Donna lives there. Donna is the opposite of me, physically. She's short and skinny and has dark brown hair. She has the family boobs though. She weighs one hundred five pounds and the joke is that fifty pounds of it is in her chest. She's in nursing school and she said I could get a job at the hospital. I never wanted to be a nurse but she said there were lots of jobs in a hospital and I could stay with her. I got a job in the kitchen which was fine. The hospital is the Cleveland Clinic which is probably the world's biggest hospital. It's a lot bigger than Lancaster. Not in square miles, but I'd bet more people work at Cleveland Clinic than live in Lancaster, Ohio. It's really modern. Lots of buildings with green glass. Rich foreigners like sheiks come there when they're sick. The kitchens have to make all sorts of food. Diabetic food, low-protein food, low-fat food, Muslim food, Jewish food. It was a lot more interesting than McDonalds.

I'd never worked with so many black people before. There are black people in Lancaster, but not so many of them. The black people at the Cleveland Clinic, a lot of them were real ghetto. Sometimes if they were talking to each other I couldn't understand what they were saying. I'd always liked country, for one thing. I didn't like hip-hop.

Donna was great about me living there, but it was a pain. I thought about going back to Lancaster. In a lot of ways, living in Cleveland wasn't a whole lot different than living in Lancaster, except it took a lot longer to get to work. My marriage had been annulled. It turned out sex didn't have anything to do with it.

Chris kept calling me and asking me to come home. I asked if he could take me out on a date. He showed up at Donna's with a dozen roses and got down on one knee. Then he called collect when he was drunk and cried.

I was talking to my dad one night—I called him every Tuesday—and complaining about Chris and my dad said, "Well, Kayla, what did you expect?"

"I expect him to act like a man," I said.

My dad chuckled and I knew he was thinking that was too much to expect of Chris. It occurred to me that maybe my dad had figured out what Chris was like a long time ago. "Do you like Chris?" I asked.

"It doesn't matter now, does it?" my dad said. I could just picture him, sitting in the recliner. My dad lives in Chauncy. He used to work for Diamond, before they closed the mill, then he worked at Lancaster Correctional. So I grew up in Lancaster. But when he had to stop working on account of his back, he moved back to Chauncy with my grandmother. Chauncy is about the size of one floor of one building of the Cleveland Clinic. When he said that, I knew he hadn't ever really thought much of Chris. Although he was always nice enough to him and they joked around.

"Why didn't you tell me?" I asked.

He sighed. I thought he was going to say that he didn't want to interfere. "I thought you wanted to wear the pants," he said.

I've always wanted a strong man. Or I thought I did. Maybe I thought a pick-up truck and talking about the army meant Chris was a strong guy. Or maybe my dad was right. Maybe I wanted to wear the pants.

Maybe I hadn't been really fair to Chris. But when he called, I would say to myself, be fair, Kayla. And the sound of his voice would make this feeling rise up in me, like the feeling of teeth scraping together, or like the weird rubbing noise that my car was making. Kind of a clicking noise. It was kind of hard to hear and so I found myself listening to it and getting more and more tense as I drove to work. That was what talking to Chris was like. I got tenser and tenser while he talked.

My car was sounding like my relationship with Chris, so of course, one day it stopped working altogether. It was the timing belt. It cost me seventy-four dollars to get it towed. Then they told me that it would cost more than six hundred to get it fixed, and that I was lucky I was on Euclid and not the highway because if it had been on the highway it might have thrown a rod and then I might as well just get a new car.

I don't even know what "throwing a rod" is but I sort of picture pieces of metal flying through the hood or something. The next time Chris called I told him about it and for the first time in a long time he perked up. "Yeah, yeah, you could have been in big trouble."

"I am in big trouble," I said. "I'm taking the bus to work. The bus is creepy and it takes forever. It's going to cost six hundred dollars to get it fixed." I was trying to save money to get a place of my own and let poor Donna have her apartment back. But I didn't have six hundred dollars and I was going to have to put it on my credit card. My credit card still had stuff on it from the wedding. Donna was paying for nursing school and only working two days a week at the hospital.

"So are you going to come home?" he asked.

"I'd rather die," I said.

Donna's dad, my Uncle Jim, loaned me the money to get my car fixed and I promised to pay him back, a hundred dollars a month.

One of the girls in the kitchen told me about medical studies. How she got paid a hundred dollars to take cough medicine every day for two weeks. She told me where to check out the list of studies and during my dinner break I went about six blocks to the building where she told me. I got lost once—I know how to get to where I park and then to where I work, but the rest of the place is still a maze.

There was a list of stuff, but nothing like the cough medicine study. It was all weird stuff—studies on depression, on taking estrogen. I looked over the whole list and couldn't find a thing I could qualify for. While I was looking, a guy came up to look, too. He looked healthy. He was a couple of years older than me. Short. Built like he wrestled, if you know what I mean.

He wrote down the info on the psoriasis study.

"What is that?" I asked.

"It's a skin problem," he said. "Your skin gets dry and flaky."

That sounded vaguely possible, although mostly my skin is too oily. "My feet get that way," I said. "Would that be enough?"

"To be psoriasis?" he said. "Probably not. But you don't have to have psoriasis to be in the study. They need healthy people for comparison. Tell Lisa you want on the list."

I did. She asked me about my psoriasis and I told her I didn't have it. She nodded and put me down. Two weeks later I got called to be in the control group.

And that was my first medical study.

Psoriasis studies are pretty good. I got a hundred fifty dollars to put cream on and be examined once a week for twelve weeks. Fifty dollars a month toward what I owed Uncle Jim helped a lot.

I got a job in a catering hall as a cook and left the Clinic, but I kept doing medical studies. A study on asthma got me enough to cover the deposit on an apartment. Which was good because Donna had met Ted and they were talking marriage and they sure didn't need me around the apartment. She graduated from nursing school and one November day, as I walked from the parking garage at the Clinic, I realized that I had lived in Cleveland for three years. The wind cut between the buildings the way it always does. The streets were a mess of slush. I was looking for a study so I could save money for a trip to Cancun in February.

The idea for the trip had started in the fall, when I called Sarah, who had been my maid of honor, and she told me Chris was getting married again. I knew I shouldn't care, but I wasn't even seeing a guy. Not that I wanted Chris. And I had a great life. Good friends. Four of us were going—two girls I worked with and another friend I had met at Weight Watchers. Weight Watchers hadn't been much of a success for me or for Melinda, but we started going out to movies and hanging out. We call ourselves the Fat Fab Four. Mel started it and she really is Fab. She wears jeans and skirts and I can remember her taking off like four hundred silver bracelets to get weighed. I love her style. Everybody had heard the story of how I didn't get to go to Cancun on my honeymoon. Mel had a friend who was a travel agent and she got us a great deal—seven days, all inclusive, for fourteen hundred dollars a piece. So it was the Fat Fab Four Not-A-Honeymoon Vacation.

Lisa was still working the desk. She said, "Hi Kayla, I haven't seen you for awhile." I hadn't done a study for ages. I could still use the money, but I'd been busy with the FF4.

I studied the list, but nothing looked good. Some things I just won't do. Anything that looks like it will hurt. I did a burn cream study once where they actually gave me a little burn on my butt. Hurt like hell. So now I'm more careful.

I was frowning.

Lisa said, "What about the pulmonary study?"

I shook my head. "I'm going out of town." The pulmonary study required that I be available for four months. The whole point of doing a study was to help pay for Cancun, not cancel it.

"This just came in," Lisa said. "Have you ever done a Phase 1 drug trial?"

I had done some drug trials, but they were all for stuff like psoriasis and the burn study. This paid two thousand dollars. It was for a leukemia drug. I'd never done something where you had to take a serious drug. But two thousand dollars was a lot. The whole trip and spending money. They only wanted twelve people.

She handed me the fact sheet. It had all the usual warnings. This drug is untested on humans … risk …

Normally I wouldn't have done anything like this. But the chance to make two thousand dollars seemed too good to pass up. Like it was almost fate, you know? I don't know that I believe in fate, especially now, but it seemed that way at the time. So I signed up.

The trial was on a Thursday afternoon. To get the day off I had to swap with someone else which meant working a double on Saturday—wedding in the morning and another wedding in the evening. At least in the evening I'd be doing bar, which wasn't so bad. Handing out glasses of wine and beer to happy drunken wedding guests.

Thursday I went to a medical lab out on Cedar Rd.

The Cleveland Clinic has three zones and it's all about patients. The front zone where the patients first see the hospital—the lobbies and the doctor's offices—is really nice. Nice carpeting, nice wood, nice chairs and tables. Plants. Art work. Then there's the middle zone, places like the surgical staging areas and the hospital rooms. The hospital rooms try to be nice but they have to have all this equipment and its not like television. It's kind of cluttered and busy and there will be stacks of blankets, boxes of latex gloves. Everything feels a little crowded. There's no art on the walls of the ER or the outpatient staging and recovery areas.

Then there's the back zone. Maintenance and the kitchen, offices and the places where the actual technicians do the lab work. Basements and closets. Hard light or not enough light. Notices and memos stuck on the wall. Employees Must Wash Hands

Before Returning to Work. * Mandatory Meeting on Health Coverage Changes * Waste Stock tracking sheets. That was the kind of place where the drug trial took place.

It was a pretty large room with no windows and a linoleum floor. It had one of those long folding tables like you see in a school cafeteria. On the table were vials and cotton swabs, syringes and gloves. A nurse was sitting in a folding chair reading a paperback.

There were ten of us, all guys except for me and one other woman. A lab tech checked us off a clipboard and we all had a packet sitting on a plastic chair. "Please sit in the chair with your packet," the guy with the clipboard said. "The dosages have been calculated based on your weight and if you sit in someone else's chair that could compromise the study." Then he came to each of us and asked us our name and our birthdate and gave us each a hospital bracelet with all that and an ID number on it. He explained how we would be asked the same thing again before receiving the injection and that was just to make sure that there were no slip-ups.

Then he explained about double-blind trials. No one in this room, he explained, knew which of us were getting the drug for testing and which were getting the placebo which was just an injection of saline. He explained Phase 1 testing. The point of this test, he explained, was not to determine if the drug worked, but just to confirm that it was safe for people. This drug, the one we were getting, had been extensively tested on rabbits and monkeys. Rabbits and monkeys, of course, could not report adverse effects, so we were to report any adverse effects we experienced. We would be getting a much smaller dose than the rabbits and monkeys.

I was the second person in the line of chairs. The guy sitting next to me was wearing a plaid shirt and thermal undershirt and work boots. He looked like he did construction. "Have you ever done this before?" I asked.

He nodded. "I've done two others, but they didn't pay as good as this."

A nurse came and asked him his name, date of birth, and ID number. She took a blood sample from him and then wrote his ID number on a label and stuck it on. Then she did the same thing to me.

As she moved down the chairs, I looked in my packet. The drug we were taking didn't have a real name. It was just called GNT1146. It was for leukemia, lupus and MS. Which, I will tell you, made me feel a little glad. It's hard to think you're doing much for humanity when you're getting paid to not have psoriasis in a psoriasis study. But what if this drug really cured people with MS? I said that to the guy in the flannel shirt.

He kind of looked at me. He made me think a little of Chris, I don't know why. Maybe because he was wearing a Ford cap.

"Is that why you're doing this?" he asked me.

"Hell no," I said. "I need the money to go to Cancun."

That made him grin. "Yeah, that sounds good," he said. He didn't know what he was going to do with the money. He's heard about it from his cousin's girlfriend who worked somewhere doing some kind of paperwork for medical stuff. He figured he should pay down his credit card but he was also thinking of saving it toward a down payment on a motorcycle.

The guy with the clipboard started talking so we shut up, although all he did was tell us the same thing that was in the packet and make us all sign that we understood the risks. It was just like school. I underlined *Phase 1 Drug Trial: Ten to Twenty healthy adults.* Phase 2 is something like fifty sick people. If the stuff doesn't seem to be as good as what people get anyway, then they stop. Otherwise they go to Phase 3. (I wondered what it would be like to have leukemia and find out that the experimental drug you are taking didn't do as good as what normal people get. I decided I was probably not brave enough for Phase 2, if I ever got leukemia.) Phase 3 has a couple of thousand sick people in it. Most drugs never get beyond phase 2, the guy with the clipboard explained.

About that time, I admit, I zoned out. One of the fluorescents was in the flicker-before-dying stage and it was annoying me. We had been there over an hour before the nurse finally started giving us injections.

The guy in the flannel shirt took off his shirt and rolled up his thermal undershirt. Then the nurse wrote down the time and his ID number. She asked me my name and birthdate and ID number but didn't give me the shot. I asked why.

"We wait two minutes between injections," she said.

"Watching for green and purple spots?" said the guy putting back on his flannel shirt.

"Purple and pink," she said.

We all three grinned.

Finally I got my shot.

Then I had to sit there while they gave the next eight people the shot wondering if my growing headache was a drug effect or the result of the bad fluorescent light. After the last person had gotten the shot, I thought we would maybe fill out some more paperwork and be told when to come back for follow-up. But we still sat there. I figured we'd been told how long we would sit there some time after I stopped paying attention. I was embarrassed to admit I had so I sat there, thinking about where I was going to eat when I left.

I finally decided I could ask Mr. Green and Purple Spots. I started to say something just as he said, "I don't feel so good."

"What's wrong?" I asked.

"I feel sick," he said. "Like I've got a fever." He was shaking.

"Hey," I said, to get the nurse's attention. "This guy doesn't feel good."

He took off his flannel shirt. "I'm burning up," he said, and rubbed his head, hard.

She came over and asked him to describe how he felt.

"Is this an adverse effect?" he asked.

"I don't know," she said.

Just our luck, I thought. We get a nurse who doesn't know what she's doing. But now I wonder if they weren't allowed to say anything. Or probably she really didn't know if he just happened to be sick or not.

"Can I have an aspirin or something?" he asked.

"Let's wait a bit," she said.

I didn't know what to do. Everyone else was leaning forward, looking at us. Looking at the sick guy.

"What's wrong with him?" someone asked the clipboard guy.

"I don't know," the clipboard guy said.

After a few minutes, the guy on the other side of me said, "I feel sick."

The nurse came over and laid her hand against his forehead. I was surprised she didn't have one of those temperature thingies that they stick in your ear. This guy was shaking, too. "I'm gonna be sick," he said. The nurse ran and grabbed the trash can and he vomited into it.

My stomach rose and I looked away. I thought maybe we weren't supposed to leave our seats, but when the flannel shirt guy threw up I got up and walked over to the wall.

"Are you all right?" the clipboard guy asked me.

"I think so," I said, although I didn't know.

Then the fourth person started throwing up.

"God," said the first guy. "My head feels like it's exploding!"

Everybody who wasn't throwing up was looking at me, or looking at the fifth person, who was the other woman. She was a black woman, maybe in her thirties? She looked scared.

"Can I have something for the pain, please!" said the first guy.

The third guy was lying on the floor now and the nurse was kneeling next to him. "He's dizzy," she said. "I think from spiking a fever." She pointed to the table where the cotton swabs and stuff was and said to the guy with the clipboard, "There's packets of Tylenol over there, give him one."

Clipboard guy said to her, "Should I call EMTs?"

"I don't know," she said. "This is your protocol."

"She's not sick," he pointed to the black woman.

"She might be a placebo," the nurse said. "How many placebos are there?"

"I don't know," he said.

"God!" said the first guy. "Oh, God, please! My head!"

The nurse got him a Tylenol which by this time seemed a little like pouring a glass of water on a house fire.

"I want to go home," the first guy said. "Call my girlfriend. I don't care about the money, I just want to go home."

"You stay here," the nurse said. "You're better here than home."

The clipboard guy was on his cell phone to someone. "I think you better send a doctor," I heard him say and then he saw me watching him and turned his back to us so he was facing the wall.

The black woman didn't get sick. The guy next to her didn't get sick, either. And then the guy next to him seemed okay, although I hadn't been watching the time so I didn't know how long it had been. Time was going so slow.

Then that next guy said, "Oh man, I feel it."

It was like that story in the Bible, where the Israelites want to leave Egypt and they smear blood on their doors and God sends the angel of death to slay all the firstborn but passes over the houses marked with lamb's blood. Except we didn't know who had been marked and who had been saved.

A doctor showed up in about half an hour, but by that time they had called EMTs. Six people had gotten the drug and four were placebos and we placebos were all standing around not looking at each other or looking at the sick guys. They loaded the sick ones into ambulances. The nurse was standing there in the hallway, holding her fist to her mouth like she was trying not to cry. I wanted to ask her if anything had ever happened like this before, but it was pretty clear no one had a clue.

I drove home.

I stopped on the way home and got a hamburger, but it seemed strange to eat it. I felt like I should be so upset I couldn't eat. Like that ever happened. When I got home I thought to check my cell phone—I had turned it off when I got to the medical trial because at Cleveland Clinic we weren't supposed to have our cell phones on inside the building. There was a message from a representative of the company that was doing the study asking me to call. I called my friend Mel instead and told her what had happened and she said she'd come over as soon as she got off work.

The phone rang as soon as I hung up and it was NewsChannel5. I told them I didn't know if I was allowed to talk, but when they asked me if I could confirm that six people had gotten sick I said that was true. Then the newspaper called. My cell kept ringing and ringing, until finally I shut it off and turned on the TV.

Mel got there just about the time that it came on the news, so I almost missed the first part. Not that it was very exciting. This news woman with really stiff, unmoving newscaster hair said that six people went to the hospital in a drug trial that went horribly wrong. The six men were hospitalized in criti-

cal condition with multiple organ failure. Then they showed the outside of a hospital—not Cleveland Clinic, maybe University Hospital?

"Fuck," Mel said, "that's so stupid."

I didn't know what she meant.

"Showing the outside of the hospital. It's just a building."

I said, "It's where they are."

"So?" she said. "What does showing you the hospital tell you? It's like when they are talking about a car accident and they show you this perfectly normal stretch of road with cars whizzing by."

Mel was really mad. It seemed a weird thing to be mad about.

"It's wrong," she said. When she lifted her hands, her bangles jingled. "It makes everything seem normal."

"They have to show something," I said, although that sounded lame.

"No they don't," she said. "We could go back to Miss My-Hair-Wouldn't-Move-in-a-Hurricane."

She shook her head. "I don't know. Are you okay?"

"Yeah," I said. "Nothing happened to me."

"I don't know why it pisses me off so much," she said. "It's just the news."

The next day they had an interview with the girlfriend of one of the guys who got sick. She said that her boyfriend was in a coma and his head had swelled up to three times its normal size and he looked like the Elephant Man. I didn't think she should have said that. She should have given him his dignity. All day at work I told people what had happened. People wanted to know if I was going to sue. For what? They had told us that there was a risk. They've got to test drugs or people would still be dying of plague and polio. It wasn't anybody's fault. It was just something that happened. I explained it over and over again. But people kept saying to me, "Are you going to sue?"

On Saturday I was so tired of the whole thing, I didn't want to talk about it anymore.

I wished I could find out what happened to the construction guy, the guy in the flannel shirt. Four of the guys were out of the ICU in a couple of days and I hoped he was one of them. I hoped he wasn't the guy whose girlfriend had said his head swelled up.

Then the news stopped talking about it.

It was almost like it had never happened. I got a check from the company that did the drug trial and I put it in my bank account. It was weird because in some ways it was a bigger deal when Chris and I got our marriage annulled. People talked about that for a long time, and not just in Lancaster. But even Mel didn't talk to me about the drug trial thing unless I brought it up.

It didn't bother me, not really. I think about it sometimes. I'm not doing any more medical trials. I figure I gave my all for science already. But other than that, it's just something that happened.

We went to Cancun, my Not-A-Honeymoon-Trip to Cancun. We stayed in a resort hotel with a pool that went halfway around the hotel and had two swim up bars. Being in Mexico, I thought everything would be more foreign, but in Cancun things felt a lot the same. There was McDonalds and KFC, Pizza Hut, even Wal-Mart. Mel said it looked just like Florida only more people speak Spanish in Florida.

Still, it was incredibly fun. You walk out of the hotel and down to the road and this bus comes along. There's no schedule because they just take you from the *zona hotelera* to the downtown. It costs fifty cents. We partied a lot because even if we got trashed it didn't matter.

There was this one club that sold drinks that were two feet tall. We'd been to Coco Bongo the night before which was great but too crowded to dance, so we just picked this place at random because it had a dance floor. They had these long skinny glasses, red and blue plastic. I was sick of margaritas but all you could get were margaritas and daiquiris so I was on my third daiquiri. Usually I could drink pretty much. I started to feel kind of sick—Cancun catching up to me, I figured. I found the bathroom. I rinsed my face off, careful to keep my mouth tightly closed. I didn't want to get Montezuma's revenge.

I overheard these two girls talking. They were thin and blond and it was clear they had never worked in McDonalds in their lives. The one was saying to the other, "I don't know if I want to come back here anymore."

The other one asked where she wanted to go instead and they talked about Hawaii or Miami something.

I hated them. I don't know why; they were probably nice enough. But I just hated them. I thought, I almost died to get here. I still felt a little sick and dizzy and I went in one of the stalls and sat on the edge of the toilet. Usually I don't want to touch anything in a public bathroom.

Maybe it just hit me, I don't know.

I had heard that all the guys lived, although I suspected none of them was exactly ready to come to Cancun. I had specks dancing in front of my eyes. I put my head down on my knees and took deep breaths and I tried not to think about my head swelling up so that I couldn't open my eyes.

I'm okay, I thought. I'm okay.

Someone called, "Are you all right?" It was Mel, jingling with bracelets.

"Yeah," I said. "I'm fine."

"Are you sick?"

I was actually feeling better. I stood up and flushed the toilet and came out. "It's okay," I said. "I think I've just been drinking too fast."

The music was disco. The beat was thumping. I went out and I started dancing, too. My head was still kind of light and as I was dancing I felt lighter and lighter. Not in a bad way, but in a good way. I thought about those girls in the bathroom. And what it would be like to be able to decide to go to Hawaii. About what it would be like to be them, or to have gotten the other kind of injection.

I thought about luck.

I could think about that or I could dance. Right now I wanted to dance. It didn't seem like a bad choice.

Alex Shvartsman is a writer, translator, and game designer, with more than 30 short stories to his credit. He is currently editing the hilarious Unidentified Funny Objects *series of anthologies. This is his third appearance here.*

※ *Flash!* ※

Alex won the WSFA Small Press Award for Best Short Story with "Explaining Cthulhu to Grandma." (October 2014)

FATE AND OTHER VARIABLES

by Alex Shvartsman

An angry drug dealer was waving a gun in my face, and it was all Greg's fault.

I raised my hands, palms-up, very slowly. "Whatever he did this time, I'm sure we can work it out."

"Sure we can," said the man my brother called Coins. He invaded my personal space, his face uncomfortably close to mine, the stink of tobacco heavy on his breath. "Pay me the three large this weasel owes me, and I'll be on my way."

I turned to Greg, mostly to disengage from the unsavory character in front of me.

Greg looked at me with that same guilty expression on his face I'd seen so many times while growing up.

I screwed up again, his expression was saying. *But it's all right, because Big Brother Mike is going to make everything better, fix things, like he always does.* It was the look I'd seen whenever our parents found pot hidden in his room. The same look he'd given me whenever I came to bail him out of jail, or whenever he would show up on my doorstep in the middle of the night, asking for cash. Some things never change.

"I don't keep that kind of money on hand."

"Well then, we'll just have to see what you *do* have." The man went through the house looking for valuables. Greg and I followed, but gave him plenty of space. My heart raced like an over-clocked CPU, then skipped a beat when he found my office.

An L-shaped workbench stood at the center of the room. Three large monitors were lined up on top

of it. A wireless keyboard and mouse rested upon piles of printouts and handwritten notes. And along all four walls of the room, stacked up to the ceiling on metal shelving units, were dozens of networked computers.

"What are you, some kind of hacker?"

Computers are logical and predictable. They don't make irrational choices, and they never let you down, unless you mess up the code. Growing up around Greg, it's no wonder I liked them better than people. I understood them better, too.

So yes, I was a hacker, and a damn good one, too. But it wouldn't do to advertise the fact to two-bit criminals.

"I'm an IT consultant."

The man with the gun smiled. "I bet these will fetch a few bucks."

"Listen pal, I'll get you your money. I'll pay Greg's debt in full, so long as you promise to cut him off. But I can't have you messing with my equipment."

He grabbed fistfuls of my t-shirt.

"Don't you ever threaten me, nerd," he hissed, spittle flying from his mouth.

"Excuse me," sounded the voice from the door.

Another stranger stood in the doorway. He was an older man with a thick, graying beard. He wore a black wool coat and held a wide-brimmed hat in his hand, his head covered with a small skullcap.

"You are done here," he told Coins, his voice calm and facial expression a picture of serenity. "Get out."

Coins let go of me and advanced on the older man, the pistol aimed squarely at his belly.

The stranger pointed at the gun, and it began to melt.

What had once been a pistol lost its form and the resulting goo slid down the drug dealer's fingers like ice cream from a cone that was left out in the sun. His eyes went wide as he tried to shake off the viscous substance. Some of it clung to his hand, like gunmetal-colored honey.

"Leave," the old man repeated, "before I do the same to you."

The drug dealer's lip trembled as he stared at what used to be his weapon. He gave me an evil look, a promise of future retaliation strongly implied, but he didn't push his luck. He shuffled out the door subdued. I couldn't blame him. A large part of me wanted to flee as well, my rational brain struggling to accept whatever had just occurred. Greg looked more miserable than ever, but he stayed also, hovering in the farthest corner of the room.

I heard the front door slam. The stranger just stood there, studying me closely. I opened my mouth to speak but after a long moment closed it again.

"I believe 'thank you' are the words you're looking for," he said, a hint of a smile hidden in his beard.

"Who are you?" I asked instead.

"My name is Nathan Adler," he said. "I'm a kabbalist."

I'd vaguely heard of Kabbalah before. It was an obscure form of mysticism and, as such, mattered little to my scientific worldview.

"Is that how you did … that?" Greg spoke up. I was a little surprised that he recognized the term.

"Yes," said Adler matter-of-factly, without a hint of pride or boasting. "You and I have a lot to talk about, Michael," he added. "I find myself in need of your skill set."

✿

"No offense, but I don't believe any of this. Whatever you did to melt that guy's gun was a very neat trick, but the rest of it is way over the top. And even if it were real, how does one hack a metaphysical book?"

We were sitting in my living room, Greg banished to elsewhere in the house. Adler was telling me stuff that sounded like it came straight out of a fantasy novel.

"You must understand," he said, "that Kabbalah is, at its heart, an exact science. Talmudic scholars used a lot of metaphors to describe things the modern scholars are only now beginning to explore at the most sophisticated levels of theoretical physics. The Almighty designed the universe to operate under strict logical rules, like a computer program. Think of Kabbalah as a developer toolkit that can modify small subroutines within that program."

"All right," I said, "let's say for the moment that you're right and shelve the argument as to whether the universe has an intelligent designer of any kind." I shifted in the armchair. "You're saying there is this Book of Fate and that angels spend one week every year writing down the destiny of every human being in the world, and that whatever they write down is locked in for the next year. Did I get that right? And, if so, how is this even remotely related to science?"

"Again, much of that is metaphor. Many of the ancient cultures were aware of this phenomenon and explained it using whatever imagery their contemporaries could understand." Adler laid things out patiently, like a parent explaining to his kid that there's no such thing as Santa Claus. Except this was, pretty much, the exact opposite of that. "The important thing for us is that there's a record—think of it as a database—of people's fates, determined a year in advance. And there's a ten-day-long window during which this record can be altered."

I felt like a film crew for one of those "gotcha" reality shows should burst from the bedroom at any moment. Still, I'd seen him do the impossible with my own eyes. Also, he'd extricated Greg and me from a very hairy situation. Least I could do was entertain his theories.

"What about free will? I seem to recall that being an important tenet of Judeo-Christian philosophy."

"Free will isn't limitless," said Adler. "For example, you can't fly out the window, no matter how much you may want to. Free will manifests in dozens of smaller decisions you make every day. Those choices won't alter what's written in the Book of Fate, though many believe that they have a direct effect on what is to be written down for next year."

"And you want us to get in there and rewrite your future so that you can become what, a king of the world?"

"Nothing like that," Adler said. "We'll introduce small changes that should fly under the radar, lest they're discovered and corrected. For instance, you could alter your brother's life trajectory by eliminating his drug addiction."

Adler said this almost casually, but the bastard knew exactly which buttons to push, knew that the possibility alone would force me to consider his proposal even while it still sounded more than a little crazy.

"Why me?" I asked. "Why not some hacker or hardware whiz who already buys into all this stuff?"

"Because you're both a hacker and a hardware whiz. You're the best there is," Adler said. "I checked. Also, as an atheist you shouldn't have as much difficulty with the philosophical implications of my plan." Which begged another question.

"What about *him*?" I asked, pointing upward. "How can you, as a religious man, justify going against the wishes of the guy upstairs?"

For the first time since we met, Adler didn't have a smooth, ready-made answer. He sat on my couch, silent, but his mind was somewhere else entirely. Finally, he spoke so quietly that I barely understood the words, "I have my reasons."

I let the matter drop.

☼

I slammed the dusty old volume shut and tossed it onto the table in frustration.

"I need a break," I said, rubbing my temples.

"Careful," Adler said a bit louder than usual. After a few months of working together I'd learned to decipher the subtle hints of emotion hidden behind the man's calm façade. I was fairly sure that I detected a tiniest bit of annoyance in his voice. "Sorry," he added. "We're taught to revere books in my culture."

"My bad." I got up to stretch and massaged the back of my neck. A glance at the wall clock confirmed what my weary body already knew; we'd been at it for most of the day.

When I'd signed on to Adler's mad scheme, the first order of business had been for me to learn the bastardized version of Hebrew the kabbalists used as their programming language. Each of the twenty-two hieroglyphs was a letter, but it was also a concept, and a number, and contained far more meaning than anyone should expect from a single character. Learning to comprehend this stuff was slow going, to say the least.

And while I was learning it, however slowly, I made no progress at all at deciphering Adler himself. I researched the man online the minute he left my house on the day we met. There was a famous kabbalist named Nathan Adler in Europe a few hundred years ago, and a number of our contemporaries shared that name, but my new acquaintance wasn't among them. He used an alias, which meant that he had something to hide. Such as, perhaps, the alterations he intended to make to this Book of Fate.

After a short break, we delved back into the study session, only to be interrupted by the chime of a cell phone. Adler fished the device from the inner pocket of his jacket. I perked up. In all the time we'd spent together, his phone had never rung before.

Adler picked up and listened intently to whomever was at the other end of the line, his jaw clenched. At times he replied in brief bursts of Yiddish, his voice monotone as ever. The conversation lasted less than a minute.

"Something's come up. I have to go," Adler said once he'd hung up the phone. "We'll pick this up again, tomorrow."

Adler departed in a hurry. I was left sitting in the empty house. Greg was out, working his shift at the part-time job he'd found, stocking the produce section at a local supermarket. Greg had managed to stay off drugs and out of trouble since our close encounter with Coins, and was genuinely trying to put his life back on track. So I sat in the living room alone, trying to figure out what Adler was up to.

On impulse, I ran outside and dragged my Honda CBR out of the garage. I got on the bike and sped down the street, hoping to catch Adler before he reached the highway.

Adler drove a twenty-year-old Buick Estate Roadmaster, a station wagon with stripes of simulated wood grain on the sides. There aren't many of those on the road, which made Adler a lot easier to follow while keeping my distance. It also helped that the tinted shield of my bike helmet completely obscured my face.

Adler got onto Route 9 and took it all the way north to Outerbridge Crossing, across Staten Island and into Brooklyn. He parked in front of the Maimonides Hospital and rushed inside.

At the front desk, Adler had to sign in. I watched him go up the elevator before I walked up and, with a friendly nod to the guard, signed in as a visitor myself and scanned the previous entry for the name and room number.

Breaking into the hospital network was a breeze, once I found a courtesy Internet terminal in one of the waiting areas. I learned that the sole occupant of the room in question was Mrs. Sheila Horowitz, sixty-four years of age and recuperating from surgery.

Sheila's prognosis wasn't good: stage four pancreatic cancer. A malignant tumor had grown on her liver, unnoticed until it was too late. Doctors had removed the primary tumor in surgery but it had already metastasized. She likely had between six months and a year to live—and that's assuming she recovered from the invasive surgery. It was still touch and go, for the moment.

Adler—or was it Horowitz?—was beginning to make sense to me now. He wasn't out to cheat the universe of its plan for some sort of personal gain; he was trying to save his wife. There aren't a lot of things in life powerful enough to cause a man of faith to go against what he saw as the wishes of his creator, but love certainly qualifies.

I sympathized with their plight and was ashamed because, in some conflicted way, I was comforted by the knowledge of it. This meant Adler's reasons and motivations were only human, after all.

Adler and I spent the summer working feverishly to prepare ourselves. According to the kabbalist, the window of opportunity to alter the Book of Fate was coming up in late September. The next year's fortunes would be written down between the Jewish holidays of Rosh Hashanah and Yom Kippur. Adler couldn't wait another year, and now that I had figured out his reason, I understood why. Frankly, I couldn't take another year of preparations myself. As difficult as it was to learn the language, that was child's play compared to mastering Kabbalah's practical applications and building the hardware.

Greg seemed content working his menial job, watching sports on TV, and chasing after women. He was doing well in that last department, if any of his constant bragging was to be believed. He never brought anyone over to the house, but he stayed out overnight at least once a week. Greg's wasn't a life I would find fulfilling, but he appeared to be happy and that was good enough for me.

So when he didn't come home one morning, I wasn't worried. But he didn't show up the next day either, and didn't return my phone calls. By then I became concerned enough to go look for him at work.

I spotted Jose, Greg's co-worker and buddy, stocking shelves in one of the aisles. I walked over. "Hey, is Greg around?"

Jose wiped the sweat off his forehead with a sleeve. "Nah, man. I haven't seen him in a while—not since he got canned."

"What? When was this?"

Jose gave me a surprised look. "You mean you don't know? It was just over a week ago. One of the supervisors walked in on him shooting up heroin in the stock room."

"Shit."

Greg was using again and, like any resourceful junkie, he was hiding it pretty damn well. I'd tried everything I could think of to help my little brother—from dragging him to AA meetings, to paying for fancy detox clinics. There was literally nothing I wouldn't do to help him get clean. But I couldn't spend my life watching over his every move. He was an adult now, and he always found a way to screw up.

Jose patted my shoulder. "Sorry you had to hear it from me, man. Greg's a decent sort. I hope he works everything out. Tell 'im the guys at work are wishing him all the best. We didn't get a chance to say goodbye, the way the management booted him that day. At least they didn't call the cops on him, so that's somethin'."

I thanked Jose and headed out. I rode around town, checking some of Greg's favorite haunts, but there was no sign of him. His phone must've been off—the calls went straight to voicemail. By the time I exhausted my options and returned home, it was a little past noon.

"Where have you been?" Adler said to me in lieu of a greeting. "We have less than a month left and you're wasting half a day on who-knows-what."

I told him.

"I'm so sorry, Michael," Adler said. "Addiction is a powerful thing. It's all too easy to relapse. Things will be much better for him once we succeed."

If we succeed. And even then, that was a month away. Greg needed help now.

"I have a better idea," I said. "Why don't you fix him? Melt away his cravings like you did that gun."

"I would if I could." Adler frowned.

"If you're concerned over my motivation, then I assure you—"

Adler cut me off. "You should have a better understanding of Kabbalah by now than to expect this of me. It's not some fairy tale magic. I can't wave a wand and change the man's soul. There's only one method that I know of to cheat fate, and we're already working on that."

I growled in frustration and punched the wall hard enough to leave a small indentation in the sheetrock. Was Adler truly powerless to help Greg, or was he holding back in order to keep the stakes high for me, keep me focused on his scheme? Ultimately, it didn't matter. Unlike any kind of a higher power, I had no influence or control over Greg's destiny. And the best way to help him was for Adler's plan to succeed. I rubbed my sore knuckles and sat down to work.

☼

The machine we built was a thing of beauty.

Well, not exactly. It was a jumbled mess of wires and microchips fused with equal parts solder and magic, a do-it-yourself project if there ever was one. It was a labor of love and countless hours of hard work and, to me, that made it beautiful.

Adler and I jury-rigged a spell-casting interface. I could input and store the complex symbols of power and the computer would convert them into the metaphysical programming language of the universe. The Buddhists had the right idea with automated prayer wheels powered by water and wind. This was taking the same concept to another level. Cutting-edge processors would fire off incantations exponentially faster than a human being ever could. If any manmade device could pick the locks on heaven's door, this was it.

We finished it with a couple of days to spare. We did as much theoretical testing as we could and the results were promising. Until the ten-day-long window Adler referred to as the Days of Awe opened, all we could do was wait.

I was decompressing and enjoying some much-needed time apart from Adler when my cell rang and Greg's name popped up on caller ID. This was the first time Greg had bothered to touch base since he'd disappeared nearly a month ago. I worried about him constantly, even though this wasn't the first time Greg had gone AWOL.

"Hello?" I picked up the phone with a mixture of relief and indignation.

"Hello, Michael." I did not recognize the voice on the other end of the line.

"Who is this? Where's Greg?"

"Gregory sends his regards. He would very much like for you and I to meet." There was a hint of an accent I couldn't quite place. "Please join me at the coffee shop on the corner of Main and Tyson."

"Put Greg on the phone."

"Coffee shop. Fifteen minutes." The line went dead, and no one picked up when I called back.

Ten minutes later I was at the café, nervously shuffling my phone from one hand to the other and studying the other patrons from the corner table. I knew the place well. It was only a few blocks from my house, and I frequented it in the mornings. I wondered if the caller had known that.

A tall bearded man in his forties approached my table with a foam cup in each hand. "Medium French Vanilla, light and sweet." He set the cup containing my usual order on the table in front of me.

"Where's Greg?"

"My associates have him," the man said cordially, as if he were discussing a piece of furniture. "He's safe and secure. Relatively speaking, of course." I still couldn't place the man's accent. His skin tone and facial features hinted at Middle Eastern or Persian ancestry.

My first instinct was to lash out at him verbally, demanding answers. Instead I remained silent. I didn't want to give him the satisfaction.

"You've made quite an impression on the local criminal element," the man continued in the same conversational tone. "A man who calls himself Coins had some fascinating stories to tell about an encounter at your residence. Stories that ultimately reached the ears of my associates and piqued our interest."

The man sat down across the table from me and sipped his drink. "Coins was surprisingly subtle and creative in his revenge scheme against you. He tracked down your brother and reintroduced him to the world of narcotics. As I understand it, the first dose was administered under duress. After that, Gregory's inner demons took care of the rest."

He took another sip. "In no time at all, your brother was willing to share with us every little detail he knew about your plan. In exchange, we had Coins ply him with whatever pills and powders he desired."

Before I knew it, I was on my feet, leaning across the small wooden table, my jaw tightened and my fists clenched.

The bastard didn't even flinch.

"Easy," he said as I struggled to control my temper, to stop myself from lunging at him. "Let's not forget that we still have Gregory. You'll have to play nice, if you want him back."

I stood there for a long moment, awash in the smell of roasted coffee and the sounds of the early afternoon crowd. Ordinary people were going about their everyday lives, unaware of the terrible cruelty of this stranger's soft-spoken words. He had my brother. Taking a swing at him wasn't going to change that. The fight left me and I slid back into the seat.

"Who are you and what do you want?" I said through my teeth.

"My name is Ajit Singh," he replied, "and I'm a mystic, just like the one who calls himself Nathan Adler. I'm no admirer of the man, but I must give credit where it's due. His idea is daring and ingenious. Visionary, even. In fact, my associates and I like it so much, we're going to annex it."

He produced a sheet of paper with names and notes handwritten neatly in tiny block letters.

"If your machine succeeds at affecting what's etched onto the Pillar of Destinies, we want you to make the following changes—and nothing else. You may aid your brother and even help yourself to a modest amount of fame or fortune, but you are not to enact any of the alterations Adler asks of you. Understand?"

"The man's wife is dying of cancer," I said. "All he wants is to save her."

"Is that what he led you to believe?" Singh laughed in my face. "Adler hasn't been married for over two hundred years."

☼

Adler and I scheduled our attempt for the day before Yom Kippur, the Day of Judgment.

As I mulled over what Singh had told me, I read up on the subjects of destiny and kismet. I found references to a pre-ordained recording of future events in almost every ancient faith. An obscure splinter group of Singh's people, the Sikhs, believed that Guru Nanak etched what's to come in marble upon a pillar that rose to the heavens. The Islamic concept of Taqdeer spoke of "The Preserved Tablet," adjusted annually by Allah based on one's deeds and performed rituals. Other traditions were bursting with stories of people's futures recorded by deities or spirit guides or blind scribes. But none of it held the answers I sought.

Singh demanded that I say nothing to Adler. I needed the kabbalist's help in the final preparations for the ritual, which forced Singh's people to keep their distance. Even as we made painstaking preparations, I agonized over what to do. I still hadn't made up my mind by the time we were ready to begin.

With a heavy heart, I launched the incantation program. The spell-casting machine whirred to life, lines of code and lines of arcane symbols scrolling down my monitor screens. I worked feverishly, activating various scripts and making on-the-fly adjustments. For a time, I was able to push everything but the pure challenge of the code out of my mind.

Even in a strange situation like this one, I felt in my own element. Computers and codes are logical, predictable. They aren't swayed by emotion, by desire, by addiction. I always knew where I stood with code, because I was capable of understanding its nature.

One by one, the layers of arcane protections fell aside like so many network firewalls. My scripts tore relentlessly through the veil of the physical universe. Then the last of the protections gave in, and I had full access. Interpreted by my computer, I could see spread before me the fate of every living being in the cosmos.

"We did it!" I shouted. "We're in."

"I knew you could do it, my friend," Adler said. "Make these modifications quickly now, before our meddling is noticed." And he handed me a list of his own.

There were a dozen names on the page. People I didn't know, faceless individuals whose future Adler wanted altered and whose fate was now literally in my hands. I scanned through the list. Sheila Horowitz wasn't on it.

Adler hadn't lied to me, not exactly. He must've let me follow him that time so that I'd draw my own conclusions. Still, he was a devious and underhanded man, just like Singh said. Then again, he didn't kidnap my brother and hold him hostage to secure my cooperation.

I tried to decide between the two lists as precious moments ticked away. Adler or Singh—the man who'd obtained my help by cunning, or the man who'd done so by the unsubtle threat of force—whose vision of the future did I dare unleash upon the world?

In the background, Adler was saying something, urging me on. I ignored him. Whatever supernatural forces controlled our lives, our fates, this decision was mine to make alone. Free will—my will—truly mattered in that one moment, perhaps the most important moment of my existence.

So I used the hard-won access to do the only thing that made sense to me. I crashed the system.

Billions of records, a multitude of pre-ordained paths, were permanently erased. I had no way to know if God, or angels, or whatever passed for an intelligent designer in this universe, would eventually rebuild the fate database. I hoped not.

There was very little time before Adler would realize what I'd done. I used it to get rid of the scripts and programs I wrote. I had no way of knowing what Adler would do once he found out. Would I survive his reaction? Would Singh release my brother or kill him out of spite? I'd taken a terrible risk to do the right thing and I could only hope for the best, knowing that whatever happened, the future was in flux, no longer predetermined by anyone.

If he survived, my brother would find the inner strength to overcome his addiction, or he would not. Sheila's cancer would go into remission, or it would not. Adler and Singh and billions of others would make everyday decisions, struggle and scheme, win and lose, and do all of it on their own. They truly had free will now.

And as I reformatted the spell-casting machine's hard drive so that no one could ever use it again, I took a small comfort in the hope that my decision was the last choice ever forced upon humanity by somebody else.

Jack Skillingstead is the author of more than 30 stories, plus 2 novels. A finalist for both the Theodore Sturgeon and Philip K. Dick awards, his work has appeared in four Year's Best anthologies. This is his first appearance in Galaxy's Edge.

DEAD WORLDS

by Jack Skillingstead

A week after my retrieval, I went for a drive in the country. I turned the music up loud, Aaron Copland. The two-lane blacktop wound into late summer woods. Sun and shadow slipped over my Mitsubishi. I felt okay, but how long could it last? The point, I guess, was to find out.

I was driving too fast, but that's not why I hit the dog. Even at a reduced speed, I wouldn't have been able to stop in time. I had shifted into a slightly banked corner overhung with maple—and the dog was just there. A big shepherd, standing in the middle of the road with his tongue hanging out, as if he'd been running. Brakes, clutch, panicked wrenching of the wheel, a tight skid. The heavy thud of impact felt through the car's frame.

I turned off the digital music stream and sat a few moments in silence except for the nearly subaudible ripple of the engine. In the rearview mirror, the dog lay in the road.

I swallowed, took a couple of deep breaths, then let the clutch out, slowly rolled onto the shoulder, and killed the engine.

The door swung smoothly up and away. A warm breeze scooped into the car, carrying birdsong and the muted purl of running water—a creek or stream.

I walked back to the dog. He wasn't dead. At the sound of my footsteps approaching, he twisted his head around and snapped at me. I halted a few yards away. The dog whined. Bloody foam flecked his lips. His hind legs twitched brokenly.

"Easy," I said.

The dog whimpered, working his jaws. He didn't snap again, not even when I hunkered close and laid my hand between his ears. The short hairs bristled against my palm.

His chest heaved. He made a grunting, coughing sound. Blood spattered the road. I looked on, dispassionate. Already, I was losing my sense of emotional connection. I had deliberately neglected to take my pill that morning.

Then the woman showed up.

I heard her trampling through the underbrush. She called out, "Buddy! Buddy!"

"Here," I said.

She came out of the woods, holding a red nylon leash, a woman maybe thirty-five years old, with short blond hair, wearing a sleeveless blouse, khaki shorts, and ankle boots. She hesitated. Shock crossed her face. Then she ran to us.

"Buddy, oh Buddy."

She knelt by the dog, tears spilling from her blue eyes. My chest tightened. I wanted to cherish the emotion. But was it genuine, or a residual effect of the drug?

"I'm sorry," I said. "He was in the road."

"I took him off leash," she said. "It's my fault."

She kept stroking the dog's side, saying his name. Buddy laid his head in her lap as if he was going to sleep. He coughed again, choking up blood. She stroked him and cried.

"Is there a vet?" I asked.

She didn't answer.

Buddy shuddered violently and ceased breathing; that was the end. "We'd better move him out of the road," I said.

She looked at me and there was something fierce in her eyes. "I'm taking him home," she said.

She struggled to pick the big shepherd up in her arms. The dog was almost as long as she was tall.

"Let me help you. We can put him in the car."

"I can manage."

She staggered with Buddy, feet scuffing, the dog's hind legs limp, like weird dance partners. She found her balance, back swayed, and carried the dead dog into the woods.

I went to the car, grabbed the keys. My hand reached for the glove box, but I drew it back. I was gradually becoming an Eye again, a thing of the Tank. But no matter what, I was through with pills. I wanted to know if there was anything real left in me.

I locked the car and followed the woman into the woods.

She hadn't gotten far. I found her sitting on the ground crying, hugging the dog. She looked up.

"Help me," she said. "Please."

I carried the dog to her house, about a hundred yards. The body seemed to get heavier in direct relation to the number of steps I took.

It was a modern house, octagonal, lots of glass, standing on a green expanse of recently cut lawn. We approached it from the back. She opened a gate in the wooden fence, and I stepped through with the dog. That was about as far as I could go. I was feeling it in my arms, my back. The woman touched my shoulder.

"Please," she said. "Just a little farther."

I nodded, clenched my teeth, and hefted the dead weight. She led me to a tool shed. Finally, I laid the dog down. She covered it with a green tarp and then pulled the door shut.

"I'll call somebody to come out. I didn't want Buddy to lie out by the road or in the woods where the other animals might get at him."

"I understand," I said, but I was drifting, beginning to detach from human sensibilities.

"You better come inside and wash," she said.

I looked at my hands. "Yeah."

I washed in her bathroom. There was blood on my shirt and she insisted I allow her to launder it. When I came out of the bathroom in my T-shirt, she had already thrown my outer shirt, along with her own soiled clothes, into the washer, and called the animal control people, too. Now wearing a blue shift, she offered me ice tea, and we sat together in the big, sunny kitchen, drinking from tall glasses. I noted the flavor of lemon, the feel of the icy liquid sluicing over my tongue. Sensation without complication.

"Did you have the dog a long time?"

"About eight years," she said. "He was my husband's, actually."

"Where is your husband?"

"He passed away two years ago."

"I'm sorry."

She was looking at me in a strange way, and it suddenly struck me that she knew what I was. Somehow, people can tell. I started to stand up.

"Don't go yet," she said. "Wait until they come for Buddy. Please?"

"You'll be all right by yourself."

"Will I?" she said. "I haven't been all right by myself for a long, long time. You haven't even told me your name."

"It's Robert."

She reached across the table for my hand and we shook. "I'm Kim Pham," she said. I was aware of the soft coolness of her flesh, the way her eyes swiveled in their wet orbits, the lemon exhalation of her breath.

"You're an Eye," she said.

I took my hand back.

"And you're not on your medication, are you?"

"It isn't medication, strictly speaking."

"What is it, then?"

A lie, I thought, but said, "It restores function. Viagra for the emotionally limp, is the joke."

She didn't smile.

"I know all the jokes," she said. "My husband was a data analyst on the Tau Boo Project. The jokes aren't funny."

The name Pham didn't ring any bells, but a lot of people flogged data at the Project.

"Why don't you take your Viagra or whatever you want to call it?"

I shrugged. "Maybe I'm allergic."

"Or you don't trust the emotional and cognitive reality is the same one you possessed before the Tank."

I stared at her. She picked up her ice tea and sipped.

"I've read about you," she said.

"Really."

"Not you in particular. I've read about Eyes, the psychological phenomenon."

"Don't forget the sexual mystique."

She looked away. I noted the way the musculature of her neck worked, the slight flushing near her hairline. I was concentrating, but knew I was close to slipping away.

"Being an Eye is not what the public generally thinks," I said.

"How is it different?"

"It's more terrible."

"Tell me."

"The Tank is really a perfect isolation chamber. Negative gravity, total sensory deprivation. Your body is covered with transdermal patches. The cranium is cored to allow for the direct insertion of the conductor. You probably knew that much. Here's

what they don't say: The process kills you. To become an Eye, you must literally surrender your life."

I kept talking because it helped root me in my present consciousness. But it wouldn't last.

"They keep you functioning in the Tank, but it's more than your consciousness that rides the tachyon stream. It's your *being*, it's who you are. And somehow, between Earth and the robot receiver fifty light years away, it sloughs off, all of it except your raw perceptions. You become a thing of the senses, not just an Eye but a hand, a tongue, an ear. You inhabit a machine that was launched before you were born, transmit data back along a tachyon stream, mingled with your own thought impulses for analysts like your husband to dissect endlessly. Then they retrieve you, and all they're really retrieving is a thing of raw perception. They tell you the drugs restore chemical balances in your brain, vitalize cognitive ability. But really it's a lie. You're dead, and that's all there is to it."

The animal control truck showed up, and I seized the opportunity to leave. The world was breaking up into all its parts now. People separate from the earth upon which they walked. A tree, a doorknob, a blue eye swiveling. Separate parts constituting a chaotic and meaningless whole.

At the fence, I paused and looked back, saw Kim Pham watching me. She was like the glass of ice tea, the dead weight of the dog, the cold pool on the fourth planet that quivered like mercury as I probed it with a sensor.

Back in the car, I sat. I had found the automobile, but I wasn't sure I could operate it. All I could see or understand were the thousand individual parts, the alloys and plastics, the wires and servos and treated leather, and the aggregate smell.

A rapping sounded next to my left ear. Thick glass, blue eyes, bone structure beneath stretched skin. I comprehended everything, but understood nothing. The eyes went away. Then: "You better take this." Syllables, modulated air. A bitter taste.

Retrieval.

I blinked at the world, temporarily restored to coherence.

"Are you all right?" Kim was sitting beside me in the Mitsubishi.

"Yes, I'm all right."

"You looked catatonic."

"What time is it?"

"What time do you *think* it is?"

"I asked first."

"Almost seven o'clock."

"Shit."

"I was driving to town. I couldn't believe you were still sitting here."

I rubbed my eyes. "God, I'm tired."

"Where are you staying?"

"I have a charming little apartment at the Project."

"Do you feel well enough to drive there?"

"Yeah, but I don't want to."

"Why not?"

"They might not let me out again."

"Are you serious?"

"Not really."

"It's hard to tell with you."

"Did they take care of Buddy okay?"

"Yes."

I looked at her, and saw an attractive woman of thirty-five or so with light blue eyes.

"You better follow me back to my house. Besides, you forgot your shirt."

"That's right," I said.

I parked my car in the detached garage and stowed the keys under the visor. The Project had given me the car, but it was strictly for publicity purposes and day trips. We Eyes were supposed to have the right stuff.

There was a guest room with a twin bed and a window that admitted a refreshing breeze. I removed my shoes and lay on the bed and listened to hear if she picked up the phone, listened for the sound of her voice calling the Project. She would know people there, have numbers. Former associates of her husband. I closed my eyes, assuming the next face I saw would be that of a Project security type.

It wasn't.

When I opened my eyes the room was suffused with soft lamplight. Kim stood in the doorway.

"I have your pills," she said, showing me the little silver case.

"It's okay. I won't need another one until tomorrow."

She studied me.

"Really," I said. "Just one a day."

"What would have happened if I hadn't found you?"

"I would have sat there until somebody else saw me, and if no one else happened by, I would have gone on sitting there until doomsday. Mine, at any rate."

"Did you mean it when you said the Project people wouldn't let you leave again?"

I thought about my answer. "It's not an overt threat. They'd like to get another session out of me. I think they're a little desperate for results."

"Results equal funding, my husband used to say."

"Right."

"My husband was depressed about the lack of life."

I sat up on the bed, rubbing my arms, which felt goosebumpy in spite of the warmth.

"How did he die?" I asked.

"A tumor in his brain. It was awful. Toward the end he was in constant pain. They medicated him heavily. He didn't even know me anymore." She looked away. "I'm afraid I got a little desperate myself after he died. But I'm stronger now."

"Why do you live out here all by yourself?"

"It's my home. If I want a change there's a cottage up in Oregon, Cannon Beach. But I'm used to being left on my own."

"Used to it?"

"It seems to be a theme in my life."

It was also a statement that begged questions, and I asked them over coffee in the front room. Her parents were killed in a car accident when Kim was fourteen. Her aunt raised her, but it was an awkward relationship.

"I felt more like an imposition than a niece."

And then, of course, there was Mr. Pham and the brain tumor. When she finished, something inside me whimpered to get out but I wouldn't let it.

"Sometimes, I think I'd prefer to be an Eye," Kim said.

"Trust me, you wouldn't."

"Why not?" She was turned to the side, facing me on the couch we shared, one leg drawn up and tucked under, her face alive, eyes questing.

"I already told you: Because you'd have to die."

"I thought that was you being metaphorical."

I shook my head, patted the case of pills now replaced in the cargo pocket of my pants.

"I'm in these pills," I said. "The 'me' you're now talking to. But it isn't the me I left behind when I climbed into the Tank." I sipped my coffee. "There's no official line on that, by the way. It's just my personal theory."

"It's kind of neurotic."

"Kind of."

"I don't even think you really believe it."

I shrugged. "That's your prerogative."

For a while we didn't talk.

"It does get lonely out here sometimes," Kim said.

"Yes."

Her bedroom was nicer than the guest room. With the lights out, she dialed to transparency three of the walls and the ceiling, and it was like lying out in the open with a billion stars overhead and the trees waving at us. I touched her naked belly and kissed her. Time unwound deliciously, but eventually wound back up tight as a watch spring and resumed ticking.

We lay on our backs, staring up, limbs entwined. The stars wheeled imperceptibly. I couldn't see Tau Boo, and that was fine with me.

"Why did you do it, then?" she asked.

"Because it felt good. Plus, you seemed to be enjoying yourself as well."

"Not that. Why did you want to be an Eye."

"Oh. I wanted to see things that no one else could see, ever. I wanted to travel farther than it was possible for a man physically to travel. Pure ego. Which is slightly ironic."

"Worth it?"

I thought of things, the weird aquamarine sky of the fourth planet, the texture of nitrogen-heavy atmosphere. Those quicksilver pools. But I also recalled the ripping away of my personality, and how all those wonders in my mind's eye were like something I'd read about or seen pictures of—unless I went off the pill and allowed myself to become pregnant with chaos. Then it was all real and all indistinguishable, without meaning.

"No," I said, "it wasn't worth it."

"When I think about it," Kim said, "it feels like escape."

"There's that too, yes."

In the morning, I kissed her bare shoulder while she slept. I traced my fingers lightly down her arm, pausing at the white scars on her wrist. She woke up and pulled her arm away. I kissed her neck, and we made love again.

Later, I felt disinclined to return to the Project compound and equally disinclined to check in, which I was required to do.

"Why don't you stay here," Kim said.

It sounded good. I swallowed my daily dose of personality with my first cup of coffee. In fact, I made a habit of it every morning I woke up lying next to Kim. Some nights, we fell asleep having neglected to dial the walls back to opacity, and I awakened with the vulnerable illusion that we were outdoors. Once, I felt like I was being watched, and when I opened my eyes, I saw a doe observing us from the lawn.

I began to discover my health and some measure of happiness that I hadn't previously known. Before, always, I'd been a loner. Kim's story was essentially my story, with variations. It was partly what had driven me to the Tau Boo Project. But for those two weeks, living with Kim Pham, I wasn't alone, not in the usual sense. This was something new in my world. It was good. But it could also give me that feeling I had when I woke up in the open with something wild watching me.

One morning, the *last* morning, I woke up in our indoor-outdoor bedroom and found Kim weeping. Her back was to me, her face buried in her pillow. Her shoulders made little hitching movements with her sobs. I touched her hair.

"What's wrong?"

Her voice muffled by the pillow, she said, "I can't stand any more leaving."

"Hey—"

She turned into me, her eyes red from crying. "I *mean* it," she said. "I couldn't stand any more."

I held her tightly while the sun came up.

At the breakfast table I opened the little silver pill case. There were only three pills left. I took one with my first cup of dark French roast. Kim stared at the open case before I snapped it shut.

"You're almost out," she said.

"Yeah."

"Robert, it's not like what you said. Those pills aren't you. They allow you to feel, that's all. You can't always be afraid."

I contemplated my coffee.

"Listen," she said. "I used to be envious of Eyes. No more pain, no more loneliness, no more fear. Life with none of the messiness of living. But I was wrong. That isn't life at all. This is. What we have."

"So I'll get more pills." I smiled.

Only it wasn't like a trip to the local pharmacy. There was only one place to obtain the magic personality drug: The Project. I decided I should go that day, that there was no point in waiting for my meager supply to run out.

Kim held onto me like somebody clinging to a pole in a hurricane.

"I'll come with you," she said.

"They won't let you past the gate."

"I don't care. I'll wait outside then."

We took her car. She parked across the street. We embraced awkwardly in the front seat. I was aware of the guard watching us.

"You've hardly told me anything personal about yourself," she said. "And here I've told you all my secret pain."

"Maybe I don't have any secret pain."

"You wouldn't be human if you didn't."

"I'll spill my guts when I come out. Promise."

She didn't want to let go, but I was ready to leave. I showed the guard my credentials and he passed me through. I turned and waved to Kim.

"She's a pretty one," the guard said.

I sat in a room. They relieved me of my pill case. I was "debriefed" by a young man who behaved like an automaton, asking questions, checking off my answers on his memorypad. Where had I spent the last two weeks? Why had I failed to communicate with the Project? Did I feel depressed, anxious? Some questions I answered, some I ignored.

"I just want more pills," I said. "I'll check in next time, cross my heart."

A man escorted me to the medical wing, where I underwent a thorough and pointless physical examination. When it was over, Orley Campbell, assistant director of the Tau Boo Project, sat down to chat while we awaited the results of various tests.

"So our stray lamb has returned to the fold," he said. Orley was a tall man with a soft face and the beginnings of a potbelly. I didn't like him.

"Baaa," I said.

"Same old Bobbie."

"Yep, same old me. When do I get out of here?"

"This isn't a jail. You're free to leave any time you wish."

"What about my pills?"

"You'll get them, don't worry about that. You owe us one more session, you know."

"I know."

"Are you having misgivings? I've looked over your evaluation. You appear somewhat depressed."

"I'm not in the least bit depressed."

"Aren't you? I wish I could say the same."

"What time is it? How long have I been here, Orley?"

"Oh, not long. Bobbie, why not jump right back on the horse? If you'd like to relax for a couple of weeks more, that's absolutely not a problem. You just have to remember to check in. I mean, that's part of the drill, right? You knew that when you signed on."

I thought about Kim waiting outside the gate. Would she still be there? Did I even want her to be? I could feel my consciousness spreading thin. Orley kept smiling at me. "I guess I'm ready," I said.

A month is a long time to exist in the Tank. Of course, as an Eye, you are unaware of passing hours. You inhabit a sensory world at the far end of a tachyon tether. I've looked at romanticized illustrations of this. The peaceful dreamer at one end, the industrious robot on the other. In between, the data flows along an ethereal cord of light. Blah. They keep you alive intravenously, maintain hydration, perform body waste removal. A device sucks out the data. It's fairly brutal.

I recouped in the medical wing for several days. I had my pills and a guarantee of more, all I would require. I had put in the maximum Tank time and could not return without suffering serious and permanent brain damage.

My marathon Tank session had yielded zip in terms of the Project's primary goal. The fourth planet was dead.

Now I would have money and freedom and a future, *if* I wanted one. I spent my hours reading, thinking about warm climates. Kim Pham rapped on my memory, but I wouldn't open the door.

A week after my retrieval, I insisted on being released from the medical wing, and nobody put up an argument. I'd served my purpose. Orley caught up to me as I was leaving the building. I was hobbling on my weak legs, carrying my belongings in a shoulder bag. Orley picked up my hand and shook it.

"Good luck to you," he said. "What's first on the agenda, a little 'Eye candy'?"

I wasn't strong enough to belt him. He looked morose and tired, which is approximately the way I felt myself. When I didn't reply he went on:

"Cruising a little close to home last time, weren't you? That Pham woman was persistent. She came around every day for two weeks straight. Nice-looking, but older than the others. I guess you would get tired of the young ones after a while."

The smirk is what did it. I found some ambition and threw a decent punch that bloodied his nose.

A cab picked me up at the gate. On impulse, I switched intended destinations. Instead of the airport, I provided sketchy directions, and we managed to find Kim's house without too much difficulty.

The house had an abandoned look, or at least I thought so. A mood can color things, though, and my mood was gloomy. The desperation of the Tau Boo Project had rubbed off on me. There was no life on the fourth planet, no life on any of the planets that had thus far been explored by our human Eyes. When the receiver craft were launched decades previously, it was with a sense of great purpose and hope. But so far, the known universe had not proved too lively, which only made our own Earth feel isolated, lonely—doomed even.

The windows of Kim's house were all black. I knocked, waited, knocked again. I knew where she hid the spare key, on a hook under the back porch.

The house was silent. Every surface was filmed with dust. I drifted through the hollow rooms like a ghost.

Gone.

I pictured all the ways, all the ugly ways she might have departed this world. Of course, there was no evidence that she had done anything of the sort. An empty house did not necessarily add up to a terminated life. Probably I was giving myself too much credit. But the gloom was upon me. I could see the white scars on her wrists.

I sat on the carpeted floor of the master bedroom, still weak from the Tank. Hunger gnawed at me, but I didn't care. I let time unravel around the tightening in my chest, and, as darkness fell, I dialed the walls and ceiling clear, and lay on my back, and let exhausted sleep take me.

Lack of nourishment inhibits the efficacy of the pill. In the morning, I opened my eyes to dark predawn and a point of reference that was rapidly growing muddy. The pills were in my bag, but my interest in digging them out was not very great. Why not let it all go? Become the fiber in the rug, the glass, the pulse of blood in my own veins. Why not?

I lay still and began to lose myself. I watched the dark blue sky pale toward dawn. At some point, the blue attained a familiar shade. Kim cradling her dead dog, the fierceness of her eyes. *I can manage.*

A sharp bubble of emotion formed in my throat, and I couldn't swallow it down. So I rolled over. Because maybe I could manage it, too. Maybe. I reached for my bag, my mind growing rapidly diffuse. The interesting articulation of my finger joints distracted me: Bone sleeved within soft flesh, blood circulating, finger pads palpating the tight fibers of the rug. Time passed. I shook myself, groped forward, touched the bag, forgot why it was so important, flickeringly remembered, got my hand on the case, fingered a pill loose onto the rug, belly-crawled, absently scanning details, little yellow pill nestled in fibers, extend probe (tongue), and swallow.

One personality pill with lint chaser.

I came around slowly, coalescing back into the mundane world, an empty stomach retarding the absorption process. Eventually, I stood up. First order of business: food. I found some stale crackers in a kitchen cabinet. Ambrosia. Standing at the sink, gazing out the window, I saw the garage. I stopped chewing, the crackers like crumbled cardboard in my mouth. I'd thought of ropes and drugs and razors. But what about exhaust?

I walked toward the garage, my breathing strangely out of sync. I stopped to gather my courage or whatever it was I'd need to proceed.

Then I opened the door.

There was one car in the double space. My Mitsubishi, still parked as I'd left it. I climbed into the unlocked car and checked for the keys under the visor. They fell into my lap, note attached. From Kim.

It wasn't a suicide note.

Copyright © 2003 by Jack Skillingstead

Ralph Roberts is a jack of all trades in the lit biz. He has written and sold more than 100 books, has sold 4 screenplays, and as a publisher he has produced more than 300 titles. And if that isn't enough, he also runs an annual film festival.

THE ORPHAN TRACTORS

by Ralph Roberts

Rain slashed down through lush foliage on the jungle planet Gamu. In the distance, one of the giant trees, roots unable to hold in the mud, crashed to the ground. Wind whipped the trees and undergrowth back and forth. Lightning flashed, thunder cracked.

In the only town, called Gamuville, Bobby Campbell splashed through a third major puddle on his short run from the rusty taxibot to the tractor dealership's entrance with his one piece of luggage. Quite an impression he would make, his only formal business coveralls mud-splattered, hair plastered to his head.

Running toward him through the rain was Master Salesman Oliver Schmid, formerly supreme representative of the Field King Atomic Tractor Company in this sector but now that was Bobby's punishment. Bobby started to introduce himself but Schmid slowed only enough to push some key cubes into his hand.

Schmid muttered, "It's all yours." He dashed off rapidly to catch the taxibot, great gouts of water spewing up as his feet pounded through the muddy puddles.

He watched Schmid get into the taxibot and leave. A police hovercar slid by slowly in the other direction. He'd seen only those two vehicles since leaving the starport, not much action happening around here.

Bobby looked at the wet front of the dealership. Water coursed down its walls. Mold, moss, and unidentified vegetation clung to the walls and obscured the Field King logo of a stylized tractor in a field with a crown over it.

Clumps of something orange and thick slowly slid down the plasticlear of the door *on the inside.*

He now remembered the same glop being in Oliver Schmid's hair.

Soaked, Bobby looked sadly at his new kingdom. Once the Chief Engineer of Field King's main plant on New California and indeed of the whole company, he was now a mere sales representative. Okay, a Master Salesman, but it was that or lose his employment entirely.

Of course, "sales" was not really a part of it. His instructions were to sell or scrap the inventory as quickly as possible. Do that and they might, just might, have another assignment for him.

The door automatically slid aside and he stepped through it.

Blap!

A flimsy bulb of orange glop burst against his chest, adding a colorful but runny highlight to his already filthy suit. The vending machine in one corner of the huge showroom lay on its side, contents spilled onto the dirty floor with tractor tracks in random profusion.

Engines roared, lights strobed, beeps sounded as big red tractors and other farm equipment cavorted around the room. One of the tractors—a boxy affair with no cab or seat for human control—picked up another bulb of what Bobby now recognized as Orange Shako with a manipulator arm and cocked back to throw it, then suddenly stopped.

"Daddy!" it yelled in delight with a two-year-old's shrill tones and not an inside voice either.

The other machines—there were a total of five although they had sounded like a lot more as they wheeled and zoomed around the showroom—also rocked to a stop.

"It's Daddy!" another screamed, raising and lowering the bucket of its front-end loader in glee.

"Daddy, we in trouble," the seeder said.

"We need help," came from the fueler up near the ceiling. Fuelers didn't have wheels, they had antigrav and floated out to feed the tractors in the field more energy so that they could keep working all day and all night.

"6F is down in the dark mud, he scared!" the seeder said.

Bobby let his bag drop to the floor. Autonomous tractors—he was in trouble! He sighed. The very reason he no longer had an engineering position and was exiled out here to the backside of nowhere—that was his punishment for creating them.

He held up his hands to shush the chattering pieces of farm equipment. It worked but he knew it would not last for long.

"Let me get situated and I'll solve your problem. Ah … where is my office?"

A2291A-W, the tractor with the front-end loader, waved a manipulator arm toward a door on the back wall. Lettering on the door read "Oliver Schmid, Manager"—or did so as much as he could tell through all the splatters of Orange Shako.

Bobby sighed. What a dump. How the mighty had fallen. Now why was this place so filthy? He looked around and saw a couple of cleaning bots hiding under a display. Ah ha, they were afraid to clean while tractors might roll over them—very smart little machines.

"First, let's have an inspection," he said, his tone firm.

"Daddy—" the machine he thought of as 1A started in a plaintive voice. The convention used by Field King employees to refer to the machines was the last number of their serial and the letter of their model designation—every sentient being needed a name.

"Now!" he said.

With a clashing of gears, engines revving, and beeps of backup warnings, four pieces of massive agricultural equipment jockeyed around and backed into their display spots. Colorful signs hung over each, detailing their purpose and specs.

"You, too," Bobby said, pointing a finger at the floating fueler.

The fueler sulkily wafted down from the ceiling and hovered in its spot.

Bobby looked them over. The "A" at the beginning of all their serial numbers stood for "Autonomous," his brainchildren. The numbers were their serial and "[letter]-W" their model and specialization, "W" for "Wheat."

He didn't question the fact they were on a jungle world where maybe some log skidders might be saleable. He knew Field King was hiding the machines anywhere they could and cooking the books to make up for the biggest blunder in the company's history.

Yeah, they blamed him—but he'd told them the concept needed more development and not to rush the autonomous tractors into production!

"Daddy," 2B, the seeder, tried again, "6F is—"

"In a minute," Bobby said, standing and looking at them with hands on his hips.

They were autonomous but with the intellect of human two-year-olds, and also possessing a bunch of other 'terrible twos' traits. Like the rebellious sniffling going on right now from a couple of them.

Autonomous machines were not robots—those common servants of these past several centuries. You *programmed* robots and, while they exhibited varying degrees of artificial intelligence, the underlying code from human programmers guided them.

These babies were not artificially intelligent—they were truly sentient. Like humans, they required training, the instilling of morality, and everything else that human infants had to learn. No built-in Three Laws of Robotics like that old scientist Asimov had formulated—you had to teach them right from wrong. Proper training took longer than the company was willing to wait.

If you toss thousands of these self-centered brats out into the galaxy before they're ready, you achieve as many torn up farms and a once respected old company like Field King driven to the edge of bankruptcy. *Yes*, he had warned his bosses!

"1A," Bobby said, trying to moderate his tone a little, "where are the other people?"

"Mean old Oliver fired them, said the company was broke."

Great—no sales people, no mechanics, no admin, no finance, no parts clerks, no—

"Daddy?" 1A prompted.

Bobby took a deep breath and started to ask what the problem was with 6F when a woman's voice interrupted his thoughts.

"Excuse me. I have an appointment."

Bobby quickly turned around to find a young woman in form-fitting wheat-colored coveralls with utility pouches on her belt. He was glad to see that the torrential rains of Gamu had left her as bedraggled as him. Although the mud on her coveralls did not stand out as badly as on his white and—

"Hi pretty lady," 2B said.

4D made an appreciative whistle. These guys might have the mentality of two-year-olds but they were smart and sophisticated two-year-olds, even if having about the same maturity.

Bobby found her far beyond "pretty" and struggled to say something … something witty and yet endearing that would impress her and—

She was impatient. "I'm Proprietor Anna Holm, Paradise Hills Farms, planet of Wheat's Glory."

Bobby swallowed. The words "Paradise Hills" were on the coveralls above her left breast, how very descriptive and—

She looked around the showroom. "Did the storm get in here? What a mess!" Then, glaring directly at him, "Are you Oliver Schmid?"

"Ah, no—are you here to buy a tractor?" he asked, hoping against hope.

Anna snorted. "I am secretary of the Wheat Growers Association. Mr. Schmid convinced us the Field King autonomous tractors were the answer to our problem. He promised us several hundred units."

Bobby suddenly tasted instant redemption. It was delicious. "… Er … Yes. Mr. Schmid is no longer with us but I can certainly help. First, let me explain how the tractors—"

"No need for that," she said, "Mr. Schmid kindly sent me a memory cube by their creator, Doctor Robert Campbell—it was very succinct. We are sold."

"Ah, I'm Doctor Robert Campbell but call me Bobby."

Her eyebrows rose and she again surveyed the wrecked showroom.

"But you were Chief Engineer of the entire company."

"Daddy got *de-moted*," 3C said.

Bobby glared at him and no more helpful comments came from the equipment.

"Ah, I was offered a field position," he said. What a disastrous start to impressing the most attractive female he'd met in years.

She snorted again. "I see you've got most of the models we're interested in lined up. Introduce me, if you will."

"Ah, yes … of course. May I call you 'Anna'?"

"No. Proceed."

Sinking fast here, Bobby, he told himself.

He indicated 1A.

"This is the first machine in our six-unit wheat series."

Anna looked down the line. "I see only five and a big empty spot."

Bobby loosened the collar of his soiled suit. "I'll get to that in a minute, just got here myself."

She looked down at the muddy piece of luggage by his feet. "Evidently—get on with it."

"Yes. This is the 'A' unit. Its purpose is multifold. Note the front-end loader, one of many attachments available and the manipulator arms—all six models in the wheat unit have manipulator arms. This one performs everything from removing rocks and stumps to pulling a grain wagon during harvest—a jack-of-all-trades. Just tell it what needs doing."

"My name's 1A," 1A said, "and I like you. Are you going to be our mommy?"

Now it was Anna's turn to be flustered. "Er …"

Bobby smiled. "You'll need to be a mother figure to complete their training."

"No!" 1A said. "Daddy needs to find a Mommy so we have two parents now that he's found us again."

He quickly beckoned her to move on to the next machine—another big boxy tractor with huge hoppers on top.

"2B is a seeder and can plant huge fields in a matter of a few hours. He also dispenses fertilizer, anti-weed chemicals, and so forth—and pulls a grain wagon at harvest time. Basically, except for our refueling solution, all units double as regular tractors of varying sizes."

2B giggled shyly when Anna smiled at the tractor. Bobby found himself yearning for her to smile at *him* like that.

They moved along to the huge 3C, which towered above them.

"The combine unit harvests the wheat when ready. He's quick, too, and it takes all four of the other tractors to keep a stream of grain wagons coming."

She looked at the hologram, part of the descriptive sign above the unit. It showed a combine trundling at high speed through an endless wheat field, a golden stream of grain filling wagons as fast as the tractors could get them underneath its spout.

"No human intervention needed," Bobby said, "as you will note there are no seats or cabs on these first three models."

Anna looked awed with the machines—another look Bobby would give a lot to see directed his way. He didn't need sales experience to see she was in a buying mood.

In the corner of his eye, out though the showroom window, Bobby saw the same police hovercar from earlier cruise by again. He didn't mention it, continuing with his sales spiel.

"Here's 4D, our refueling solution and the only unit not on a tractor chassis."

They looked at the fueler, a big tank floating just above the floor. There was a rudimentary seat and handholds on its top but no controls at all.

"The seat is for if you need to get out into the field to check on one of the other machines or just to look at how the crop's coming along," Bobby said. "It's fun to fly around on, too."

"Zoom, zoom!" 4D agreed.

They walked to the last machine.

"There are two really big tractors completing the unit," he told her. "5E is actually the smaller of the two, 6F is—"

"6F is in the gooey dark, Daddy. He wants out," 5E said.

Bobby held up his hand. "In a moment, 5E. … Ah, note he does have a cab for convenience of riding along in all sorts of weather. Air-conditioned and heated and with a complete entertainment center. Slightly smaller than the 'F' model—it has extra power for plowing. The 'E' is optimized for harrowing and cultivation, although the 'F' assists in those tasks, too."

"So, where is this last machine?"

"6F wants you to rescue him, Daddy, before he runs out of energy."

"I'll check," Bobby assured him.

He looked at Anna and shrugged. "Let's go into the office and discuss your order and I'll find out what happened to the other tractor."

"Hurry, Daddy!" 3C yelled as Bobby picked up his bag and they went toward the office door.

✧

Schmid's office was as messy as the showroom. It was small and cramped even more by clutter. A holographic computer terminal in standby mode was fighting a losing battle for room on the littered desk.

A chair behind the desk showed signs of wear but the visitor's seat in front seemed little used. Trash decorated the floor; a cot with unmade bedding crookedly paralleled the back wall. Against a side wall were stacked boxes of cheap food and carton upon carton of Orange Shako. Looked like Schmid had been living here, too—times were hard.

"Guess he liked Orange Shako," Bobby said.

"Can't abide that crap," Anna said.

"Me either," Bobby replied, hoping they had finally found a point in common.

She looked at the orange stain on the front of his once-formal coveralls. "Yeah?"

Bobby brushed crumbs and stuff off the seat of Schmid's chair, sat, and motioned her to the visitor's chair. She looked at it in distaste but gingerly lowered herself onto it.

Looking out the big window on the office's front wall into the showroom, he saw the tractors moving around, trying to peer into the office. Bobby made an emphatic pointing motion with one hand and they reluctantly returned to their display spots.

Bobby sighed and looked down at the desktop. Schmid had left a steno pad on which were a brief resignation and the computer password. He activated the dealership's computer, logged in, and scrolled through the records appearing in midair with hand gestures.

"Uuuuuph … Only one sale made this whole year. Three days ago."

Anna nodded. "6F, right?"

"Yeah, sold to a logging company—on credit, down payment deposit bounced, no other payment recorded. Schmid did not attempt repossession. Poor kid, he'd be lost at logging. Only knows wheat farming."

Anna leaned forward, finally showing a little interest in him. "The ones out there seem very glad to see you. Do you remember them?"

Bobby smiled. "Vaguely, but I trained hundreds."

"They love you," she said, as if in deep thought.

"Okay, I need to find out what's happening with 6F and get him back," Bobby said, trying for a more businesslike tone. "Let's help you first, however. You're looking for a wheat unit?"

"First, what's your experience with wheat farming?" It was obvious Schmid had none.

Bobby sat up straight and spread his hands expansively—he was on firm ground here, so to speak.

"I was born and raised on New Kansas. Corn, cattle, lots and lots of wheat—our farm was fifteen thousand acres of wheat. I know wheat."

Anna relaxed and crossed her legs, Bobby regretting the desk kept him from really seeing it.

"So, why did you leave the farm and become an engineer?"

Bobby shrugged. "I was the fifth of five boys. The others wanted to stay. We had some old Field King tractors I kept running. My parents sent me off to university on a Field King scholarship to learn all about designing better tractors. … I do miss the farm life though."

Anna's smile was warmer now.

Bobby returned it. "So, you want to buy some tractors? I can make you a deal today on this unit. I'll either retrieve 6F or find you the same model in our inventory. Can I write you up for one unit or more?"

"Several hundred units, actually," Anna said, grinning as Bobby's mouth fell open in shock. "You should have Mr. Schmid's quote there."

Bobby swallowed hard and flipped through the correspondence folder floating over the computer. There it was! A *three hundred million credit* quote! Notes in the file showed all the details of pulling the units from scores of dealerships across the galaxy and shipping instructions to Wheat's Glory.

All he had to do was enter the sale with cash payment in advance since their credit was not sufficient. A returned message from Anna accepted these terms and related she and the treasurer of her organization, a certain Roman Kucharski, were on the way, bringing enough credit blocks for payment in full!

Moreover, the Master Salesman's commission was ten percent. *Thirty million credits!* He could retire and buy a farm somewhere, like Wheat's Glory maybe and—

"Why do you need so many?" he asked.

"Do you know where Wheat's Glory is?"

Bobby brought up a galactic map on the computer, nudging the display of it around where they could both see it and zoomed it down to show the right area.

Anna pointed. "We're in the Earth Federation but in that narrow arm between the Aleph Empire and the Hegemony of Soujudu, which were recently at war."

"Short war," Bobby said. "The Federation forced them to end hostilities in quick order."

"Yes," Anna said, "But we got all our farm laborers from Aleph—lots of overpopulation there and they work really cheaply—and both the Hegemony and the Aleph Empire bought lots of our wheat as well as the Federation markets. We are *very* profitable when we can grow wheat."

Bobby smiled encouragingly.

"So," she continued, "When war broke out the Aleph Navy surged through and conscripted all our laborers. Then the Hegemony pushed back, taking all our machinery on the way through since they needed scrap for their war effort and—"

"The Federation came in and stopped it all, leaving you without labor or tractors?"

Anna sighed. "Not only that but the Feds won't let the laborers return and are not pushing the Hegemony, which was broke to begin with, to reimburse us for the equipment they took."

"But we had lots of credits. I read an article about Field King's autonomous tractors. They were the answer to our problem! Tractors that did not need farm workers to run them and get the harvest in. I contacted the nearest dealership. And here I am."

A sizzle like ice water dousing a flame was suddenly inside his head. Why had Schmid run away in such haste from a deal like that?

"Ah …"

She slumped, suddenly dejected, gazing down at her clasped hands. "Well … soon after we arrived two weeks ago I had to tell Mr. Schmid that we no longer had the funds for payment."

"But he already had authorized some shipments."

Anna groaned. "He was very upset and, I could see, scared."

"No wonder they sent me so quickly," he said, "What happened?"

She looked up, angry now. "That cretin Kucharski spent most of the trip here on the starliner trying to hit on me. Then, as soon as we landed, he grabbed some logger's personal truck and took off with the credit bars."

Bobby immediately understood. Hackers kept financial transactions via faster-than-light radio unreliable. So shipping physical credit bars between worlds was the best means of moving large sums. However, the normal practice was to use the bank's heavily armed and bonded couriers rather than lug it around personally.

"He made off with the entire three hundred million?"

Anna sighed. "Yes, we had high denomination bars for ease of transport. A good-sized case but one person could carry it."

"Where was he going? This is the only town on Gamu—nothing out there but muddy logging roads?"

"He was pretty stupid. I called the police. After forcing me to pay them what ready funds I possessed, they took off in immediate pursuit. Some short time later, they caught up with him.

"It was at the bottom of a hill in a sharp curve. He lost control. The truck skidded, sailed into the air, and sank into a mudflat. No retrieval possible; those things are sometimes bottomless."

Bobby nodded. "So Kucharski is dead then?"

"No such luck. He jumped and the police have him in jail, but the funds are gone. The police also tried to charge me for his upkeep in jail! Corrupt sons of—"

"I'm sorry, Proprietor Holm—"

"Oh, call me 'Anna'," she said, calming down but dejected.

"Right, ah, Anna. … There is nothing I can do—the tractors en route now will surely be cancelled since payment has not been made."

She moved her head miserably in understanding.

Bobby stood. "In the meantime, I need to take care of the 6F problem."

He grabbed his bag and put it on the desk, waving his hand to undo the locks. Anna, curious, leaned over to see what he carried. Not so many clothes but various gadgets—well, he was an engineer after all.

Anna gasped in surprise as Bobby took out an energy weapon and put it in his belt.

"I *am* going out into the jungle," he said, and got out two devices, placing them in his belt pouch.

She got to her feet also.

"I want to help," she said, "I need to feel like I'm accomplishing something."

"Sure," Bobby said. "Yes, good idea."

She opened one of her utility pouches and showed him a nasty-looking palm-sized blaster.

"Girl has to have protection," she said.

Bobby nodded and hesitated a moment. "Er, later, I could, ah, maybe buy you dinner?"

It looked like her reflex was to say "no" but she shrugged. "Sure, why not?"

Bobby beamed. "Okay, let me see about 6F and—"

She smiled at him and it was a real smile.

In the showroom, Anna told the tractors a children's story—the one about the little rocket that could. They loved it, giggling and begging for more.

Meanwhile Bobby made several trips back to the parts department. Most of the equipment went into a large durasteel box with a lid. He finally brought out a huge heavy-duty winch on an antigravity flat and pushed it up to 5E.

"Put this on, big guy," he said.

5E deftly used his manipulator arms to attach the winch to his front and plugged its power cord into one of his auxiliary power sockets. He gave it a brief test, playing out and retrieving the big hook on the end of the cable.

Bobby patted him. Then he looked at 5E again and indicated the box. 5E rolled over, picked it up, and clicked it in place on his rear.

"You see," Bobby said, grinning at Anna, "All sorts of useful attachments and accessories—standard with the wheat unit, by the way."

"How do you know we'll need the winch?"

"If the kids here say 6F is down in a dark place then he is and we'll have to pull him out. We're taking 5E to do the heavy work and 4D because as a fueler he has the circuits to locate the other tractors precisely."

"Okay, I'm impressed," Anna said, "You make things happen."

"Ah, you sure you want to go along? We'll be riding in 5E's one-person cab. It'll be kind of crowded."

"I can stand that," she said and gave him another smile.

My! Things were looking up.

"Okay," Bobby said, "1A, 2B, 3C—we're off to rescue 6F. 1A, you are in charge and you *will* let the cleaning bots out from under the displays and help them clean this place."

1A tried to argue. "Aww, we want to—"

"No!"

"Mommy, Daddy won't let us—"

"Clean! Story time when we get back," Anna promised.

With that, Bobby and Anna squeezed into 5E's minimal cab, the big equipment access door slid up, and 5E trundled out into the rain with 4D floating in the lead.

Sheets of wind-driven water surged across the street as they headed for the edge of town. That was a short trip—the entire town was seven or eight blocks long and the dealership only a block from the jungle's edge.

The police car from before swung out of a parking spot and followed along behind until the edge of the jungle loomed. Then it turned and rapidly headed back into town.

Bobby and Anna, with Anna quite pleasantly wedged into Bobby's lap, were watching through the back window of the tractor cab.

"Someone seems to be taking an interest in us," Anna said.

Turning his head, Bobby saw the pavement end as 5E entered the tunnel of trees and underbrush marking the rudimentary logging road. It was not much more than a trail and 5E skidded briefly on the slick surface then gained traction again.

Bobby opened a small storage area and handed Anna a communicator button. They clipped the buttons to their collars.

"Sorry, Daddy," the tractor said, his voice coming through the communicator, "Lots of dirty old mud."

Bobby looked out the back again.

"The police are not following us in here."

"They don't go out in the jungle unless they have to," Anna answered, "and the fact they bother watching us at all indicates they still hope for some gain."

"Smart police work, not going out into this mess, I'd say."

5E and 4D had bright lights on so whatever animals lurked out there saw two small suns moving through the dank forest.

"Powerful work lights on the wheat unit," he said. "They can work all night, no matter how dark it gets."

Anna squirmed around on his lap trying to get comfortable in the cramped cab.

"Powerful," Bobby said, trying to keep his mind on the rescue.

✿

Soon enough they came to the portion of the logging trail down the hill to the sharp curve with the steep bank overlooking the mud flat. 5E needed no warning to be careful. He inched down the hill, staying as far from the mudflat side as possible, stopping just before the curve, the expanse of the mud flat to his front.

4D, floating along, had no such worries. He zoomed out over the mud flat and slowed to hover over a spot not all that far from the bank, directly in front of them.

"6F is down there, Daddy," he piped through their communicators.

"That would be an exact position then?" Anna asked.

"Yes, fuelers locate tractors precisely," Bobby said.

In the curve, there were still signs where both 6F and the truck Kucharski was in had broken down small trees in their skids over the bank and into the mud.

"6F, are you here?" Bobby called.

"Daddy! Yes! 6F way down in the mud and can't find the way out, bank too steep under here."

"Hold on, big fellow. It won't be long now."

"Thanks, Daddy," said the voice of 6F. "I loves you, Daddy."

"And me loves Daddy, too!" said 1A over the radio link from back in the dealership. The other tractors and 4D all chimed in as well.

Anna looked at Bobby, a hint of tears in her eyes, and then out over the mud flat in the driving rain. "I really hope you can do this, Bobby."

Bobby smiled at her. "We're both going to get really muddy and wet but I have a plan. Now, as much as I like you in my lap, we have things to set up."

They climbed down from the cab. Anna's feet almost went out from under her on the road's slick surface but Bobby steadied her.

Then Bobby called 4D to float over to where he was opening the durasteel box on 5E's rear. He first took a small device from his belt pouch and attached it to 4D's underside.

"Take this," he said, hauling a large pulley out of the box. "Attach it to the limb of that big tree over there and come back here."

4D used his manipulator arms to take the pulley and flew to the tree. While 4D was on his way, Bobby pulled another device from his pouch and looked at its screen.

"Three-dimensional ground penetrating radar," he explained to Anna, "Ah ha, that's a relief. Not very deep here—if 6F puts up a manipulator arm, it will be above the surface."

"You must have some other really interesting devices in that bag," Anna observed.

"Well … ah … I spent time in Naval Intelligence before going to work for Field King. Still design the occasional gadget for them."

"Smart men really turn me on," Anna said, wiping rain from her face.

Bobby grinned. *Wow! Was he making progress or what?*

Anna looked around at the mud and soaked jungle. "Doubt I'll find any out here, though."

"Uh, yeah," Bobby said, properly deflated.

While 4D was hanging the pulley, Bobby had 5E back up enough to have room to pull 6F out of the mud. 5E helped him pull two thick cables and heavy-duty clamps from the box and attach them behind the tractor to sturdy trees on both sides of the road. Then he had 5E pull the cables taut, anchoring the tractor in place.

5E revved his powerful engine a couple of times. "Ready to get 6F out of the dark place, Daddy," he said.

4D came back and Bobby gave him the end of the cable from the winch on the front of 5E, which had a large hook attached. He instructed 4E to run the cable over the pulley.

4E did so and again hovered over where 6F lay beneath the surface of the mud flat.

Anna rubbed rain from her eyes and surveyed the rig, looking at the anchor cables and the pulley high in the tree.

"Think it will work?" Bobby asked.

"Of course it will," Anna said. "… If these trees hold and the cable does not break and …"

She saw the look on Bobby's face and stepped up to hug him. "It'll work," she said.

He nodded and took a deep breath. "6F, stick one of your arms up and 4D will guide a hook to you. Put the hook into your center lift point."

One of 6F's manipulator arms eagerly broke the surface of the mud and 4D guided the hook into his grasp. The arm and hook disappeared and a moment later 6F said, "Ready, Daddy!"

Bobby made a circling motion with his hand to 5E.

The tractor's engine roared, the trees anchoring him groaned, as did the big tree the pulley swung from. Nothing else happened—there was no movement of the cable.

"6F, spin your wheels and use your manipulator arms to push against the bottom. We need to break the suction!"

Now the cable moved, slowly at first and then a little faster. A very huge and muddy tractor broke out of the mud with a loud sucking sound and into the air, swinging back and forth.

An ominous cracking came from the tree holding the pulley. Before Bobby could give an order, 4D blasted into 6F as he swung toward the bank, giving him an extra boost. As 6F passed over the edge of the bank and was now above the road, 5E suddenly slackened the winch cable.

With a mighty *splat* 6F impacted the road, throwing great gouts of mud on them all. He yanked the hook from the lift point as the tree came apart and fell into the mud flat. 5E reeled the winch cable back in and 4D managed to swoop around the falling tree and snatch the pulley out of midair.

Bobby laughed, wiping mud from his face. He turned to Anna. "You *see*? That's what *autonomous* means. They reacted to the emergency and responded as a team. Robots wouldn't have had a clue."

"They had a smart designer," she said.

6F bashfully moved up a little and stuck out one of his manipulator arms. From it swung a large case.

"The money!" Anna said in awe.

"The meanies who swindled dumb old Schmid into selling me made me go into the dark mud to find this," 6F said and gave it to Bobby.

Bobby put it down and pushed the mud-encrusted case over to Anna. She squatted and opened the lid just enough to peek inside but not let the rain in.

"The credit bars," she said, almost breathless, "Looks like they're all there." She carefully closed the lid and stood up, grinning. "Still want to sell some tractors?"

"Ummm," Bobby said, thinking, "How many cops on the Gamu police force?" as he put the case in the durasteel box on 5E.

"Just three," she said, "and they all have got to be in on this, along with Kucharski. It's an immense amount of money and you can bet Roman's made a deal."

"How many banks are there in town?"

"Just have the one—First Planetary Lumberjacks Bank."

"If we can get the credits deposited, there's nothing they can do."

Anna sighed. "But they'll be guarding the bank to keep us out. With Kucharski, all they have to do is grab the cash, let Roman deposit it, and split the proceeds. Bobby, I don't want to get you or the tractors hurt."

"Problem is, if I can't sell the tractors by next week, they get scrapped," Bobby said. "The order has gone out to the other dealerships. Field King wants out of the autonomous tractor business in the worst way, the idiots. If they'd only let me properly train—"

"No! We can't let that happen to the kids," Anna said.

"That three hundred million buys them all. I'd say we have to get it deposited. Once in the bank, we use their couriers and it's all secure."

"6F don't mind squishing bad men who leave him in dark," 6F said. "Mad about that and being taken away from my brothers."

"Police will have heavy weapons available and they'll arm Kucharski also. That's what I would do."

"Run over like bugs," 5E said.

"Now it occurs to me," Bobby said, tapping his muddy chin in thought with an equally muddy finger, "a smart man, especially one with naval combat experience, still might just be able to slide those credits into the bank."

Anna looked at him for a moment and simply nodded. That meant more than anything that had ever happened to him.

"Okay, let's plan as we go back to town." He looked at 6F's slowly draining mud-filled cab. "5E's cab is so cramped I'll ride in 6F."

"No," Anna said. "Now that I've found a smart man, I want to sit on him so he can't get away."

"Ooooh," 5E said, "Looks like Daddy has found us a Mommy!"

☼

Bobby had sent 4D up through the trees to fly back the fastest way. The fueler had orders for himself, 1A, 2B, and 3C—spelling out their parts in the coming battle.

He and Anna, again scrunched into 5E's cab with 6F lumbering along behind, were almost back to the tree line at the outskirts of Gamuville. Bobby reluctantly slid from under Anna and was now on the outside of the cab in the unrelenting rain, clinging to 5E's side with one hand and looking at the small screen of the device in his hand.

He leaned into the cab and showed it to Anna. "4D is floating over town getting us some good intelligence."

"Only one cop where we come out of the woods?" she asked.

"Poor tactics, that's the choke point, but the rest are close to the bank—guess they're keying on keeping us out for sure if we get by this guy."

"That's a big gun he has, Bobby."

"Model 34 Energy Assault Rifle, same thing our Space Commandos used when I was in the Navy."

"Bobby, I don't think—"

The end of the woods was coming up and they could see the cop outside the vehicle, pointing his rifle at them as they came out of the trees.

"He'll hesitate, won't want to damage the credits." Bobby activated his communicator, "Charge, boys!"

5E and 6F roared out of the woods, splitting and increasing speed as they closed rapidly with the suddenly panicked police officer.

He loosed a bolt of energy as a warning shot over the two careening tractors, but the time for warnings was over. 1A suddenly burst from between two houses, the bucket of his front-end loader full of mud as he came at the cop. The cop, screaming now, whirled and fired at 1A, the dirt and tough stuff of the bucket making the beam harmless.

1A rocked to a stop, raised his bucket, and dumped the load on the cop before he could fire again.

6F skidded around the pile, got traction again, and ran over the police vehicle, pancaking it into the mud.

5E stopped as Bobby slid off, followed by Anna, and ran to the mud pile. He dug into the mess frantically, came out with the energy weapon, and handed it to Anna. Digging a bit more, he pulled the cop out and helped him to his feet, confiscating his sidearm in the process.

The cop took one quick look around at the tractors loudly revving their engines and the two muddy creatures in front of him, then took to his heels toward the lush rain forest.

"One down," Bobby said.

"Three to go," Anna said.

1A didn't wait for further orders but took off into town, as did 6F.

Bobby and Anna climbed back onto 5E. "To the bank but slow," Bobby said.

☼

"This is fun, Daddy!" 5E said as he moved up the street, at a sedate speed. Even so, they were soon at the bank.

The two remaining cops had their vehicles across the street roadblock style, one facing them and the other guarding the other approach. The cop facing away from them had spun and was running up to reinforce his partner. Both had energy rifles. Behind them was the bank on one side and a deserted building on the other side of the street.

Over 5E's engine, they could hear the other tractors' engines roaring and some crashing, but did not see any of them.

"What about the back?" Anna yelled.

"Locked up tight, I'm sure," Bobby said, "and we don't want to break into the bank. They don't like new customers doing that."

Suddenly 6F sailed through the front of the deserted building, pieces of the building spraying from him like water, and flattened the police vehicle nearest to Bobby and Anna.

The cops backed away quickly, raising their rifles.

3C, the big wheat combine, zoomed out of an alley and rode down the vehicle behind the cops.

As they aimed at Bobby and Anna, who had their weapons out also, the seeder, 2B, pushed out of the old building 6F had opened up. He had filled himself with mud and exploded it out at the cops, knocking both off their feet.

Bobby and Anna quickly ran forward, covering the cops, and secured their rifles and side arms.

"How about we say this never happened?" the higher ranking cop—a sergeant—asked.

Bobby tapped his weapon thoughtfully in his other hand. The tractors revved their engines.

"On the other hand," the sergeant said, "looks like a good day for a walk in the woods."

Bobby nodded and watched as they ran off through the puddles in the street. He waved the tractors quiet.

"Where's Kucharski?" Anna asked.

"Just inside the bank I would imagine; let's go see."

Bobby went behind 5E and retrieved the case of credit bars. Then he and Anna walked up to the bank's front entrance.

Just before they got there, Roman Kucharski stepped out holding an energy rifle.

"Set the case down and leave," he ordered.

4D floated down from out of the rain and started speed-pitching bulbs of Orange Shako with unerring aim. In a burst of thick orange glop, Kucharski went down, his rifle flying away.

✿

Dr. Robert Campbell, formerly employed by the Field King Atomic Tractor Company, now a farm owner on Wheat's Glory, walked out of the main house on the Paradise Hills Wheat Farm. He handed Anna one of the two cups of coffee he carried.

Through their communicator buttons, 6F happily piped, "Look at me, Mommy and Daddy, I'm plowing!"

This was not a major revelation, since he had been doing just that day and night for the last three days. Between Paradise Hills and the old Jacobs farm next door that Bobby had bought, they had several thousand acres of soon-to-be wheat.

The three hundred million had bought every autonomous tractor Field King had in inventory, so just about every farm on Wheat's Glory had them.

Bobby had gotten a ten percent commission, thirty million credits, and a generous severance settlement. With that windfall he had bought three things. That was the old Jacobs place, the rights to the autonomous tractors—now rebranded Farm Delight Autonomous Tractors—and a ring for his new partner in *everything*, Anna!

Business was bustling since their new company now supported and properly trained autonomous tractors. With a little love and motivation, the tractors *delighted* in working for farmers, hence the new company name.

4D zoomed up. "Daddy, going out to refuel 5E where he's harrowing—Daddy want to ride me?"

Bobby smiled. "Sorry, Mommy and I have some important coffee drinking to do."

4D floated off, humming happily.

Bobby looked at Anna and, careful not to spill his coffee on her—for he really was a smart man—leaned over for a kiss.

Original (First) Publication
Copyright © 2014 by Ralph Roberts

Jack McDevitt is a Nebula winner (and 16-time Nebula nominee) as well as a multiple Hugo nominee. He is the author of 21 novels, 5 collections, and 80 short stories.

CRYPTIC

by Jack McDevitt

It was at the bottom of the safe in a bulky manila envelope. I nearly tossed it into the trash with the stacks of other documents, tapes, and assorted flotsam left over from the Project.

Had it been cataloged, indexed in some way, I'm sure I would have. But the envelope was blank, save for an eighteen-year-old date scrawled in the lower right hand corner, and beneath it, the notation "40 gh."

Out on the desert, lights were moving. That would be Brackett fine-tuning the Array for Orrin Hopkins, who was then beginning the observations that would lead, several years later, to new departures in pulsar theory. I envied Hopkins. He was short, round, bald, a man unsure of himself, whose explanations were invariably interspersed with giggles. He was a ridiculous figure, yet he bore the stamp of genius. And people would remember his ideas long after the residence hall named for me at Carrollton had crumbled.

If I had not recognized my own limits and conceded any hope of immortality (at least of this sort), I certainly did so when I accepted the director's position at Sandage. Administration pays better than being an active physicist, but it is death to ambition.

And a Jesuit doesn't even get that advantage.

In those days, the Array was still modest: forty parabolic antennas, each thirty-six meters across. They were on tracks, of course, independently movable, forming a truncated cross. They had, for two decades, been the heart of SETI, the Search for Extra-Terrestrial Intelligence. Now, with the Project abandoned, they were being employed for more useful, if mundane, purposes.

✧

Even that relatively unsophisticated system was good. As Hutching Chaney once remarked, the Ar-

ray could pick up the cough of an automobile ignition on Mars.

I circled the desk and fell into the uncomfortable wooden chair we'd inherited from the outgoing regime. The packet was sealed with tape that had become brittle and loose around the edges. I tore it open.

It was a quarter past ten. I'd worked through my dinner and the evening hours, bored, drinking coffee, debating the wisdom in coming out here from JPL. The increase in responsibility was a good career move; but I knew now that Harry Cooke would never lay his hands on a new particle.

I was committed for two years at Sandage, two years of working out schedules and worrying about insurance, two years of dividing meals between the installation's sterile cafeteria and Jimmy's Amoco Restaurant on Route 85. Then, if all went well, I could expect another move up, perhaps to Georgetown.

I'd have traded it all for Hopkins's future.

I shook out six magnetic disks onto the desk. They were in individual sleeves, of the type that many installations had once used to record electromagnetic radiation. The disks were numbered and dated over a three-day period in 2001, two years earlier than the date on the envelope.

Each was marked "Procyon."

In back, Hopkins and two associates were hunched over monitors. Brackett, having finished his job, was at his desk with his head buried in a book.

I was pleased to discover that the disks were compatible to the Mark VIs. I inserted one, tied in a vocorder to get a hard copy, and went over to join the Hopkins group while the thing ran. They were talking about plasma. I listened for a time, got lost, noted that everyone around me (save the grinning little round man) also got lost, and strolled back to my computer.

The trace drew its green-and-white pictures smoothly on the Mark VI display, and pages of hard copy clicked out of the vocorder. Something in the needle geometry scattering across the recording paper drew my attention. Like an elusive name, it drifted just beyond reach.

Beneath a plate of the Andromeda Galaxy, a coffee pot simmered. I could hear the distant drone of a plane, probably out of Luke Air Force Base. Behind me, Hopkins and his people were laughing at something.

There were patterns in the recording.

They materialized slowly, identical clusters of impulses. The signals were artificial.

Procyon.

The laughter, the plane, the coffee pot, a radio that had been left on somewhere: everything squeezed down to a possibility.

More likely Phoenix, I thought.

☼

Frank Myers had been SETI Director since Ed Dickinson's death twelve years before. I reached him next morning in San Francisco.

"No," he said without hesitation. "Someone's idea of a joke, Harry."

"It was in your safe, Frank."

"That damned safe's been there forty years. Might be anything in it. Except messages from Mars. ..."

I thanked him and hung up.

It had been a long night: I'd taken the hard copy to bed and, by 5:00 a.m., had identified more than forty distinct pulse patterns. The signal appeared to be continuous: that is, it had been an ongoing transmission with no indication of beginning or end, but only irregular breaches of the type that would result from atmospherics and, of course, the long periods during which the target would have been below the horizon.

It was clearly a reflected terrestrial transmission: radio waves bounce around considerably. But why seal the error two years later and put it in the safe?

Procyon is a yellow-white class F3 binary, absolute magnitude 2.8, once worshiped in Babylon and Egypt. (What hasn't been worshiped in Egypt?) Distance from Earth: 11.3 light-years.

In the outer office, Beth Cooper typed, closed filing drawers, spoke with visitors.

The obvious course of action was to use the Array. Listen to Procyon at 40 gigahertz, or all across the spectrum for that matter, and find out if it was, indeed, saying something.

On the intercom, I asked Beth if any open time had developed on the system. "No," she said crisply. "We have nothing until August of next year."

That was no surprise. The facility had booked quickly when its resources were made available to the astronomical community on more than the limited basis that had prevailed for twenty years. Anyone wishing to use the radiotelescope had to plan far in advance. How could I get hold of the Array for a couple hours?

I asked her to come into my office.

Beth Cooper had come to Sandage from San Augustin with SETI during the big move twenty years before. She'd been secretary to three directors: Hutching Chaney, who had built Sandage; his longtime friend, Ed Dickinson; and finally, after Dickinson's death, Frank Myers, a young man on the move, who'd stayed too long with the Project, and who'd been reportedly happy to see it strangled. In any case, Myers had contributed to its demise by his failure to defend it.

I'd felt he was right, of course, though for the wrong reason. It had been painful to see the magnificent telescope at Sandage denied, by and large, to the scientific community while its grotesque hunt for the Little Green Man signal went on. I think there were few of us not happy to see it end.

Beth had expected to lose her job. But she knew her way around the facility, had a talent for massaging egos, and could spell. A devout Lutheran, she had adapted cautiously to working for a priest and, oddly, seemed to have taken offense that I did not routinely walk around with a Roman collar.

I asked one or two questions about the billing methods of the local utilities, and then commented, as casually as I could manage, that it was unfortunate the Project had not succeeded.

Beth looked more like a New York librarian than a secretary at a desert installation. Her hair was silver-gray. She wore steel-rimmed glasses on a long silver chain. She was moderately heavy, but her carriage and her diction were impeccable, imbuing her with the quality that stage people call presence.

Her eyes narrowed to hard black beads at my remark. "Dr. Dickinson said any number of times that none of us would live to see results. Everyone attached to the program, even the janitors, knew that." She wasn't a woman given to shrugs, but the sudden flick in those dark eyes matched the effect. "I'm glad Dr. Dickinson didn't live to see it terminated."

That was followed by an uncomfortable silence. "I don't blame you, Doctor," she said at length, referring to my public position that the facility was being underutilized.

I dropped my eyes and tried to smile reassuringly. It must have been ludicrous. Her severe features softened. I showed her the envelope.

"Do you recognize the writing?"

She barely glanced at it. "It's Dr. Dickinson's."

"Are you sure? I didn't think Dickinson came to the Project until Hutch Chaney's retirement. That was '13, wasn't it?"

"He took over as Director then. But he was an operating technician under Dr. Chaney for, oh, ten or twelve years before that." Her eyes glowed when she spoke of Dickinson.

"I never met him," I said.

"He was a fine man." She looked past me, over my shoulder, her features pale. "If we hadn't lost him, we might not have lost the Project."

"If it matters," I added gently.

"If it matters."

She was right about Dickinson. He was articulate, a persuasive speaker, author of books on various subjects, and utterly dedicated to SETI. He might well have kept the Project afloat despite the cessation of federal funds and the increasing clamor among his colleagues for more time at the facility. But Dickinson was twelve years dead now. He'd returned to Massachusetts at Christmas, as was his custom. After a snowstorm, he'd gone out to help shovel a neighbor's driveway and his heart had failed.

At the time, I was at Georgetown. I can still recall my sense of a genius who had died too soon. He had possessed a vast talent, but no discipline; he had churned through his career hurling sparks in all directions. He had touched everything, but nothing had ever ignited. Particularly not SETI.

"Beth, was there ever a time they thought they had an LGM?"

"The Little Green Man signal?" She shook her head. "No, I don't think so. They were always picking up echoes and things. But nothing ever came close. Either it was KCOX in Phoenix, or a Japanese trawler in the middle of the Pacific."

"Never anything that didn't fit those categories?"

One eyebrow rose slightly. "Never anything they could prove. If they couldn't pin it down, they went back later and tried to find it again. One way or another, they eliminated everything." Or, she must be thinking, we wouldn't be standing here having this conversation.

✧

Beth's comments implied that suspect signals had been automatically stored. Grateful that I had not yet got around to purging obsolete data, I discovered that was indeed the case, and ran a search covering the entire time period back to the Procyon reception in 2011. I was looking for a similar signal.

I got a surprise.

There was no match. There was also no record of the Procyon reception itself.

That meant presumably it had been accounted for and discarded.

Then why, two years later, had the recordings been sealed and placed in the safe? Surely no explanation would have taken that long.

SETI had assumed that any LGM signal would be a deliberate attempt to communicate, that an effort would therefore be made by the originator to create intelligibility, and that the logical way to do that was to employ a set of symbols representing universal constants: the atomic weight of hydrogen, perhaps, or the value of pi.

But the move to Sandage had also been a move to more sophisticated, and considerably more sensitive, equipment. The possibility developed that the Project would pick up a slopover signal, a transmission of alien origin, but intended only for local receivers. Traffic of that nature could be immeasurably difficult to interpret.

If the packet in the safe was anything at all, it was surely of this latter type. Forty gigahertz is not an ideal frequency for interstellar communication. Moreover, the intercept was ongoing, formless, no numbered parts, nothing to assist translation.

I set the computer working on the text, using SETI's own language analysis program. Then I instructed Brackett to call me if anything developed, had dinner at Jimmy's, and went home.

✧

There was no evidence of structure in the text. In English, one can expect to find a 'U' after a 'Q', or a vowel after a cluster of consonants. The aspirate is seldom doubled, nothing is ever tripled, and so on. But in the Procyon transmission, everything seemed utterly random.

The computer counted 256 distinct pulse patterns. Eight bits. Nothing recurred at sufficient intervals to be a space. And the frequency count of these pulse patterns, or characters, was flat; there was no quantitative difference in use from one to another. All appeared approximately the same number of times. If it was a language, it was a language with no discernible vowels.

I called Wes Phillips, who was then the only linguist I knew. Was it possible for a language to be structured in such a way?

"Oh, I don't think so. Unless you're talking about some sort of construct. Even then—." He paused. "Harry, I can give you a whole series of reasons in maybe six different disciplines why languages need high and low frequency letters. To have a flat 'curve,' a language would have to be deliberately designed that way, and it would have to be non-oral. But what practical value would it have? Why bother?"

Ed Dickinson had been an enigma. During the series of political crises that engulfed the nation after the turn of the century, he'd earned an international reputation as a diplomat, and as an eloquent defender of reason and restraint. Everyone agreed that he had a mind of the first rank. Yet, in his chosen field, he accomplished little. And eventually he'd gone to work for the Project, historically only a stepping-stone to serious effort. But he'd stayed.

Why?

Hutching Chaney was a different matter. A retired naval officer, he'd indulged in physics almost as a pastime. His political connections had been instrumental in getting Sandage built, and his assignment as Director was rumored to have been a reward for services rendered during the rough and tumble of congressional politics.

He possessed a plodding sort of competence. He was fully capable of grasping, and visualizing, extreme complexity. But he lacked insight and imagination, the ability to draw the subtle inference. After his retirement from Sandage, Chaney had gone to an emeritus position at MIT, which he'd held for five years.

He was a big man, more truck driver than physicist. Despite advancing age—he was then in his 70s—and his bulk, he spoke and moved with energy. His hair was full and black. His light gray eyes suggested the shrewdness of a professional politician, and he possessed the confident congeniality of a man who had never failed at anything.

We were in his home in Somerville, Massachusetts, a stone and glass house atop sweeping lawns. It was not an establishment that a retired physicist would be expected to inhabit. Chaney's moneyed background was evident.

He clapped a big hand on my shoulder and pulled me through one of those stiff, expensive living rooms that no one ever wants to sit in, into a paneled, leather-upholstered den at the rear of the house. "Martha," he said to someone I couldn't see, "would you bring us some port?" He looked at me for acquiescence.

"Fine," I said. "It's been a long time, Hutch."

Books lined the walls, mostly engineering manuals, a few military and naval histories. An articulated steel gray model of the Lance dominated the fireplace shelf. That was the deadly hydrofoil which, built at Chaney's urging, had contributed to a multipurpose navy that was simultaneously lethal, flexible, and relatively cheap.

"The Church is infiltrating everywhere," he said. "How are things at Sandage, Harry?"

I described some of the work in progress. He listened with interest.

A young woman arrived with a bottle, two glasses, and a plate of cheese. "Martha comes in three times a week," Chaney said after she'd left the room. He smiled, winked, dipped a stick of cheese into the mustard, and bit it neatly in half. "You needn't worry, Harry. I'm not capable of getting into trouble anymore. What brings you to Massachusetts?"

I extracted the vocordings from my briefcase and handed them across to him. I watched patiently as he leafed through the thick sheaf of paper, and saw with satisfaction his change of expression.

"You're kidding, Harry," he said. "Somebody really found one? When'd it happen?"

"Twenty years ago," I said, passing him the envelope and the original disks.

He turned them over in his hands. "You're not serious? There's a mistake somewhere."

"It was in the safe," I said.

He shook his head. "Doesn't much matter where it was. Nothing like this ever happened."

"Then what is it?"

"Damned if I have any idea."

We sat not talking while Chaney continued to flip pages, grunting. He seemed to have forgotten his wine. "You run this yourself?" he asked.

I nodded.

"Hell of a lot of trouble for somebody to go to for a joke. Were the computers able to read any of it? No? That's because it's gibberish." He stared at the envelope. "But it *is* Ed's handwriting."

"Would Dickinson have any reason to keep such a thing quiet?"

"Ed? No. Dickinson least of all. No one wanted to hear a signal more than he did. He wanted it so badly he invested his life in the Project."

"But could he, physically, have done this? Could he have picked up the LGM? Could he have done it without anyone else knowing? Was he good enough with computers to cover his tracks?"

"This is pointless. Yes, he could have done it. And you could walk through Braintree without your pants."

A light breeze was coming through a side window, billowing the curtains. It was cool and pleasant, unusual for Massachusetts in August. Some kids were playing halfball out on the street.

"Forty megahertz," he said. "Sounds like a satellite transmission."

"That wouldn't have taken two years to figure out, would it? Why keep the disks?"

"Why not? I expect if you go down into the storeroom you'll find all kinds of relics."

Outside, there was a sound like approaching thunder, exploding suddenly into an earsplitting screech. A stripped-down T-Bolt skidded by, scattering the ballplayers. An arm hung leisurely out the driver's side. The car took the corner stop sign at about forty-five. A couple of fingers went up, but otherwise the game resumed as though nothing had happened.

"All the time," Chaney said. His back to the window, he hadn't bothered to look around. "Cops can't keep up with them anymore."

"Why was Dickinson so interested in the Project?"

"Ed was a great man." His face clouded somewhat, and I wondered if the port hadn't drawn his emotions close to the surface. "You'd have to know him. You and he would have got along fine. He had a taste for the metaphysical, and I guess the Project was about as close as he could get."

"How do you mean?"

"Did you know he spent two years in a seminary? Yes, somewhere outside Philadelphia. He was an altar boy who eventually wound up at Harvard. And that was that."

"You mean he lost his faith?"

"Oh, yes. The world became a dark place, full of disaster. He always seemed to have the details on the latest pogrom, or viral outbreak, or drive-by murder. There are only two kinds of people, he told me once: atheists, and folks who haven't been paying attention. But he always retained that fine mystical sense of purpose that you drill into your best kids, a notion that things are somehow ordered. When I knew him, he wouldn't have presumed to pray to anyone. But he had all the drive of a missionary, and the same conviction of—." He dropped his head back on the leather upholstery and tried to seize a word from the ceiling. "—Destiny.

"Ed wasn't like most physicists. He was competent in a wide range of areas. He wrote on foreign affairs for *Commentary* and *Harper's*; he wrote on ornithology and systems analysis, on Malcolm Muggeridge, and Edward Gibbon."

He swung easily out of his chair and reached for a pair of fat matched volumes in mud-brown covers. It was *The Decline and Fall of the Roman Empire*, the old Modern Library edition. "He's the only person I've ever known who's actually read the thing." He turned the cover of volume one so that I could see the inscription:

For Hutch,

In the fond hope that we can hold off the potherbs and the pigs.

Ed

"He gave it to me when I left SETI."

"Seems like an odd gift. Have you read it?"

He laughed off the question. "You'd need a year."

"What's the business about the potherbs and pigs?"

He rose and walked casually to the far wall. There were photos of naval vessels and aircraft, of Chaney and President Fine, of the Sandage complex. He seemed to screw his vision into the latter. "I don't remember. It's a phrase from the book. He explained it to me at the time. But …" He held his hands outward, palms up.

"Hutch, thanks." I got up to go.

"There was no signal," he said. "I don't know where these recordings came from, but Ed Dickinson would have given anything for a contact."

"Hutch, is it possible that Dickinson might have been able to translate the text? If there had been one?"

"Not if *you* couldn't. He had the same program."

✧

I don't like cities.

Dickinson's books were all out of print, and the used bookstores were clustered in Cambridge. Even then, the outskirts of Boston, like the city proper, were littered with broken glass and discarded newspapers. Surly kids milled outside bars. Windows everywhere were smashed or boarded. I went through a red light at one intersection rather than learn the intentions of an approaching band of ragged children with hard eyes. (One could scarcely call them children, though I doubt there was one over 12.) Profanity covered the crumbling brick walls as high as a hand could reach. Much of it was misspelled.

Boston had been Dickinson's city. I wondered what the great humanist thought when he drove through these streets.

I found only one of his books: *Malcolm Muggeridge: Faith and Despair*. The store also had a copy of *The Decline and Fall*. On impulse, I bought it.

I was glad to get back to the desert.

We were entering a period of extraordinary progress, during which we finally began to understand the mechanics of galactic structure. McCue mapped the core of the Milky Way, Osterberger developed his unified field concepts, and Schauer constructed his celebrated revolutionary hypothesis on the na-

ture of time. Then, on a cool morning in October, a team from Cal Tech announced that they had a new set of values for hyperinflation.

In the midst of all this, we had an emergency. One night in late September, Earl Barlow, who was directing the Cal Tech groups, suffered a mild heart attack. I arrived just before the EMT's, at about 2:00 a.m.

While the ambulance carrying Barlow started down the mountain, his people watched helplessly, drinking coffee, too upset to work. The opportunity didn't catch me entirely unprepared. I gave Brackett his new target. The blinking lights of the emergency vehicle were hardly out of sight before the parabolas swung round and fastened on Procyon.

But there was only the disjointed crackle of interstellar static.

✧

I took long walks in the desert at night. The parabolas are lovely in the moonlight. Occasionally, the stillness is broken by the whine of an electric motor, and the antennas slide gracefully along their tracks. It was, I thought, a new Stonehenge of softly curving shapes and fluid motion.

The Muggeridge book was a slim volume. It was not biographical, but rather an analysis of the philosopher's conviction that the West has a death wish. It was the old argument that God had been replaced by science, that man had gained knowledge of a trivial sort, and as a result lost purpose.

It was, on the whole, depressing reading. In his conclusion, Dickinson argued that truth will not wait on human convenience, that if man cannot adapt to a neutral universe, then that universe will indeed come to seem hostile. We must make do with what we have and accept truth wherever it leads. The modern cathedral is the radiotelescope.

Sandage was involved in the verification procedure for McCue's work, and for the already controversial Cal Tech equations. All that is another story. What is significant is that it got me thinking about verifications, and I realized I'd overlooked something. There'd been no match for the Procyon readings anywhere in the data banks since the original reception. But the Procyon recordings might themselves have been the confirmation of an earlier signal!

It took five minutes to run the search. There were two hits.

Both were fragments, neither more than fifteen minutes long; but there was enough of each to reduce the probability of error to less than one percent.

The first occurred three weeks prior to the Procyon reception.

The second went back to 2007, a San Augustin observation. Both were at 40 gigahertz. Both had identical pulse patterns. But there was an explosive difference, sedately concealed in the target information line. The 2007 transmission had come while the radiotelescope was locked on Sirius!

✿

When I got back to my office, I was trembling.

Sirius and Procyon were only a few light-years apart. My God, I kept thinking, they exist! And they have interstellar travel!

I spent the balance of the day stumbling around, trying to immerse myself in fuel usage reports and budget projections. But mostly what I did was watch the desert light grow hard in the curtains, and then fade. The two volumes of Edward Gibbon were propped between a *Webster's* and some black binders. The books were thirty years old, identical to the set in Chaney's den. Some of the pages, improperly cut, were still joined at the edges.

I opened the first volume, approximately in the middle, and began to read. Or tried to. But Ed Dickinson kept crowding out the Romans. Finally I gave it up, took the book, and went home.

There was duplicate bridge in town, and I lost myself in that for five hours. Then, in bed, still somewhat dazed, I tried *The Decline and Fall* again.

It was not the dusty rollcall of long-dead emperors that I had expected. The emperors are there, stabbing and throttling and blundering. And occasionally trying to improve things. But the fish-hawkers are there too. And the bureaucrats and the bishops.

It's a world filled with wine and legionnaires' sweat, mismanagement, arguments over Jesus, and the inability to transfer power, all played out to the ruthless drumbeat of dissolution. An undefined historical tide, stemmed occasionally by a hero, or a sage, rolls over men and events, washing them toward the sea. (During the later years, I wondered, did Roman kids run down matrons in flashy imported chariots? Were the walls of Damascus defiled by profanity?)

In the end, when the barbarians push at the outer rim of empire, it is only a hollow wreck that crashes down.

Muggeridge had been there.

And Dickinson, the altar boy, amid the fire and waste of the imperial city, must have suffered a second loss of faith.

We had an electrical failure one night. It has nothing to do with this story except that it resulted in my being called in at 4:00 a.m., not to restore the power, which required a good electrician, but to pacify some angry people from New York, and to be able to say, in my report, that I had been on the spot.

These things attended to, I went outside.

At night, the desert is undisturbed by color or motion. It's a composition of sand, rock, and star; a frieze, a Monet, uncomplicated, unchanging. It's reassuring, in an age when little else seems stable. The orderly mid-twentieth century universe had long since disintegrated into a plethora of neutron galaxies, colliding black holes, time reversals, and God knows what.

The desert is solid underfoot. Predictable. A reproach to the quantum mechanics that reflect a quicksand cosmos in which physics merges with Plato.

Close on the rim of the sky, guarding their mysteries, Sirius and Procyon, the bright pair, sparkled. The arroyos are dry at that time of year, shadowy ripples in the landscape. The moon was in its second quarter. Beyond the administration building, the parabolas were limned in silver.

My cathedral.

My Stonehenge.

And while I sat, sipping a Coors, and thinking of lost cities and altar boys and frequency counts, I suddenly understood the significance of Chaney's last remark! Of course Dickinson had not been able to read the transmission. That was the point!

✿

I needed Chaney.

I called him in the morning, and flew out in the afternoon. He met me at Logan, and we drove toward Gloucester. "There's a good Italian restaurant," he said. And then, without taking his eyes off the road: "What's this about?"

I'd brought the second Gibbon volume with me, and I held it up for him to see. He blinked.

It was early evening, cold, wet, with the smell of approaching winter. Freezing rain pelted the windshield. The sky was gray, heavy, sagging into the city.

"Before I answer any questions, Hutch, I'd like to ask a couple. What can you tell me about military cryptography?"

He grinned. "Not much. The little I do know is probably classified." A tractor-trailer lumbered past, straining, spraying water across the windows. "What, specifically, are you interested in?"

"How complex are the Navy's codes? I know they're nothing like cryptograms, but what sort of general structure do they have?"

"First off, Harry, they're not codes. Monoalphabetic systems are codes. Like the cryptograms you mentioned. The letter 'G' always turns up, say, as an 'M'. But in military and diplomatic cryptography, the 'G' will be a different character every time it appears. And the encryption alphabet isn't usually limited to letters; we use numbers, dollar signs, ampersands, even spaces." We splashed onto a ramp and joined the Interstate. It was elevated and we looked across rows of bleak rooftops. "Even the shape of individual words is concealed."

"How?"

"By encrypting the spaces."

I knew the answer to the next question before I asked it. "If the encryption alphabet is absolutely random, which I assume it would have to be, the frequency count would be flat. Right?"

"Yes. Given sufficient traffic, it would have to be."

"One more thing, Hutch. A sudden increase in traffic will alert anyone listening that something is happening even if he can't read the text. How do you hide that?"

"Easy. We transmit a continuous signal, twenty-four hours a day. Sometimes it's traffic, sometimes it's garbage. But you can't tell the difference."

God have mercy on us, I thought. Poor Dickinson.

☼

We sat at a small corner table well away from the main dining area. I shivered in wet shoes and a damp sweater. A small candle guttered cheerfully in front of us.

"Are we still talking about Procyon?" he asked.

I nodded. "The same pattern was received twice, three years apart, prior to the Procyon reception."

"But that's not possible." Chaney leaned forward intently. "The computer would have matched them automatically. We'd have known."

"I don't think so." Half a dozen prosperous, overweight men in topcoats had pushed in and were jostling each other in the small entry. "The two hits were on different targets. They would have looked like an echo."

Chaney reached across the table and gripped my wrist, knocking over a cup. "Son of a bitch," he said. "Are you suggesting somebody's moving around out there?"

"I don't think Ed Dickinson had any doubts."

"Why would he keep it secret?"

I'd placed the book on the table at my left hand. It rested there, its plastic cover reflecting the glittering red light of the candle. "Because they're at war."

The color drained from Chaney's face, and it took on a pallor that was almost ghastly in the lurid light.

"He believed," I continued, "he really believed that mind equates to morality, intelligence to compassion. And what did he find after a lifetime? A civilization that had conquered the stars, but not its own passions and stupidities."

A tall young waiter presented himself. We ordered port and pasta.

"You don't really know there's a war going on out there," Chaney objected.

"Hostility, then. Secrecy on a massive scale, as this must be, has ominous implications. Dickinson would have saved us all with a vision of order and reason. ..."

The gray eyes met mine. They were filled with pain. Two adolescent girls in the next booth were giggling. The wine came.

"What has the *Decline and Fall* to do with it?"

"It became his Bible. He was chilled to the bone by it. *You* should read it, but with caution. It's capable of strangling the soul. Dickinson was a rationalist. He recognized the ultimate truth in the Roman tragedy: that once expansion has stopped, decay is constant and irreversible. Every failure of reason or virtue loses more ground.

"I haven't been able to find his book on Gibbon, but I know what he'll say: that Gibbon was not writing only of the Romans, nor of the British of his own time. He was writing about us. Hutch, take a look around. Tell me we're not sliding toward a dark age. Think how that knowledge must have affected him."

We drank silently for a few minutes. Time locked in place, and we sat unmoving, the world frozen around us.

"Did I tell you," I said at last, "that I found the reference for his inscription? He must have had great respect for you." I opened the book to the conclusion, and turned it for him to read:

The forum of the Roman people, where they assembled to enact their laws, and elect their magistrates, is now enclosed for the cultivation of potherbs, or thrown open for the reception of swine and buffaloes.

Chaney stared disconsolately at me. "It's all so hard to believe."

"A man can survive a loss of faith in the Almighty," I said, "provided he does not also lose faith in himself. That was Dickinson's real tragedy. He came to believe exclusively in radiotelescopes, the way some people do in religions."

The food, when it came, went untasted. "What are you going to do, Harry?"

"About the Procyon text? About the probability that we have quarrelsome neighbors? I'm not afraid of that kind of information; all it means is that where you find intelligence, you will probably find stupidity. Anyway, it's time Dickinson got credit for his discovery." And, I thought, maybe it'll even mean a footnote for me.

I lifted my glass in a mock toast, but Chaney did not respond. We faced each other in an uncomfortable tableau. "What's wrong?" I asked. "Thinking about Dickinson?"

"That too." The candle glinted in his eyes. "Harry, do you think *they* have a SETI project?"

"Possibly. Why?"

"I was wondering if your aliens know we're here. This restaurant isn't much further from Sirius than Procyon is. Maybe you better eat up."

Copyright © 1983 by Davis Publications

A Classic Revived
Includes the prequel story,
"The Ballad of Lost C'Mell"

On Sale Now

Marina J. Lostetter was a 2013 Writers of the Future quarterly winner, and has recently sold to a number of magazines, including Penumbra *and* Orson Scott Card's InterGalactic Medicine Show. *This is her third appearance in* Galaxy's Edge.

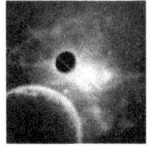

a

Sargasso Containment

story

www.SargassoLegacy.com

SONG OF THE SARGASSO

by Marina J. Lostetter

Aye, aye, m'lady,
There's a dragon down below.
Aye, aye, m'lady,
Yet exploring we shall go.
Don't give your heart to the red-dusted man,
Don't give your heart to the Sea.
Please stay steady-on by the dock,
And save your heart for me.
—Chorus. Last transmission
from the *Illico One.*

Victor Carvalho couldn't hear Kira's scream, but he sure as hell could *see* it.

It was plastered on her face, frozen there beneath her space helmet.

The image would be forever seared into his memory. He crouched down on the barren deck of the *Illico* and reached a shaking hand toward her supine form. She didn't move—how could she, with her body twisted like that?

We shouldn't have come here. We shouldn't have reached into God's domain.

☼

Nineteen Hours Before

"All right everyone, we're about to cross into Sargasso space. If you feel the need to vomit, or strap yourself in tight, maybe say a few prayers, no one will hold it against you."

Victor made a slight course adjustment, then buckled himself into the nav chair. His cat, a short-haired calico with 'Starbuck's limp,' curled herself up on his lap.

"Ready, Dinah?" he asked, running his fingers through her soft fur. "Hold onto your hairballs."

Though he joked, he didn't think anything was funny about the extra-solar Sargasso Sea—or the Sargasso Grid, as it was called by those who'd never dare travel out beyond the planets. He watched the computer count down as it estimated their position, and his heart beat faster with every light-second gained. *Just remember the money, you can't beat the money*, he told himself. A lot of hazard pay came with venturing into the Sea, and Victor ticked off all the things he could buy when he got back to Mars.

An entire biodome all for himself.

A sports-class racing ship.

A million swimming pools' worth of cat food.

… Diapers. Lots of diapers.

There were as many stories about the Sea as there once had been about the edge of the world. *Here there be drag-ions*, went the old astronaut's joke. Mythical beasts, mythical particles, it didn't matter—the region, forming a globe around the solar system starting at 1,260 AUs from the sun, was a very real borderland. Did something swallow the ships out this far, or shut them down? Did they fall into micro black holes, or drop out of existence altogether? No one really knew what happened out in the Sargasso. But one thing was for sure: no one who'd gone more than three light-hours in had ever come back.

Their ship, the *Basilisk*, was on an intercept course with a planetoid in the region—three point three light-hours in. Traveling at one-fourth light speed—more commonly known as 0.25c—and accounting for slowdown, that was sixteen hours travel time.

Almost there, almost. He cringed, gripping his armrests with sweaty palms as the edge of the Sea approached. It wasn't that he expected turbulence, or chaos, or the instrumentation to go wiggy—it was the unknown that sent waves of queasiness through his stomach.

"Three … two … one …"

They'd breached the Sea. The computer kept counting on, oblivious to the monumental moment.

Nothing changed. Victor's hair hadn't turned blue, the stars hadn't realigned themselves outside the forward shield, and Dinah still had the right number of eyes. Satisfied that all was normal, at least for the moment, he opened up the comm channels. "All right, we're in. If all you *maracujás de gaveta*—" he loved insulting them in Portuguese—"are A-OK, lemme know. Press your locator badges, please—light up my dash."

The panel marked *Crew Locations* sprang to life, revealing four red dots. One lit up in the mess, two in the bunks, and one in Service Vent Three. Each carried a name tag and title: Aadesh Dutta, Payload Specialist; Jonas Boudreaux, Biochemical Engineering Specialist; Shandra Tesh, Mining Specialist; and Kira Miyagi, Ship's Specialist.

"Thank you," Victor said.

"We will be arriving at our destination within the next twenty-four-hour period. For your safety, and the safety of those around you, please get some shut-eye. Over and out."

Following his own advice, he tucked Dinah into her safety carrier. The two of them traipsed through hatchway after hatchway toward the bunk arm, and he hummed the old sailor's *Song of the Sargasso* as he went.

When he passed the mess, a gruff voice, like rattling bits of glass and metal, snapped at him. "Don't you be humming that!" Jonas stepped out, tube of reconstituted pea-mush in one hand, and barred Victor's path. "Song's cursed. Singing it sent the crew of the *Ill*—of *that ship*—into oblivion. Don't you go dooming us, too."

Jonas was a throwback if Victor had ever encountered one—the man acted like they were conscripts on a seventeenth-century sailing rig rather than space-faring freelancers.

The *Illico* had been the first manned craft to aim for another solar system. Six hours into the Sea it had disappeared, leaving nothing but questions and a snippet of song behind. For someone like Jonas, speaking its name once you were in the Sea was akin to breathing "Macbeth" in a playhouse.

Victor let the last bar in the chorus die on his lips.

Satisfied, the big man ducked back into the mess pod.

A *clang!* and a grunt drew Victor's attention to an open panel a few steps away. Kira slid out of the service vent—face covered in grease—onto the corrugated floor. "Lights in nav should stop flickering now," she said, wiping her hands on her jumper. Clearly she hadn't been worried about the Sea—she'd worked right through the transition.

Kira was good people. This was her first time as head caretaker of a ship, and she carried the position with pride.

She and Victor had grown close over the trip. He thought of her as a true friend.

"Wanna play some cards?" she asked.

"Nah. I—" He paused, catching a whiff of lilac and vanilla, a scent he hadn't encountered in months. It had no place aboard the *Basilisk*. When Kira raised an eyebrow at him, Victor shrugged off the anomaly and continued. "I better rest up. Need to be sharp for the approach."

He stepped over the lip into his bunk pod, latching the hatchway behind him. The pressure seal made a half-hiss, half-sucking sound as it locked into place.

Gently, he placed Dinah's carrier on the floor and let her out. She meowed softly, curling up on the foot of his cot. He tucked himself in, still feeling the tingle of perfume in his nose.

Only one person he knew wore that fragrance, and she was light-weeks away. When he finally fell asleep he dreamed of the day he'd last seen her. They stood together in a garden dome, under the calm Martian sky. She'd taken his hand—oh so platonically—and explained why she'd bowed out of the mission.

Parts of the memory were interspersed with dream-phantoms. Another person, a dark entity, seemed to be crouching behind the orchids near the stone path, watching and giggling.

The woman's words came out garbled, and the expression on her face was unclear. She said a lot of things, seemed to talk for hours. "Presence. Listening. Feeling."

"I don't understand," Victor said at last.

She placed her palm over her stomach. "I can't go to the Sea like this. You'll have to tell me all about it when you get back."

"But, I … Lily."

"When you get back … get back … get back … get back!"

Victor awoke with a start, the echo of a mini-blast ringing in his ears. His hatch swung outwards, smoking slightly. All four of his crewmates stood there.

"Thank God!" said Kira, rushing in.

Groggy, Victor threw aside the covers and tried to stand. "What the hell are you guys—?"

Kira pushed him down. "Recirculator in your pod shut off." She hopped onto his cot to reach the vent in the ceiling. "No alarms sounded, nothing."

Still woozy with sleep, Victor slowly worked out what she meant. No recirculator meant no air in or out. It meant dwindling oxygen and rising carbon dioxide. A shiver ran up Victor's spine—he could have slept right through dying.

"Good thing you left your comm on," said Aadesh, twisting his white ball cap around backward. "Your girl here—" he scooped up Dinah—"made such a commotion I came to see what was up, but your hatch jammed."

"Yeah, good thing," Victor mumbled. But he couldn't remember the last time he'd used his bunk comm. It had to have been on for days, at least. Wouldn't someone have noticed? He glanced sideways at Dinah, wondering if she could have pressed—no. He shook off the notion.

"We're in the Sea now, boys," Shandra said. "Better stay vigilant. Never know what might crap out next."

✿

Victor tried to shake off the mishap in his bunk pod, but couldn't rid himself of the feeling that something wasn't right. A sinister fog had crept into his mind.

And why had he dreamt of Lily Silva?

That day, when she'd told him about the baby, was both his worst and best in recent memory. He'd found out the love of his life, his best friend—who had rejected his advances years ago—was pregnant by another man. But he'd also been released. A wave of relief had secretly washed over him when she'd said she couldn't go to the Sargasso. He'd dreaded the idea of being confined to five-hundred cubic meters of living space with her—no means of escape,

no means of release—the constant proximity would have killed him.

So he'd put on a smile and told her he was happy for her, told her he couldn't wait to meet the baby when he got back.

Lies, lies, lies.

He loved her so much he had to forget her, and her absence from the mission was the perfect opportunity. Time and distance could ease the pain away.

"How you doing down there, Aadesh?" he asked over the comm. Victor had initiated braking two hours previously. The unnamed planetoid loomed in the distance, not much more than a speck, but growing all the time.

"Rovers will be ready. You concentrate on not crashing and we'll be fine," Aadesh replied from the bay. "And remember to breathe."

"Oh, har har—very funny."

Spectrometer readings said the planetoid was rich in carbon, hydrogen, and oxygen. The thing was a ball of sugar. Nothing like it had been seen before in either the asteroid belt or the Kuiper Belt. It should be great for making an outer-system carbohydrate depot, as long as everything checked out biochemically.

Originally, that had been Lily's job. She was a research biologist with a strong background in biochemistry. When she'd found out she was pregnant and had to cancel, Jonas had been the last-minute addition to the team.

Victor began plotting his trajectory for fast-fall into orbit. They were close enough now to get precise readings on the object's spin, course, and gravity. But some of the computer readouts weren't what Victor had anticipated.

He double-checked his baseline stats. There was a distinct wobble that hadn't been present before, like a counterweight had been thrown in.

"Anyone remember seeing data about a known satellite around this thing?"

No reply.

"I'm definitely picking up something already in orbit."

A draft moved beside him.

"*Victor?*"

He jumped. "Whoa, don't sneak up on me like …" He turned around. No one was there.

"Hello?"

Dead quiet.

"Everyone?" he asked over the comms. "Press your locator badges, please."

For a moment, five dots appeared where there should have been four. The extra light quickly blinked off again—another malfunction. The women were together in the chem lab. The men were in the payload bay.

"Thanks. Never mind."

Dinah looked up from beside his chair and meowed.

"I know," he said, scratching her between the ears. "Gotta get my head back in the game."

More calculations, more readings, more fine-tuning. He slapped the equipment a few times—damn computer was glitching. It kept insisting there were other gravitational anomalies, variances. There one minute, then gone the next: pinpricks in the fabric of space, swirling into existence like whirlpools, then out again.

Ignoring those, he zeroed in on the planetoid and its companion, and began to get a clear picture of their relationship. "Unstable retrograde orbit—heavily decaying. Whatever it is is new, and won't stay in the sky for long."

That could be bad news for their mining prospects. They wouldn't want to land their expensive rovers only to have the machines eventually sandwiched between the surface and a plummeting asteroid.

He waited impatiently for the ship to get close enough for imaging and radar. Maybe if it was a rubble-pile asteroid they could dismantle it—might even make for a good side-project if it contained valuable materials.

He calibrated the instruments and cameras, then snapped away. Moments later the pictures popped up on screen. The first were fuzzy, giving only a hint as to its shape. As they drew nearer and the magnification increased, the satellite began to look more familiar. *Too* familiar.

Black letters, each two stories high, declared the impossible across the object's side.

"I need everyone up in nav, now!" he demanded over the comm.

✿

"It's the *Illico*, I'm sure."

"No way," said Shandra, "If that ship's still out there, it's on the opposite side of the solar system. They were headed for Alpha Centauri. This can't be it. I mean, it's not where it's supposed to be, so this just can't be the *Illico*."

"This is crazy," said Kira, cycling through the images.

Fuzzy though the snapshots were, they revealed that all of the ship's airlocks had been blown. The inside of the *Illico* lay dark and cold.

On its bow, red and yellow smears formed strange, concentric circles. What may have been plasma burns scarred the area above the "Ill."

"It's going to crash into the planetoid," Victor told them. "Those early one-quarter light-speed drives were pretty unstable. It could contaminate the surface, if not deeper. And it wouldn't be cost-effective to scrub the sugar. Salvage it or divert it, we have to move that ship or else it'll make our operation useless."

"It's big—I don't think we can slap a towline on it," said Aadesh. "Gravity well's got too good a grip."

"If it's still functional, I might be able to pilot it," Victor said.

"You want to put boots on its deck?" asked Jonas, incredulous.

"Kira and I should be able to handle it," Victor said.

Kira stared at the screen for a long, silent moment. "Why are all the airlocks open?"

"Malfunction?" Aadesh suggested. "Could be why the last thing they sent was singing. If the locks all blew open, they could have been caught off guard and …"

They all nodded. It probably meant they wouldn't find any bodies on board.

"Yeah," Kira said thoughtfully. She sounded distant. "Tough angle to tell, but I think their emergency shuttle is still attached."

"In that case, should we all suit up?" Shandra suggested. "Just in case we have a similar malfunction?"

"Couldn't hurt," said Victor.

"We should leave it alone," said Jonas. "We shouldn't touch a cursed ship."

"I don't like it, either," said Kira. "But you heard Vic, we can't ignore it."

"I'll put on a suit, but I'm having no part in this. Call me when it's time to mine," he said over his shoulder, stalking out of the room.

"Ignore him," said Kira, catching Victor as he tried to go after Jonas. "Wouldn't be any good to us in ship salvage, anyway. Better to have him sulk up here than get in the way. Tell us what we need to do to board the *Illico One*."

✿

Instead of falling into geostationary orbit with the planetoid, they matched the decaying trajectory of the old exploration ship. Using one of the backup twin-booster packs for the mining rovers, Victor guided a tether through one of the *Illico*'s open airlocks and secured the two ships together.

The crew all donned their suits. Despite Jonas' previous insistence that he not be involved, he volunteered to monitor the two-man away team. To save time, Aadesh and Shandra went about scanning the planetoid's surface for the best place to land the rovers.

After loading a self-propelled trolley with any tools they might need, Victor and Kira eased themselves out of a hatch, down the tether, and into the dark belly of the ghost ship.

When they touched down on the smooth floor, they activated their magnetic boots and switched on their spotlights. The beams bored through the blackness, creating narrow tunnels of vision and leaving all else in gloom.

They found themselves in a loading dock. A huge wall of massive cupboards and drawers—packed with supplies for the long, thirty-four year journey—loomed to their right. It appeared undisturbed.

The ten-person crew hadn't been able to put so much as a dent in their non-growable rations before they disappeared. Which meant the massive ship, a skyscraper in space, had a lot to offer Victor's employers; if you wanted to build an extra-solar food depot, you couldn't get much better seed material.

"We should take some of this back," he said.

Their lights cast harsh shadows everywhere as they strode through the ship. The spacesuit and heavy magnetic boots forced Victor to take slow, deliberate actions. He kept seeing movement out of his peripheral vision, and had to remind himself that it

was the light playing tricks with his eyes, nothing more.

Even when he saw an ashen face reflected in the bowl of his helmet.

The image caught him off guard. He whirled, expecting to see a corpse floating behind him, but it was nothing. Just some white piping grouped in a strange way.

A narrow ladder took them from the bowels of the craft up into the living quarters. Victor went first. The hatchway above should have sealed off the area, but it sat open. Waiting. The climb set them at such an angle that Victor's light couldn't yet pierce the blackness beyond.

He had the sudden impression that he was squirming through a tight feeding tube and into the mouth of a giant creature. In his mind's eye he imagined a great pink tongue slithering down to greet him.

"What's that ticking sound?" Jonas asked. "I'm getting a ticking through your external microphones."

Victor looked down at Kira. She shrugged. "We don't hear anything," he said. "Jonas, we're in a vacuum."

"Something must be working down there. I definitely hear a tick."

Victor pulled himself over the top rung of the ladder, catapulting himself into the room before his magnetic boots brought him back down. The trolley followed after, then Kira. They'd entered some kind of communal area. Plush cushions lined a bench that wound around the room. Several tables dotted the floor.

"Look at this," Kira said, waving him over. One of the tables had been bent over on its stem. The bulging metal was twisted and discolored.

"These are solid steel," Victor said. "What could do that?"

She shrugged.

He remembered the gravitational anomalies his instruments had picked up. He'd thought the readings faulty, but what if the "pinpricks" in space really existed?

His beam traveled down the length of the table stem to the floor, illuminating dark blotches under their feet. It took him a moment to recognize the marks as lettering. Quickly, he gestured Kira aside, and they bent over it together.

"It's in Spanish," she noted.

"Not Spanish, Portuguese," Victor said. He'd grown up in Brazil. "It's a line from the Song of the Sargasso."

"What does it say?"

He paused before replying. "It says, *There's a dragon down below.*"

She looked up at him, but the glare of his spotlight obscured her expression. "I don't like it here."

"Me neither," he agreed. "The sooner we move the ship, the sooner we can leave."

As he stood, he caught something out of his eye. Movement, for sure. White and gauzy. He held out a hand, signaling for Kira to hold still.

"Saw something. Maybe just a cleaning bot," he said. "But something's here."

"The ticking's getting louder," Jonas said.

Victor still couldn't hear anything.

The movement had vanished, out of the common area. He took two steps forward before Kira grabbed him by the arm.

"It could be dangerous," she whispered.

"It could be a sign that parts of the ship are in fine working order," he said rationally. "Come on."

Though confident that the thing had gone this way, he couldn't find it again.

What they did find were more song verses, scrawled haphazardly, from the walls down to the floors and up the walls again.

A metal chair, like the one Victor used in the nav pod, blocked their way around one corner. At first they thought it torn from its housing, but it appeared to be cut—its bottom smooth and the connecting wires shorn neatly. One corner of the chair back had melted against the adjoining wall, ringed by red and yellow powdery circles similar to what they'd noted outside on the hull.

"What the hell happened in here?" Kira asked.

With no sign of a cleaning bot, functional or otherwise, they finally found the cockpit.

"Cross your fingers," he said, reaching for the auxiliary power switch. As it flipped, the navigation dash flickered to life. "And we have power, yes! One more—oh, look, the artificial gravity. Any guesses?

Will it, won't it? Aaaand, it will." Victor felt a familiar tug pull him to the deck.

Kira slapped him on the back.

He smiled warmly at her and felt a little thrill. He never thought he'd find himself in such a position. They were on the *Illico*!

How often did anyone get to make such a discovery? And with a friend by his side.

But for a split instant it wasn't Kira looking back at him. It was Lily. And he realized he'd much rather be sharing the moment with her.

Stupid, silly notion.

Why did he have to torture himself like that? Why couldn't he just forget her?

A faint whisper of, "*Tick, tick, tick,*" rattled through his helmet. He looked to Kira, but she either hadn't heard or was ignoring the sound.

Hurriedly, he checked the navigation record. "Shandra was right. They shouldn't be here. Last recorded position puts them right where you'd expect them, billions of miles away, shooting straight out of the neighborhood."

"How did they end up here, captured by a planetoid?"

"Your guess is as good as any."

Jonas's voice tore through Victor's speakers at deafening decibels. Victor reeled, trying to pull away from the scream that was everywhere. "Shaaaandraaaa! Aadesh! No. It's got them—it has their faces. The tick—"

Transmission from the *Basilisk* cut out.

"What's happening? Jonas?"

Kira's eyes locked with his, wide and full of dread. He could feel a similar rigor in his face, the muscles pulled taut. Bile rose in his throat.

"What was that?" he demanded again after a moment. "Jonas? Guys, answer! Anyone, answer!"

Kira spun to face the cockpit entrance, visibly shaking in her suit. On the inside of the door, *Aye, aye, m'lady* had been scrawled in English. But unlike the other verses, which had been drawn with ink, this one looked a rusty red, as though written in blood.

"Maybe Jonas is right about the song," she said, her breath shaky.

"Come in, *Basilisk*. Anyone, *come in*."

Suddenly, the entire ship jerked hard to port. The tether holding the two ships together had pulled taut. Shifting left created torque that shot the bow of the ship right. They flew to port, then banked starboard. Their magnetic boots held fast, but Victor's knees buckled and he toppled to one side. The trolley slid, bouncing off a far wall. Kira caught herself on the edge of the dash and remained upright.

"What's happening up there?" Victor yelled. They were moving now.

He couldn't guess what was transpiring aboard their ship, so he had to get control of this one. Switches flipped, dials turned, buttons depressed. He put in a gentle away course. Nothing. The main drive refused to engage. He tried the compensating thrusters—no go.

"We have to go, Vic!" a hysterical voice from the *Basilisk* broke in. Jonas. "Tick. Tick. Have to turn this ship around."

"What are you talking about? You can't go anywhere while the ships are still tethered. If you turn on the Poincaré drive, it'll tear them both apart!"

Victor banged his fist against the dash, willing the engines to work.

"Jonas, stop the ship, now! Dammit, you'll kill us! Where are the others?"

But Jonas wouldn't answer.

"We've got power, but I'm not getting any control. Kira, we have to—"

But Kira wasn't paying any attention to him. She took achingly slow steps toward the words on the door, reaching out.

"Come on, grab the trolley." He slid between her and the entrance.

Tears streamed down her face. He grabbed her by the shoulders and shook. "What's wrong? We have to finish this!"

Her gaze bore straight ahead, as though he weren't there. The ship jerked again, and they fell together on their sides.

She didn't try to get up. Instead she started to hum. Her stare was glossy, distant.

"Kira? Kira, come back to me! Kira!"

She sang quietly, her voice swollen with emotion. "Aye, aye, m'lady, there's a dragon down below. Aye, aye, m'lady, yet exploring we shall go."

The timbre of her voice horrified him—it was the sing-songy lilt of a small girl, trying to make herself feel better with a cheery tune. Surreal and out of place, it conjured up images of broken dolls and skinned knees.

Unsure of himself, sick with the sudden collapse of the crew, Victor tried to hold on to some semblance of normalcy. "You want to sing?" he asked, hefting her to her feet. "Fine. We can sing, but we have to work. Kira, do you understand?"

She nodded slightly, and Victor's heart rose with a glimmer of hope.

He let her move away toward the trolley under her own power. But as he released her, his eye caught a reflection in the forward shield. The reflection of a figure. A third person in the room.

Instinctively, he reached again for Kira, yanking her close. He twirled on the spot to face … nothing. Still nothing.

But when he looked back at the reflection, the person was still there. A woman, unmistakable, in a flowing white gown.

"Lily?"

The reflection lifted one finger to its lips.

It couldn't be. He knew it wasn't her. Knew it had to be in his mind.

And yet …

"*How?* You aren't supposed to be here. You can't. *You can't!* You said we couldn't be together, so leave me alone!"

The reflection pointed past him, toward the door.

"What is it?" Kira asked, curling into him. "Do you hear it, too? It's not real, is it? The ticking's not real."

With lungs stuttering and heart racing, Victor's gaze darted around the cockpit. Was something here with them? Or was it all in their heads? Was this what happened to the *Illico* crew? Had something invaded the ship and taken hold of their brains?

Then he heard it for sure. Faint at first, like the soft ping of a confused insect bouncing off a windowpane.

Tick, tick, tick.

Then louder, more insistent. Rocks thrown at a biodome door.

Tick, tick. Clang. Clang.

"What is that?" Kira sobbed. "*What* is *that?*"

Trepidation filled Victor up like a fuel tank. One spark and he'd go up in flames of panic. He couldn't get his lungs to work right. Spots swam before his eyes and he feared he'd pass out.

"It's nothing!" he insisted. "Don't look. Close your eyes. There's nothing there. Just don't look."

The next moment, Kira cried out. She jerked violently against his body, shoving him away. He let go, and she tripped, falling heavily to the deck.

She screamed and screamed, scooting herself slowly away from him. Legs flailing, she held up her arms as though to ward off a blow. "It's got his face!" she yelled.

Quick snaps arched and flexed her spine. The white gloves of her suit strained up for the ceiling, then fell against the floor. Her eyes rolled back in her head as tremors overtook her entire body. Every muscle seized.

"Daddy?"

A half choke, half gurgle sprang from her throat and her face knotted into utter shock.

Then the spasms stopped—but before Victor could force himself to move, the bottom half of Kira's body whipped wildly around, opposing her stationary top half. Her mouth widened in a ghastly, silent scream—her gaze fixated on the ceiling.

He couldn't hear it, but he saw her spine *snap*.

Then all was still.

"Oh God, no," he breathed.

Darting to her side, he reached out, but did not touch her supine body.

There was nothing natural about the way she lay—her spine no longer formed a smooth line through her body. Poor Kira's face was as contorted as her form, frozen in surprise.

"Kira, get up," he said weakly. She was fine, she had to be fine. She was fine a moment ago. "Kira? Come back to me. Kira."

Heat swathed his face, and his jaw muscles clenched so tightly his teeth ached. What had happened? He couldn't process it, couldn't accept it.

Lily's phantom reflection appeared once more—inside his helmet. It felt close, as though his best friend stood right over his shoulder.

I should have stayed on Mars. Everyone knew the Sargasso was dangerous. And their crew had ven-

tured too far, past the point of no return. Three-point-three light-hours. Too far.

"Go away," he moaned.

The Lily-ghost simply pointed.

But now, instead of pointing toward the door, she pointed straight up.

Tick, tick. Clang.

There's nothing there, he told himself. *There can't be any sounds because you're in a vacuum. There's nothing there—*

Except Lily, her arm held tightly by her side with just her index finger extended, rigid.

Pointing up.

Pointing at this same spot on the ceiling where the dead woman's gaze was transfixed.

Tick, tick.

"Don't look. *Don't look!*" he whimpered. "It can't get you if you don't see it." A child's reasoning—but the only thing that made sense to his muddled brain.

Sweat slid down the bridge of his nose and dropped into the bottom of his helmet. It pooled, and he glanced down.

A dark shape was refracted in the droplet. He clamped his eyes shut.

Too late.

I see you!

With a roar he threw back his head and opened his eyes.

Clutching the ceiling with four mechanical legs—each tapping out a little tick as they dithered against the paneling—was a ghastly abomination.

Slack-jawed, mask-like human faces blossomed from a fat black belly. Faces of people he knew. There was Shandra, and Aadesh, and Kira. And his grandmother and his sister. But at the forefront, bigger than the rest, was Lily. Her mouth wide, jaw unhinged, flapping haphazardly as the creature tried to speak. But no words came out.

Searing pain engulfed Victor's head. Worse than any migraine he'd ever felt. He almost threw up, except his insides felt empty, like he had no guts and no bones.

Every inch of him felt overloaded. And in that moment he knew he was going to die—seeing this thing. This thing that must have followed them throughout the ship was going to kill him just like it killed Kira.

But why did it have Lily's face?

He tore his gaze way from the ceiling, and there in front of him stood the other Lily—the gauzy reflection.

She stepped closer, still ethereal, nothing more than a two-dimensional glimmer. Closer. Closer.

With the pain rising, he didn't care. He just wanted everything to end.

Then the reflection stepped *through* him.

Instantly, the agony disappeared. In its place, the reflection left behind the ease of pure peace. Utter solace. A love and understanding like he'd never known before.

Was it all in his mind? Or had the love come from this Lily-phantom?

Victor dropped to his knees, gasping. Really breathing for the first time in hours.

Shifting out of his body, the reflection floated above him, putting itself between him and the accursed creature. Once more she pointed, and he understood.

Flee. Escape. Survive.

He was in danger, and it wanted him to live, this figment—this thing that was both the woman he loved and something else entirely. Something else intelligent.

An overwhelming urge to escape wracked his body, tugging him out of the cockpit.

He hurried for the exit, leaving the trolley and Kira's limp form.

The *tick, tick, tick* followed him.

While he dashed through the verse-covered halls, heavy vibrations shook the *Illico*. The *Basilisk* was still pulling away. "Is there anyone out there?" he asked. "You have to kill the Poincaré drive, *now!*"

He reached the loading dock in record time. Out the open airlock, he could see the *Basilisk* at the other end of the tether, trembling like a leaf in the wind. The drive had yet to fully engage, and couldn't yet compensate for the planetoid's gravity. Strain pulled the cable taut. Just as he was about to attempt the climb, a new stage in the drive kicked in, causing a massive jerk. The line stretched, went slack, then snapped tight again. If he'd been out there it would have flung him to the stars.

There was no chance he could get safely up the line and into the *Basilisk*. He was stranded in a dead

ship, hitched to a mechanical bull with no one at the helm.

He whirled back around, considering his options, and saw the abomination hanging from the ceiling. Fangs protruded from the Lily head, and the Kira head had grown larger, more dominant. Its feet tapped against the carbon-composite, but he could no longer hear their *tick, tick, tick*.

Would the creature pursue him forever? Torment him right until the end?

Fatigue hit him like a sledgehammer. *I should stop. I should give up. I should just go to sleep and let the nightmare end.*

Intense emotion, a calming love, flowed into his limbs. He looked up, out of the airlock. There stood Lily on the tether, like an angel walking on a high wire. She pointed at the *Basilisk*.

An escape pod shot away.

Someone was alive.

The sight fortified him, and the reflection willed him to keep going.

He took a deep breath. He had to get out of here—if not for himself, then for whoever was in that pod.

One foot in front of the other. You can do it.

Backing away from the open hatch, he pivoted on one foot, redirecting his efforts. With another deep breath he steeled himself against the grotesque creature. What would happen when he passed under it? Would it rocket itself from its perch, grab onto his helmet and tear inside?

Victor let out a great roar and bolted beneath, waving his hands frantically above his head to ward off an attack. His gloves brushed the doorframe, but missed the monster.

A handful of Lily's reflections popped up at once in the hall, like road signs, guiding him through the skeleton of the *Illico*. But he didn't need them to point the way. He knew where he was going.

The vibrations became more and more violent as the *Basilisk*'s thrust increased. Victor tripped over uneven sections of flooring and bounced between the walls of the narrow passageways.

Finally, he reached his destination. A sign above a sealed door proclaimed: *Emergency Shuttle Dock.*

Slipping through the hatch, he immediately put all of his weight behind the door to close it. He knew the abomination was close, though he could not hear the ticking. But the hinges were soft-close—the door shifted slowly.

Victor's heart pumped wildly in his chest.

Go away, go away, go away! I'm leaving your damn Sea. You can keep it!

One long, black leg slipped in around the frame. It looked different now, ethereal, like the reflections. It scraped through the vacuum, searching him out, trying to make contact. Victor pushed with all his might, dodging the frantic claw.

The door closed with a soft *thud* that Victor felt rather than heard. It pushed through the creature like it wasn't even there—but the leg remained. Severed from the monster, it hung for a long moment, impossibly suspended, before becoming hazy and disappearing altogether—like a dream.

Safely locked inside, Victor took note of the stasis tubes, then hurried to the pilot's seat. The shuttle wasn't simply a mini-ship. It was for emergency evacuation only, and could not store enough provisions needed to support a full crew for a long period of time. Anyone finding themselves more than one week outside of inhabited space had to use the stasis chambers. The imperfect cryo tubes did not stop aging or autonomic responses, but slowed them considerably. In theory, it slowed them enough to get an otherwise-stranded or severely injured crew to safety.

"Come on, come on!" Victor chanted through gritted teeth as he powered up the shuttle. With a deep moan and series of creaks, the craft came awake. A quick diagnostics check revealed that all systems were *go*.

The reflection smiled back at him from a glint on the helm. He knew it wasn't Lily, and he knew it wasn't his imagination. This reflection represented something else, something real.

His savior.

As he deftly piloted away from the ghost ship, he took in the bigger picture through the craft's shield. Pieces flew off both ships. Frantically, he searched for the pod.

"Where are you?"

Bits of metal sailed past, like shoals of fish or swarms of insects.

Could he spot the pod amongst all the debris?

Ah, there!

Everything around Victor appeared to slow as he approached the jettisoned pod. Time stretched out. His breaths seemed to come minutes apart. Smooth, deliberate motions brought the shuttle's entryway airlock in line with the pod's. All the while, the two big ships disintegrated in slow motion.

And the love he felt from the reflection kept increasing, growing into a splendid light in his mind. It blossomed into a feeling he could only equate with the divine. An angelic love.

He ran from the pilot's seat to the airlock and briefly hesitated before throwing open the hatch, not knowing what to expect. Would the creature still be there, clinging to the door?

Didn't matter. He had to rescue whoever was in that pod.

He eased the door open. Dinah leapt into his arms. No one else followed—not his crewmates, and not the abomination.

"Dinah, how?" Had the cat somehow escaped on her own, or was that just a madman's fancy? Someone aboard must have sealed her in. Surely. Right?

The cat purred, blinking her eyes softly at Victor. He studied her for a long moment, wondering if the Sea had changed her, too.

He was too exhausted to think on it further. Right now he was simply relieved to have her curled safely in his arms.

Laying in a trajectory for the closest inhabited body—Uranus's moon, Titania—Victor watched helplessly as the *Illico* twirled and collapsed in a stunning dance of death. The *Basilisk* matched it, and as the Poincaré drive petered out, the two bodies of debris began orbiting each other around their tethered point. Fragments rained down on the planetoid.

For a long time, Victor scanned the wreckage for his shipmates' bodies. He found none.

"Come on, Dinah. We have to sleep now." He calibrated one stasis chamber for the cat. Limping, she jumped into the cryo tube of her own accord.

After double-checking their course, he settled into a chamber himself. The glass covering whooshed into place, revealing yet another reflection of Lily. She appeared to be with him, curled up next to him in the tube.

He understood now that ships were not welcome in the Sargasso. It was guarded by an intelligence—something previously completely unknown. Victor was the only one who'd encountered it and lived. He knew it would be his job to inform the system, spread the word far and wide: the Grid—the *Sea*—is off limits.

All people who venture into the region will go insane, will be overcome by that monster.

But why had *he* been allowed to live? Why had the reflection of Lily saved him when no one else had ever escaped? He would spend a lifetime trying to decipher the clues.

As he shut his eyes, drifting off into a stasis-dream, his limbs tingled with relief and his heart swelled with adoration. Once more, the reflection bestowed upon him a loving sense of ease. The love was not from Lily, but it was better, surer, more constant than any human love.

Victor let sleep claim him, confident that when he awoke, his savior would still be there.

Please stay steady-on by the dock,
And save your heart for me.

Original (First) Publication
Copyright © 2014 by Marina J. Lostetter

Lou J. Berger lives in Denver with three kids, three Shelties, and a kink-tailed cat with odd habits. This story marks his seventh sale, and his fourth appearance in Galaxy's Edge.

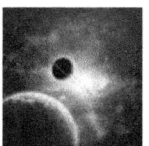

a
Sargasso Containment
story
www.SargassoLegacy.com

NIKKI DARK AND THE BLACK RUST

by Lou J. Berger

Nikki Dark piloted the *Dreadnought* to a perfect landing on Ceres' icy surface, shut down the small craft's systems, and put her helmet on.

She took a moment to just lean back and relax, anxiety washing over her like rain. Whether it was running from the Space Patrol, being shot at by rivals, or being cheated by her smuggling contacts, every moment of her life was stressful. Her ship was overdue for repairs and she simply didn't have the money. Too many things had gone wrong lately. Finally, she got up and stepped outside.

The distant sun threw stark shadows among the piles of dirty, carbonate-infused ice that made up the dwarf planet's surface. Fifty meters beneath her feet, dark water sloshed in utter blackness.

A single yellow light gleamed over the door of a corrugated iron shed connected to the end of a long row of ag domes, where all the food was grown. She trudged across the rough ice pasture to the door, then banged on it. It cracked open, and Seamus poked his helmet out, touching it to hers.

"Got my stuff?" he demanded.

"Don't I always?" she replied.

"Good." Then: "I've got something new for you to move—a new recreational drug."

She shook her head. "I don't sell drugs."

"You'll sell this one," he assured her, handing her the satchel. "And you'll make more than on your last dozen produce shipments. We call it Rust."

Nikki regarded the satchel with distaste, but she knew her son Kyle would need money for college soon.

"Rust?" she repeated. "Like on metal?"

"No, it's a type of fungus. Our bioengineer noticed it growing on the corn plants and traced it back to the water we'd pulled from under the ice. These"—he pointed to the satchel—"are two varieties: ten packages of red, seventy percent pure with some live fungus mixed in, and ten packages of black, ninety percent pure and no live fungus."

"What does it do?"

His eyes flashed with excitement. "A smooth high with no hangover. Stuff usually goes a kilocredit each for the red, and three kilos for the black."

"That's awfully expensive for a new drug," she noted.

Seamus flashed a rare smile. "True. But it's in huge demand in the colonies."

"*All* the colonies?" she asked dubiously. "What about Earth?"

He nodded. "All of 'em. And this stuff is *hot*. Don't tell anybody where you got it. I don't need any visits from the Space Patrol."

They walked to the ship and she tucked the satchel into the *Dreadnought*'s external hold, then touched her helmet to his again. "Fine, add it to my bill. Help me move these inside?"

Together, they moved the crates into the shed, stacking them against an unused wall. Seamus closed the exterior door and threw a switch that started a vibration she felt through her feet. When the sound of the pump grew loud enough to hear, she unbuckled her helmet and removed it, inhaling the rich, fertile odors wafting from the connected domes. She shook loose her auburn hair, then tilted her head forward to hide the crinkled scar on her left cheek. She removed a gauntlet and poked her datapad, entered a password, and brought up the manifest.

"Here we go," she said, then scanned each crate's ID tag as she called out their contents. "Cigarettes, holo crystals, Earth liquor, copper tubing and silica, a case of printers, and this"—she indicated a large crate at the bottom of the stack—"is your new forge assembly. Are you thinking about changing your name to Hephaestus?"

Seamus frowned. "Who?"

Nikki took a deep breath and then let it out slowly. Nobody read the classics anymore. "Never mind. It's all here. Sign my receipt and then let's grab some dinner."

Together they walked through the linked domes, moving between spinning hydroponic cylinders. The warm, fetid stench of well-fertilized plants circulated throughout the mining colony's interior. They continued walking until they reached the dining hall, nestled in the colony's hub. Dirty prisoners, all with bar codes tattooed on their arms, stood in line, awaiting the chow bell. It rang, and each of them surged forward to grab trays and utensils. Nikki leaned close to Seamus and whispered: "Those tomatoes were a big hit on Callisto. So were the beans. Do you have any more?"

Seamus nodded. "And we also have a metric ton of potatoes crated. Ten percent upcharge?"

"Throw in fifty bushels of kale and it's a deal."

"I'll see what I can do."

When it was her turn in line, she ladled double helpings of blotchy, white beans onto her tray, then added a large spoonful of pale, steamed spinach. She took three ears of corn, which prompted some grumbling down the line. The vegetables looked smaller, more pale than they had the last time she'd visited. Even the ears of corn were half-sized.

She sat down at a large table across from Seamus, staring at her tray in disgust.

"What's up with the food?"

He ignored her and shoveled white beans into his mouth.

She looked around. All the prisoners looked a little off, as if they were medicated. The normal chatter was absent, and the only sound that filled the hall was the scraping of utensils against plastic trays.

"What's going on?" she whispered through clenched teeth.

"Later. Eat now."

She ate, thinking about how much things had changed. Normally, she looked forward to eating the fresh produce on Ceres; it was the highlight of her smuggling triangle. The food she bought on the little ice planet was for her next destination, the high-priced restaurants of Callisto.

Later, back in the shed, she took stock of the inventory that Seamus had assembled for her. She stared in dismay at the wilted kale, the blotchy tomatoes, and more half-sized ears of corn.

"What the hell, Seamus?" She glared.

"It's what we've got. Take it or leave it."

"I can't sell this crap to my clients! They pay top dollar, and they expect the best. Take this junk back and bring me something I can move!"

Seamus crossed his arms, his mouth set in stone. "Don't push it, Nikki. This is what we have to offer."

She drew her weapon and pointed it at him. "I'm not going to ask you again."

"I can't give you anything better. We don't *have* anything better!"

"Why the hell not?"

He rubbed his hand across his half-shaven face. "We've been working on keeping up with the demand for the Rust, getting it prepared. Some of it must have contaminated the grow houses. You can still eat it."

"Then I want a discount. A serious discount."

His shoulders slumped and he finally nodded.

"What's the deal with this Rust, anyway? You guys have always prided yourself on the quality of your gardens." She indicated the crates. "Are you telling me that you've decided to become drug dealers instead?"

"Nikki, you don't understand," he said. "The Rust takes you into another dimension."

"And you're letting hardened criminals process it for you," she noted with a frown.

"We've had some trouble," he admitted. "Been a few overdoses."

She stared at him in disgust. *Well, there goes another produce supplier down the drain.*

They suited up and Seamus helped her load the crates into the *Dreadnought*. She retrieved the satchel, clambered aboard and pressurized the ship.

She tapped into the colony's wireless signal to retrieve her mail, scanned her messages, and saw one from her son. She clicked it first.

"Mom?" Kyle's recorded face filled the screen. His eyes were troubled and he kept looking away while he spoke. "I left Uncle Curtis' house. I couldn't stand it there anymore. I'm safe, but I won't go back. He's

…" The young man paused in the recording. "I wish you were here."

His image froze. Kyle was a good kid, never caused any trouble. She'd known he wouldn't be safe in the Outer Colonies, at least in the places she could afford, so she'd made arrangements for him to stay with her brother.

She bit her lip and archived the message, then clicked on the next one, from her brother Curtis. His face appeared on the display. "Hey, Nik. Kyle's gone, and I don't know where. Call me."

She rubbed her eyes and sighed. She'd been on the run for five exhausting years. Living with an unmarried uncle was no life for a kid, but she couldn't provide a better one for him. At least, not yet.

She sent a brief message to Kyle, asking him what had happened, then recorded an angry one to Curtis. She pointed out that she was paying him quite a bit of money to raise Kyle, and she damned well expected him to earn it. Then she lifted off, keeping under the base's radar until she'd cleared the nearby horizon.

As she made her way to Callisto, she thought about Kyle and, for the hundredth time, wished that things were different.

She arrived a week later and was immediately intercepted. A massive cruiser suddenly appeared as her proximity alarms began screeching.

"Attention, *Dreadnought*," said a voice.

She keyed the mic and replied. "This is *Dreadnought*. Who is this?"

"Commander Warren Jain, Space Patrol. You'll be boarded and searched upon landing. Don't deviate from your flight path, Ms. O'Riley. You wouldn't like the results."

She blanched. Nobody out here knew her real name. She'd been operating as Nikki Dark for twenty years and everything she owned was registered in that name. This clearly wasn't a typical inspection. They'd been waiting for her.

"Affirmative, Commander Jain."

She guided the ship down to Callisto Station, a sprawling series of domes scattered across the blasted surface of the moon, with Jupiter looming large on the horizon. Once down, she dismantled the copilot's instrumentation board and pushed the satchel deep into a recess in the bulkhead, a storage spot she'd had constructed for just such an occasion. She reassembled the board and verified that the dummy instrumentation showed appropriate readings for a grounded ship.

A pounding on the airlock sounded at the same moment as Jain's voice came through the speakers. "Ms. O'Riley? My security detail has arrived. Please allow them access to your ship."

She deactivated the external locks and a young soldier stepped into the cramped cabin. "Sorry, ma'am, but I have orders from Commander Jain to search inside your vessel for contraband." He thumbed over his shoulder. "The other two will look outside."

Nikki scowled and waved her hand, granting permission. She'd been very careful, hiding her smuggling activities with legitimate shipments of needed goods, like the forge she'd just delivered to Ceres. For five years, ever since Mercury, she'd managed to keep a low profile. She touched a finger to the wrinkled scar on her left cheek and thought about that day. For a full minute she'd been adrift in space without a suit, the Sun's rays scorching her. It had taken twenty-one skin grafts to rebuild her face. She still shuddered at the memory.

Red lights flashed on her board as the soldiers opened the external sealed compartments. She leaped to her feet.

"Hey! I have produce in those bins! Exposure to these temperatures will ruin it!"

The soldier shrugged. "Orders, ma'am. Nothing I can do about it."

"That's not good enough!" she snapped. "Get Commander Jain online!"

Commander Jain's voice filled the cockpit. "How may I be of service, Ms. O'Riley?"

"Your gorillas are ruining my shipment! I expect you to pay me for my loss!"

"Now, Nicole, why don't you just tell us where the Rust is, and we'll stop searching your ship?"

She sat down slowly. So that's what the search was about. "I don't know about any rust, Commander. I keep a well-maintained ship—shiny and rust-free."

Jain's voice paused, then continued, silky-smooth but with an edge. "Corporal, please continue your search."

Nikki watched from the copilot's seat as the young man opened every interior hatch, then crawled behind the engine equipment, looking for a hiding place. When he approached the copilot's station, Nikki looked up at him with cold disgust, letting her hair fall away from her scar.

He flushed and turned away, ignoring the board.

After twenty minutes of fruitless searching he called Jain. "Nothing here, sir. She's clean."

Jain's voice returned. "Thank you, Corporal. Ms. O'Riley, you are free to continue. I am deeply saddened by the loss of your shipment. My condolences. Please present me an itemized bill and I'll see that it gets reimbursed, once it's maneuvered through all of our red tape. Jain out."

After the corporal had left, she suited up and went to examine the cargo. Not great to begin with, it had frozen solid upon exposure to Callisto's thin carbon-dioxide atmosphere and had been rendered inedible.

She went through the Station airlock to try to negotiate partial payment on a fast resupply, but her Callisto contact was furious and demanded a full refund. With reluctance, Nikki drained her bank account and gave him everything she had. She promised to find a new supplier, but he slammed the door in her face.

She left his restaurant and mingled with the evening crowds, walking aimlessly for hours before eating dinner alone, then went back to the ship. Eventually, she turned over and fell asleep by the dim light of the chronometer.

✧

When she awakened nine hours later, her message light was blinking. She stumbled to the pilot's chair and sat down, rubbing sleep from her eyes.

It was from Curtis.

"Nik, I got your message. You really aren't in any position, telling me what to do while you gallivant around the Jovian moons. And your kid is just as stubborn as you always were. It's no surprise he's the way he is, given your inability to obey the law."

His message ended, and the transmission froze on an image of his contorted, scowling face. Nikki punched a button and the screen went dark. He'd been clean for almost a decade when she entrusted him with Kyle, but she was sure now that he was using again. She needed to get to Earth, despite the bounty on her head.

She squared her shoulders, opened the console, withdrew the satchel of rust, and left the ship. It was time for Nikki Dark to make things right.

She headed into the seedy areas of Callisto Station, looking for the nightclubs away from the Strip, hovels without garish neon signs where the right sort of clientele might clamor for the red rust she carried instead of more traditional forms of escape like heroin and cocaine, or the tried-and-true crystal meth. They'd have money, and if she was going to take Kyle back and find a new place for him, she was going to need all the money she could get her hands on.

She found a likely spot in the corner of a filthy dome away from the main Strip. It had a dirty facade, a burly synth manning the door, and a glowing sign that read "*Shady's Shadow*" above the door.

"Can I score pharms here?" Nikki asked, sidling up to the synth.

"Who wants to know?"

She shrugged. "Nikki Dark."

"Never heard of you."

"That's due to change," she assured him. "Tell your boss that I have something he wants."

The synth chomped on his toothpick for twenty seconds while his eyes glazed over. They grew clear again. "*She* says to go inside."

Nikki pushed open the door. The interior lights were up and the cleaning robots were trying without much success to scrub the grime from the floor and walls. A young woman with bright orange hair and firefly ink tattoos sat at the bar, reading a scrolling newsfeed. She looked up, uncoiled from her stool, and walked over to Nikki.

"The *real* Nikki Dark?" she said, squinting in disbelief.

"The one and only."

"I'm Shady," said the orange-haired woman, then stuck out a hand. "You're a legend ever since Mercury."

Nikki took her hand. "You ever hear of Rust?" she asked without preamble.

Shady's eyes lit up. "You got black?"

"No," lied Nikki. "But I have ten packages of red. I just turned down an offer on the Strip. He wouldn't meet my price."

"What *is* your price?"

"Why don't you tell me what you're willing to pay for quality red?"

Shady thought for a moment, then smiled. "I'll buy all ten kilos for double your best offer. My customers have been beating my door down for it."

Nikki clenched her jaw in silent frustration. She had no idea what the drug was worth on the street, only what she had paid Seamus. Maybe she could negotiate for ten kilocredits each, for a 900% profit. "How about ten?"

Shady paled. "Ten megs? You're kidding. They offered five? I figured if the other club offered only two megs, you'd take four."

Nikki kept her face stony. Two *megs* for each package was a two thousand percent profit. Way more expensive than heroin. Had the drug become that popular in only a week? "This is red Rust, not black. We're clear, right?"

Shady inclined her head.

Nikki sighed dramatically and said "Okay. You win. The other guy offered three megs, but I knew I could do better. Pay me six and I'll deliver right now."

Shady winced but agreed and they bumped datapads. Nikki dug into the satchel and handed the ten bricks of red, paper-wrapped rust to Shady.

"What's the big deal with this drug, anyway? I'm surprised it's so popular, given the cost."

Shady sat down on the stool and a faraway look came into her eyes. "It's like nothing else, Nikki. You haven't tried it, I assume?"

Nikki shook her head. "Drugs and me aren't friends."

Shady smiled. "You really should make an exception. Rust—and especially the black stuff—is an entirely new experience. Hallucinations are great, don't get me wrong, but these *take* you somewhere … somewhere *else*. Somewhere different, you know?"

Nikki shrugged. "I don't really get it, no."

"Trust me, you need to try it. Once. It was like I was talking to an alien version of God."

"How much would you pay for the black if I could score some?"

Shady put the bricks behind the counter. "Black is super rare, and currently worth fifteen megs per kilo on the street—but it's usually cut. If you can get me some pure stuff, I'll pay thirteen each."

"I'll see what I can do," said Nikki.

She left the place and walked through the streets of Callisto Station, clutching the satchel to her chest. If the numbers were right, she had over a hundred megacredits inside it, more than enough to compensate for her cargo loss, maybe even enough to retire. She would certainly have enough to get Kyle and bring him to the Jovian moons. He could go to school there, maybe get a tutor. No more smuggling. No more running from the law.

She hurried back to the ship and stored the satchel in its hiding place. Then she filled the fuel tanks and took off, heading directly for Earth.

And Kyle.

✦

Even at full speed, it took several weeks to get from Jupiter to Earth. Exactly twenty-seven days after lifting off from Callisto, Nikki requested permission to land near Denver and was granted it, using a counterfeit transponder code.

She made her way to her brother's apartment, hugging the satchel close. It was dangerous to have with her, but it was too damned valuable to be left alone on the ship.

"What the hell, Nik?" he said, his face going pale as he opened the door. "When did you get here?"

"Never mind that," she said through clenched teeth. "Where's Kyle?"

"I don't know. He hasn't been here in weeks."

"Who does he hang out with? So help me, Curtis, if he's hurt, I will personally cut your throat."

Curtis backed away a few steps. "Now, Nik …"

She pointed a finger at him. "I've been pulling your fat out of the fire your whole life. Now I give you one job, pay you generously, and you let him run off!"

Curtis held out his hands as if to placate her. "Nik, come on! He's sixteen years old. He's probably crashing at a friend's house."

"For a month? What happened? Why did he leave?"

Curtis ran his fingers through his hair, averting his gaze. "I had to be a little strict with him. I didn't give him his allowance for a couple months."

Part of the money she sent every month was to go directly to Kyle. "What did you do with his cash?"

She glared at him and noticed the tremor in his fingers, the pallor of his skin. His shirt hung loosely on him.

"Curtis, goddammit, I thought you were clean! You've been using again!"

"I can explain!"

She stepped forward and sank her fist into his pudgy gut. "You took Kyle's money to buy drugs!"

Curtis stumbled to the couch, clasping his middle, unable to look at her directly.

"Damn you!" She looked around, then walked over to his terminal. "Open this up. I want to send a message to Kyle."

He slunk over and unlocked the terminal. She sat down and looked directly into the terminal's camera. "Kyle, I'm at your uncle's. Come home. I've come to take you away with me." She terminated the message and sent it, then spun around in her chair to face a panicky Curtis.

"You can't!" he cried out, wringing his hands. "You can't just hire me to watch him and then swoop in here and take him away!"

Nikki glared. "You let him walk out of here and never tried to find him! You've been spending his money—hell, *my* money—to get high! You think this is a safe place for my son to live anymore?" Curtis blustered but Nikki held up her hand to silence him. "Never mind. Nothing you say will help your case right now. I'm going to look for Kyle."

She walked to the front door and opened it—and did a double-take. Kyle stood there, hand raised to knock. He was taller than she remembered, his hair was longer, and his face was now sprinkled with acne. But it was him.

She stepped into his embrace and wrapped both arms around him, clutching him hard. "Kyle, I …"

His own voice was husky. "I just got your message. I've really missed you, Mom!"

✦

Half an hour later, Nikki sat on the couch in Curtis' living room. Kyle kept disappearing, then reappearing with armfuls of clothes, books, and other belongings. A small pile grew larger in the middle of the floor.

"Kyle, you can't take all this with you. We can't fit it all on the *Dread*."

Curtis sat in a recliner, hunched forward, hands clasped to stop the tremors. "Why are you doing this, Nik? How can you be here? Aren't you still wanted for that thing near Mercury?"

"They don't know it was me. I'm here to get Kyle, then I'm taking him back to the Jovian moons. We're leaving Earth for good."

Curtis thought for a moment. "But what if somebody comes asking about him? What if the school wants to know why he hasn't come back?"

"He's *my* son, Curtis, not yours. He's my responsibility."

"Aren't you worried they'll find you?" Curtis sat upright in his chair. "Am I expected to lie for you?"

She stared at him and realization dawned. "For a price," she said, her voice filled with disgust. "It's not going to be for free, now, is it?"

He examined his fingernails and remained silent while Kyle walked into the room, dumped another load, then turned around and went back to his room. "You wanna share some of your fortune?"

"How much?" she said through clenched teeth.

"A megabuck?"

She looked into his eyes, and saw the raw, naked need. "No," she said after a moment. "Forget it. I'm tapped out."

Curtis stood up and stomped out of the room.

Kyle came back with a dramatic sigh, then dumped the last load on the floor. "There, that's everything."

"Let's go through this mess. You can take a third of it."

"Aw, Mom!"

She set her jaw. "Don't make me cut it down to a fourth."

For the next few hours, they winnowed through the pile, sharing memories, holding up old trophies, laughing over drawings he'd made in elementary school, until they finally had it pared down to a manageable size.

Kyle began taking his things to the rental, and Nikki followed him with an armful of his clothes. Her satchel was open in the back seat, and it had

been closed before. One of the packages of black was missing. She looked up at Curtis' bedroom window, then rushed through the front door. She went upstairs to check on him.

"Curtis, I …" She stopped just inside his bedroom door. Curtis lay in bed on his back, unseeing eyes staring at the ceiling. The missing package of black lay beside him on the bedspread. Bloody foam spilled from his gaping mouth.

She looked down at him, tears filling her eyes, at the silent body of her little brother.

"Oh, hell, Curtis," she muttered.

"Mom?" Kyle's voice floated up from downstairs. "You coming?"

"Just a minute!" She wiped her eyes, then opened his phone and called the emergency number.

"Yes?" said the voice on the other end of the line.

"There's a body here." Nikki gave the dispatcher the address. "An overdose."

"Thank you, ma'am. And what is your name?"

Nikki broke the connection and hurried downstairs. Kyle stood on the front walkway, waiting for her. "Come on! Let's get out of here!"

As she pulled away, flashing lights began converging on her brother's house.

They lifted off the next morning, having stocked the *Dreadnought* with supplies, topped off the tanks, and gotten permission for departure.

She took off and relinquished controls at 2,000 meters, allowing the automated system to guide her into orbit. A small warning signal advised her that the ship was once again under her command.

"What's this?" Kyle said, holding the satchel she'd tossed on the floor as they'd boarded.

"Give me that." She held out her hand.

Kyle hesitated. "What is it?"

"It's none of your business."

He opened the satchel and peered inside. His eyes widened. "Black? You scored some! Good for you!"

An image of Curtis' face, slathered in red foam, eyes wide open and unseeing, flashed across her mind.

"That's really dangerous stuff, Kyle—not to be messed with. Give it to me."

Reluctantly, he handed over the satchel. She opened it and counted the packages. Nine. "Thank you. I'll get rid of these when we get back to Callisto."

"Callisto? I thought we were going to Io."

She'd planned on selling the black rust and going to Io, but Curtis had changed all that.

She set her jaw. "No. Callisto is our first stop."

✿

They were greeted again by the same warship, which matched speeds with them.

"My, my," said Commander Jain. "If it isn't Ms. Dark."

"What do you want, Commander?"

There was a long silence. When Jain spoke again, his voice was reflective. "Excellent question. I want you in jail."

"I have another suggestion."

Jain hesitated. "What do you mean?"

She glanced at Kyle and then at the satchel at her feet. "Meet me at Shady's Shadow tonight at eight. Just the two of us. Nobody else." She broke the connection.

"Mom?"

She drew in a deep, ragged breath. "It's going to be okay. I think."

✿

Jain sat in the back of the bar, alone at a table. Shady smiled when she walked in and stepped forward to greet her, but Nikki shook her head in warning. Shady frowned and backed away. Nikki dropped the satchel on the table in front of Jain and sat in the other chair.

Jain looked at her for a long moment, then leaned forward and peered into the satchel. His eyes widened and his face grew serious. "That's quite a gift, Nikki," he said. "What do you expect in return for it?"

She let him see the weapon she had trained on him. "It's not a gift just yet." She stared at him. "You knew my real name. What else do you know about me?"

"I know everything. We linked you to the Mercury Coalition, where you damn near succeeded in stealing a billion credits worth of gold. Several agents were injured in that little escapade of yours. I believe your husband died?"

Nikki nodded. "Yes." She fingered the scar on her face, remembering the Sun's scorching heat, her desperate attempts to breathe in vacuum, Brian's frozen body drifting away into the blackness.

"We also know about your brother, and the black Rust we found in his home. You are looking at several lifetime sentences for smuggling, dealing in narcotics and, because of your brother, negligent homicide."

Nikki shook her head and pointed to the satchel. "If we don't reach an agreement I can sell this on the street and make enough to keep you fighting me in court for decades, always assuming I don't kill you in the next sixty seconds."

Jain leaned forward and placed his hand on the satchel. "Maybe, maybe not—but taking this off the street makes my career. You may have just handed me a promotion."

"Why haven't you arrested me before now?" demanded Nikki, staring at him. "Why leave me out there if you knew all this?"

"Nikki, we didn't arrest you because nothing you've done was that big a deal."

"But Mercury …"

He waved his hand in dismissal. "Nothing worth chasing you down for. We recovered the gold, you got a helluva scar to remind you of it, and nobody of importance got hurt."

She thought of Brian's torn body drifting away. *He'd* been important.

"So, in the end, we really didn't care what you did. Until now." He caressed the satchel.

She placed the blaster on the table and pushed it over to him, then pointed to the satchel. "There you go. I'm turning it over to you."

He lifted the satchel and set it on the floor beside his chair. "What is your suggestion?"

She took a deep breath. "I join forces with you and help you stop smuggling. You give me a suspended sentence for something minor, charge me some negligible fine, and drop all the other charges. My son is sleeping in a hotel room not far from here, and I'd like to go back to him tonight and wake up tomorrow a free woman, without looking over my shoulder anymore."

Jain pondered her over steepled fingers, then sighed. "Done. Report to me at the Space Patrol offices in the morning and I'll have the paperwork ready. I'll talk to the attorneys and have them drop all charges."

Nikki exhaled deeply and sank back into her chair. Tears stung the corners of her eyes. It was finally over.

"What made you decide to do this?" asked Jain.

"My son. He needs me."

He picked up the satchel and stood, then extended his hand. Slowly, she rose and took it.

"Where did you get the black Rust?" he asked. "Who's manufacturing it?"

She shrugged, looked him in the eye, and lied. "I got it from a woman who says it comes from a secret lab in the Sargasso."

He turned to go, then stopped.

"I look forward to working with you," he said. "The infamous Nikki Dark and me—partners! If nothing else, it's going to be interesting."

He walked through the smoke-filled bar and out the door, the throbbing music following him into the street.

After a moment Nikki left, heading back to the hotel and her sleeping son. Jain was right: starting tomorrow, her new life was going to be interesting. At the very least.

But tonight, for the first time in well over a decade, she knew peace.

Original (First) Publication
Copyright © 2014 by Lou J. Berger

Joy Ward is the author of one novel. She has several stories in print, at magazines and in anthologies, and has also done interviews, both written and video, for other publications.

THE *GALAXY'S EDGE* INTERVIEW
❧ ERIC FLINT ❧

Eric Flint, also known as the Red Bear of Baen's Bar, is a man who defies categories. So does his New York Times *bestseller writing, which varies from the far-ranging 1632 alternate history series to his fantasy and hard science fiction creations. We got the chance to visit with this icon at his home outside Chicago.*

Eric Flint: The very first piece of fiction I wrote was a hand-written military sf novel I wrote when I was 14 or 15. It was a novel about World War III. I don't think there were any main characters in it. I think it was a kid playing toy soldiers. But I discovered I liked to write, so then in high school I wrote a lot. I wrote a total of three novels, one of which I thought was good enough I paid a typist. Cost me sixty dollars, which was a lot of money for a 16-year-old kid; it was 1962 or '63. But I paid a professional to make a real manuscript out of it and I sent it in to Ace Books.

It came back rejected in three months. Thank God. I did get a very nice rejection letter from John Campbell which unfortunately I lost decades ago. But I was impressed. It was two pages long hand-written and a detailed explanation of why he was rejecting the short story. He encouraged me to keep writing. "Kid, you're talented. Keep at it."

Joy Ward: You spent about 25 years in political and union organizing. What drew you into political action?

Flint: I had been active in the civil rights movement from a very early age. I've been interested in politics since I could remember. I've always been interested in history since I could remember.

JW: What was important for you about you being involved in the civil rights movement?

Flint: It's the whole situation with race relations in America. When I was a kid my parents moved to France. I started out going to French schools. One of the things I like to tease my American conservative friends about who talk about how there ought to be more discipline in schools is you would love French schools because I used to get beaten in French schools. French schools are tough. When my dad realized that the headmaster of my school was regularly beating me, he blew his stack and went down there and chewed him out. I'm sure this French headmaster thought who is this crazy American because it is just taken for granted in France that naturally you whack kids with a ruler. My parents yanked me out of French schools. There was a very wealthy school, a very well-known private American school, the American Community School in Paris, which is still in existence. My best friend was the son of the American Ambassador to France. My sisters' best friend was the daughter of the Indian Ambassador to France because any kid who came from a place where the people spoke English, could be Indians, could be Indonesians, would send their kids there. It was a very multi-racial school. I didn't really think anything about it because kids don't. But my first conscious awareness of anything involving race I was eight years old and I learned the word "n*****s" from somebody. I wasn't really quite clear what it meant but I came home and I used it at dinner. The minute I used it I knew I was in serious trouble because there was dead silence at the table. My mother gave my father an apprehensive look. He got up and he said, "Eric, come with me." We went into the study. He pulled out a book with pictures and opened it up. It was a book about lynchings in the South. He showed me a number of these pictures of Black people being lynched. The one that I really remember, the thing that is most vivid about the picture is there was this young white boy right in the foreground, about my age, maybe eight years old pointing up at the corpse of the Black man hanging with a big smile. I remember that. It was just appalling.

But then my father said to me, "The word 'n****r' is a Nazi word." This is right after World War II. He had fought in World War II. He was a combat pilot in World War II in the Army Air Corps and he had come out with a Distinguished Flying Cross. He was quite highly decorated. He said, "This is what I fought against in World War II. This is what we were fighting. It wasn't just Germans. That's where it was worse. You can find this anywhere. That word is one of the manifestations of it." I don't even remember if he used the word racism but that's what he was talking about. And he said, "So we don't use it." And that was it.

I had decided I was going to major in history when I went to college. I pretty much had decided I was going to become a college professor in history. But I still didn't know what particular branch of history I was going to get into because I found all history interesting. In those days there was a very high-end glossy magazine called *Horizon*. One issue came in that had an article by a writer named Basil Davidson on the lost cities of Africa. It turned out that there was such a thing as African history. I wasn't aware it even existed. That was part of Davidson's point, that, one of the manifestations of the racism had been the kind of obliteration of the fact that Africans actually had a history of their own. The impression that most white Americans had, including me, was that they were a bunch of people running around in the jungle somewhere. It turned out it was an introduction to African history.

So I said, "I'll do this. I'll specialize in African history." UCLA, as it happened, was one of the three centers in the world that has African history. I was in the right place.

The single most important epiphany I ever had actually involved Chinese history. It was around the same time but I was at a friend's house. I can remember looking out over one of the hills in Los Angeles. I had been studying Chinese history. I actually was interested in non-European history. I got to thinking about all those generations of Chinese peasants that nobody remembers their names; nobody will ever know their names. Their families don't remember their names. But each one of them, just like every human being who has ever lived anywhere in the world, made some contribution to the human race. It may have been nothing more elaborate than providing food for other people as well as themselves but there was something.

Of all political philosophies the one I probably detest the most—it's not the worst, but I personally detest it—is Libertarianism, this attitude that Libertarians seem to have, that of ME. I did it on my own. Nobody ever, ever does it on their own. You come into the world as part of a species that is a quintessential social animal. You would not exist without that entire species. You cannot continue to exist. Whatever your accomplishments might be you can't ever say, "that was me." I know some part of that might have been you but you owe something. That is the basis of my own personal morality. You have a debt and you have to repay it. I leave it up to each individual to figure out what they think is the right way to try to do it. But I do think you have a debt. I think we can't say our job in life is ME, ME, Me and make as much money as you can and just screw you. Like I said, it's not the worst philosophy. It's not like the Nazis.

I just remember looking out that window thinking how connected we are not only to all other people but to our own history. I think it was Faulkner, I've forgotten who it was, said, I've forgotten the exact words he used but something like, "The past is still with us and not even past. The past isn't dead, It's not even past." I think it was Faulkner. And really that's true. So my interest in history has always been there. I can't remember a time in my life when it wasn't.

I've always thought we should try to understand the world from viewpoints different than your own. That's why I've always been interested in non-western histories. This is not multi-culturalism because I do not think cultures are equal. There are a whole lot of cultures out there that really sucked. We're probably way better off when they finally go away but you should still understand or look at them.

I think it was also tied in with my interest in science fiction. That goes back to at least when I was twelve. I've always thought about aliens and non-human intelligence as another angle to look at us. Now you can only do that in your own imagination. We never

met any but it's probably why in a lot of my novels the aliens are looking at us.

JW: What's important about looking at things from another point of view?

Flint: If nothing else to make sure you're not screwing up. One of the things that really drives me nuts when I hear is that when they talk about compassion they don't seem to understand what the word means. They seem to think it means "I am somehow a nice person." That's not what it means. It means the ability to see your kinship with anybody, including people who are really screwed up either because of objective circumstances or poverty or disease or 'cause they are just screwed up in other ways because they don't behave well. It doesn't mean you have to accept them but it does mean you should try to understand them. I run across people who seem to think that just because they are religious they automatically partake of this virtue. They don't. There are some very outstanding exceptions but I think that interest of mine is also a valuable trait if you're a writer because that is what writers are doing. Whether they realize it or not they are exercising their compassion when they write in the sense that they are seeing the world through someone else's eyes and make that make sense. It's the reason for the kinds of things I write when so much of what I write is based in history. Even things that don't look like it. *Mother of Demons*, my first novel, is really an alternate history taking modern humans and transplanting them into a Bronze Age world. How would they handle that? So I made it a Bronze Age world of aliens, not humans, so it gave them some freedom.

JW: What does that do for you to translate that into science fiction?

Flint: When I decided to become a writer I had been a political activist over twenty years, and I was kind of a little burned out. It's a pretty hard life. I had done twenty, twenty-five years of it and I figured whatever debt I had to the human race had been paid off. One other thing I really wanted to do was write. I did have to think about, what are you going to write? I've always enjoyed science fiction more than other writing but I've read a lot of other.

I've read a lot of mysteries. I've read a lot of historical fiction. The reason I picked science fiction was because it would give me the most artistic latitude. Modern literary fiction is basically a genre of its own. It's very rigidly circumscribed.

JW: What's important about that for you?

Flint: I want to write stories that I want to write and not worry about whether I'm fitting into a mold or not. I enjoy Westerns and actually I probably have been more influenced by Westerns than anything else in how I write. But I wouldn't want to write Westerns because it is too restrictive. Also the market for it has kind of blown up. I enjoy mysteries but I don't want to write mysteries because basically there are only three characters: the murderer, the victim and the detective. That's about it. All the mystery novels basically revolve around those three characters. Well, I enjoy that but I wouldn't want to spend a lifetime revolving in that narrow a line. There's a lot of romance in my writing but I don't want to write romances because there are a lot of restrictions on what you can do there when you start off. So-called literary fiction is really circumscribed. If you want to make it in literary fiction what you have to do is create a character who is some way or another pretty dysfunctional and then the plot is how he or she underachieves. I just don't want to write this because I don't care. It's not that I'm not sympathetic, it's not what I want to write. But it's very hard in literary fiction to break out plus there is an incessant concern about your prose. Science fiction gives me a lot of leeway. I could write about issues. You call it speculative fiction and you can write pretty much what you want. Actually the majority of what I write I don't think is alternate history. Alternate history is what I'm best known for and is certainly where I make the most money. Alternate history, how is that science fiction? In the case of the 1632 series, fine, it's a time traveler. In the case of the Belisarius series it's a time travel element involved. In the case of the series I've done two books, the Trail of Glory series, there's no science fiction element at all. It's just different history. But you can do that in science fiction. I can write pretty much anything I want. I can do comic fantasy, which I do.

You write books for different reasons, a different mix of reasons with each book. The book I'm writing right now with Mike Resnick, it's pretty much kooky. There's a certain serious element in it sort of in that I'm writing the alien side of the story. My aliens are all a bunch of religious fanatics. Their religion is very different from any human religion in that they are much less given to abstractions about ultimate gods and they consider human beings insanely optimistic. The idea that there is some good divine deity that created it all, this obviously flies in the face of all evidence. It should be clear that whatever gods exist are probably a bunch of assholes. I just finished a chapter in which my heroine recites the three principal prayers of her particular tenet or creed, the first one of which is seek not revelation lest ye be revealed. You don't want to call the attention of the gods to yourself because that always ends badly. The other two are along those lines so when they encounter humans it's kind of like these people are batshit crazy. That's fun to write. If I can poke some fun at some of the way human beings look at religion, God. It's a lot of fun to write because I don't have to do research. I can just sit there and I don't have to even think through the science.

JW: What does collaborative writing do for you?

Flint: Honestly on an emotional level probably the reason I do so much collaborative writing is I like it because you've got to remember I spent most of my adult life working in workforces where the work was one way or another collective. There was a lot of interaction in the workforce. On top of that I was a political activist and organizer so I had a lot of interaction with co-workers. It's a social life on the job. There's two things I don't like about being a writer. One of them is you wind up being able to read a lot less. At least in reading whatever you want to 'cause there's always something you've got to read. The other thing I don't like is my job is to go down to this room that measures 13 feet by 17 feet and talk to myself all day. This is a really weird way to make a living. The reason I go to conventions is that it's good for my mental health to get out of here and go somewhere and meet people I don't know, I didn't invent them and I can't predict what they are going to say because I don't get to do that on the job. The other way I do it, I do a lot of collaborative writing so I'm constantly interacting with other writers in all kinds of ways. I do a lot of editing, too. So the truth is I actually have at least as many friends as I ever have had in my life through the science fiction and I interact with them constantly and one of the main ways that takes place is collaborative writing. That's one reason.

The other reason is I can write a wider range of books. I can tell more stories than if I were simply working on my own because there's an old joke that in collaboration everybody does 70% of the work. Which is probably true but that's still not a hundred percent. So you can get more done collaboratively than simply by yourself. There are some things you have to do solo because you do lose a certain something with every collaboration. It's not quite as individual as something you did by yourself but the flip side of that is that you can do stories you could not do on your own.

JW: What do you look for in a co-writer?

Flint: The first thing I'm looking for is, can I get along with this person? My very first collaborative writer was David Drake. I remember David saying to me, he's done a lot of collaborative writing, "You know, Eric, it's really a bad sign when the first part of the paper you turn to each morning is the obituary section hoping you'll see the name of your co-author." He said, "But that happens." All my experiences have been good.

The second thing is do they have or are they bringing into the partnership a level of knowledge that I don't have or would be very hard for me to duplicate? The final thing is as much as possible I want them to be people whose writing skills have strengths. They may also have weaknesses, sometimes they do. Some of my co-authors are really uneven. But there's really something there.

What I don't want is a writer whose kind of, I'm trying to figure how to say this so it doesn't sound arrogant, I don't want them to be second-ringer as a co-author. I don't want them to be me. I want them to be whoever they are, whatever their strengths and weaknesses might be and we'll go from there. Some

of my co-authors like David Weber and Misty Lackey are extremely capable, accomplished, better-selling authors than I am. So that's not an issue but even there we're meshing well because we are bringing different things into it.

JW: What advice would you give to this next generation of writers?

Flint: The single biggest piece of advice I give to new writers, the same advice I give to kids trying to figure out what to major in in college, which is study what you're interested in and write what you want to write. Don't try to second-guess the market. Don't try to figure out what people want to read. Don't try to figure out what's going to sell. You do have to be practical about stuff. If you have a burning desire to tell a story that looks at the world from a viewpoint of a turnip I suggest you wait until you're a very well established writer. It takes months to write a novel, even if you're a fast writer. You're having to put a whole lot of your own self into it. Don't do that with a story you're not interested in. Do something you find interesting. Figure out a story you really feel passionately about and write about it. Let the chips fall where they fall.

Copyright © 2014 by Joy Ward

Paul Cook is the author of 8 books of science fiction, and is currently both a college instructor and the editor of the Phoenix Pick Science Fiction Classics line.

BOOK REVIEWS

by Paul Cook

Old Mars
Edited by George R.R. Martin and
 Gardner Dozois
Bantam - 2013
ISBN 978-0345537270 (Hardcover)

Old Mars, edited by George R.R. Martin and Gardner Dozois, is an anthology that intentionally takes a backward glance at the Mars of an earlier era in science fiction. As the editors state, they wanted their authors to return to the Mars of Bradbury and Burroughs to see what they could come up with. The stories gathered here differ wildly from one another, in terms of their vision of old Mars, but they tell us more about where science fiction is at the present moment rather than where it once was. True, the cities of Burroughs are here, as are varieties of Martians including those from H.G. Wells. But most of these stories have an unexpected grimness to them that belies any true relationship to the Mars of an earlier era. This is because today's authors have grown up in a different, more cynical era. The old adage still holds true: you can never go home again.

I was struck with how many stories deal with the darker side of scientific inquiry and the human pen-chant to enslave or destroy what it conquers. Several stories deal with humans looting and chewing up (literally) the Martian landscape and a lot of blood is otherwise spilled, much of it needlessly. We find this in "Martian Blood" by Allen M. Steele, "The Ugly Duckling" by Matthew Hughes, "Sword of Zar-Tu-Kan" by S. M. Stirling, and "Shoals" by Mary Rosenblum. The Stirling and Rosenblum are particularly grim stories, with the Stirling saved by the presence of a devoted and heroic Martian pet, something like a dog, whose plight I found more poignant than that of the humans. It would never have been published in any Frank Munsey pulp of the Teens, Twenties, or Thirties. *Asimov's*, yes. *All-Story Weekly*, no.

The stories that worked well in this anthology were also the stories that were just plain fun to read (as I'm sure they were to write). Foremost among them was "In the Tombs of the Martian Kings" by Mike Resnick, "The Wreck of the *Mars Adventure*" by David D. Levine, "The Sunstone" by Phyllis Eisenstein, and Howard Waldrop's *sui generis* "The Dead Sea-Bottom Scrolls." Several stories here have sea-faring motifs, including the aforementioned "The Wreck of the *Mars Adventure*" by David D. Levine, which will remind the reader of the preposterous journey to the moon in the movie *The Adventures of Baron Munchausen*.

We would recognize these stories today as mostly fantasy, but a kind that partakes of the alternate-history trope so that they only resemble science fiction. Still, it's a hard-edge brand of fantasy. The reason for this is as I mentioned above: The writers in *Old Mars* cannot escape from being what they are: creatures of the 21st century who bring to their stories all that they know of the innate viciousness in human nature. It's easier for us to envision the rape of the Martian landscape and its treasures than it is to harken back to the naive, high-fantasy Burroughs and H.G. Wells or the simplicity of Ray Bradbury's Mars. That aside, this is a fun collection, and word has it that a book on Venus is on the way. Now *that* should be a kick.

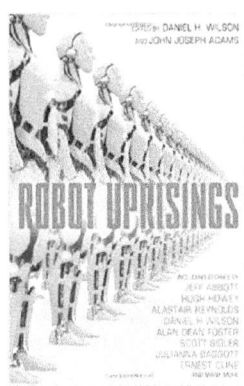

Robot Uprisings
Edited by Daniel H. Wilson and
  John Joseph Adams
Vintage - 2014
ISBN 978-0345803634

Mary Shelley's *Frankenstein* gave birth to the genre of science fiction in 1818 by giving the field its most potent metaphor, that of technology out of control. Science fiction since then has evolved in all kinds of directions, but it's never really let go of the simple idea that we, being the creatures that we are, might create something that could end up doing more harm than good.

Robot Uprisings is a collection of seventeen stories, most original to this volume, dealing with robots in all shapes and sizes, doing what they have traditionally done in science fiction: causing trouble. There are a couple of light-hearted romps in this anthology–Alan Dean Foster's "Seasoning" is the best of them. Most of these stories, though, depict humans at some level of peril with their mechanical creations. Among the best stories in this collection is Scott Sigler's "Complex God," wherein an arrogant young woman has created insect-sized robots that are engineered to remove radioactive waste from a bombed-out Detroit, one grain at a time. Her arrogance and indifference make her, oddly, one of the best "mad" scientists in science fiction I've run across in a long time. Julianna Baggott's innocently titled story, "The Golden Hour," is about a robot who helps a human survive a massive robot apocalypse that shuts down the human race in only an hour. I was deeply moved by the story-teller's voice and how much humanity Baggott managed to infuse in the robot who assists him. Cory Doctorow's "Epoch," the longest story here, concerns an intelligent robot called BIGMAC whose corporate owners want to shut him down and the human who becomes involved with him. This story and the above-mentioned "Complex God" were the two stories that also effectively dealt with corporate politics and how humans, because of their greed, ambition, or sheer stupidity, make bad decisions that ultimately cause havoc.

What I found most impressive in this collection was its broad mix of stories that expands what it means to be a "robot" and what we can do with them. In the past, as in Asimov's day, a robot was a human-shaped creation, meant to do things humans couldn't. We now know that robots can take all kinds of shapes, as well as take on the shapes of whatever system they happen to be *in* at the time, whether it's a computer network, a building, or even the human body. *Robot Uprisings* has a freshness to it that reminds us just how vibrant and relevant the *Frankenstein* metaphor continues to be … and how inventive our writers still are.

A Darkling Sea
by James L. Cambias
Tor - 2014
ISBN 978-0765336279 (Hardbound)

A Darkling Sea, a spectacular debut novel by James L. Cambias, takes place on a frozen planet called

Ilmatar which closely resembles Europa: Underneath a mile of ice is a dark oceanic world, this one teeming with life of all kinds, including intelligent beings resembling multi-limbed, multi-segmented crustaceans straight from the Burgess Shale. The Ilmatarans are farmers and harvesters (and some are bandits and thieves) and they live around deep-sea volcanic vents and mine the minerals and nutrients that come up from beneath the surface. Humans and another alien race, the Sholen, are forbidden by treaty not to have any contact with the primitive creatures at the bottom of Ilmatar's ocean. It's something like the Prime Directive, but it mostly has to do with science and scientists–human and Sholen alike–who have agreed by treaty not to pollute or taint *any* newly discovered intelligent race. They believe that these should be studied from afar until more can be known about them.

The novel begins when a narcissistic and totally reckless media star goes out one night in a stealth suit and gets within six feet of a group of Ilmatarans. Unfortunately, Ilmatarans have all kinds of senses that humans don't. They capture him and proceed to dissect him because they've never seen anything like a human before. This transgression by the humans angers the Sholen, a six-limbed species who think highly of themselves and much less so of human beings. The novel details the conflict between the Sholen and the humans as the Sholen try to shut down the research station and take all of the humans back up to the surface. The humans resist, of course, and they soon make contact with an exiled Ilmataran who tries to rally his people to fight the Sholen and help the human beings.

Cambias, like Hal Clement and Robert Silverberg before him, has put a lot of thought into the culture of the Ilmatarans, who are totally blind but perceive the world through smells and sounds and touch. They use tools but haven't developed metals technology. They have sophisticated laws and a strong sense of territoriality, but really don't know much about their world, especially what's above them. There are no philosophers among them, no religions. And Cambias doesn't make it easy for the humans and Ilmatarans to communicate. This takes a while as the action unfolds. (And typical of science fiction, the aliens in *A Darkling Sea* often are more rounded and complex as characters than the human beings.) Even so, this is a wonderful standalone novel that may or may not suggest a series, or at least a sequel. It's extremely well-written and the action never flags. This is *exactly* what a good science fiction novel is supposed to do. A terrific debut.

The Memory of Sky
by Robert Reed
Prime Books - 2014
ISBN: 978-1607014263 (Trade paperback)

The Memory of Sky is a trilogy in Robert Reed's Great Ship series which centers around a mysterious planet-sized space ship as it moves through the galaxy. The first novels in the series were *Marrow* (2000) and *The Well of Stars* (2004) and now we can add *The Memory of Sky*.

The Memory of Sky is three short novels about a boy named Diamond who lives in a fantastic tree-dwelling culture. The trees in *The Memory of Sky* are kilometers in height and are connected by walkways, rope bridges, and zeppelin-like air transports. The trees, though, exist in a world where the sun is *below* them and when it rains, it rains *upward*. The roots of the trees are embedded in a kind of rugged coral that is inhabited by a different kind of human being called the *papio*. Kilometers above them is nothing but incredibly dense canopy and misty clouds that few have penetrated. The tree-dwellers and the *papio* compete for *coronas* which they hunt. *Coronas* are giant creatures that inhabit the upper atmosphere of the "sun" just underneath the coral of this world. The humans get their metals, their rugged armor, and their sharp weapons from the *coronas*. As we learn early on, there is a connection between Diamond and the *coronas* and the novel is about that connection. Mostly the novel is about Diamond and how everyone wants a piece of him–literally.

To reveal more than that would be to spoil all the mysteries that Reed sets up. His world of trees might remind the reader of other science fiction novels taking place in a forested world (those by Bester, Niven, Le Guin, and Foster immediately come to mind), but Reed is a master of invention and creates a world that is truly *sui generis*. The three novels themselves dovetail nicely as we come to thoroughly know this massive hanging forest world and how fragile their whole society is as they wage war to capture Diamond. The action is non-stop with the second novel containing the greatest sustained battle scene I've ever read. All of the characters are poignantly drawn and the deaths of some are quite heartfelt. This is one of those rare books I literally could not put down. I was so effectively pulled into the yarn that I couldn't wait to find out who Diamond was or why everyone was fighting for him. I especially wanted to know where the novel was taking place and why no one seemed at all curious as to why things were the way they were.

Inexplicably–and much to the detriment of this beguiling novel–none of the many questions Reed puts forth are answered in the end. We learn nothing of the characters' true origins or even of the world itself. We don't learn a thing about how the tree dwelling humans are any different from the *papio*. We learn nothing about the "sun" below or the world above the tree canopy. We don't learn why this book is part of the Great Ship series. The Great Ship is mentioned once, but very obliquely and is never mentioned again. We're left wondering as to where the novel take place. Is it *inside* the Great Ship somewhere? Is it even inside of Marrow? Reed doesn't say.

Even stranger still, the ending Reed does give *The Memory of Sky* doesn't follow from any of the events in the novel. It seems tacked on, even hastily conceived. It was as if Reed couldn't decide how to end *The Memory of Sky* or that he saw that more could be milked from the story. Certainly there would be more money to be made from writing yet another trilogy about Diamond and his siblings. The fact is that Reed had more than enough room to conjure a satisfactory ending to *The Memory of Sky* but he chose not to. Whatever book he writes to answer all of the unanswered questions posed in *The Memory of Sky*, who's to say he won't pull the same stunt the next time around?

✿

Yesterday's Kin
by Nancy Kress
Tachyon Publications - 2014
ISBN: 978-1616961756 (Trade paperback)

Yesterday's Kin centers around the family of renowned geneticist Marianne Jenner and their involvement with the arrival of a group of humanlike aliens from a planet around the star Deneb. The aliens land in New York Harbor and build a heavily shielded floating pavilion called the Embassy. They claim that they are here to help humanity. It turns out that they are the ones in need of help.

Both the Earth and Deneb are about to be exposed to an approaching cloud of deadly spores drifting through the galaxy, and the aliens need the help of humanity's best geneticists to assist with finding a cure for the spores. One of the novel's mysteries is that the aliens and human beings are almost genetically identical. Thus, the cloud will affect both species. Marianne Jenner and several of her colleagues are enlisted to help the aliens with their research as the clock winds down.

Finding a cure for the spores would itself make for a good science fiction novel all on its own. Kress, however, always raises the stakes by bringing in her main character's family problems. Even though Marianne Jenner's professional life is on the upswing, the lives of her adult children aren't faring as well. The oldest children, Ryan and Elizabeth, constantly bicker with one another. Elizabeth is with the Border Patrol and has a harsh, dictatorial personality and doesn't like the aliens at all. Ryan, though more stable, is very passive and doesn't want any more boats in his life rocked.

It's the youngest of Marianne's children, Noah, who becomes central to the novel. Noah is homeless and addicted to a designer drug that, when ingested, creates a new identity for the user, giving him or her a false sense of reality. When Noah finds out that he was adopted and that he is genetically related to the aliens, he decides to join them. He moves into the Embassy, against Marianne's wishes, and much of the tension in *Yesterday's Kin* comes from what happens to Noah—and Marianne's reaction to it—as time begins to run out for the aliens and humanity.

Kress, more than anyone writing in science fiction today, understands that her fictional characters first and foremost come from families, and much of what they do and think and say reflects their family background—their wants, their needs, their ambitions. You can almost smell the Similac and the baby powder and the Gerber baby food jars on the kitchen counter in her stories … even as aliens are landing outside and Mom has to do something about it. Kress understands the poignancy of biological bonds and I don't think I've ever read a story of hers where this did not play a major role. *Yesterday's Kin* is another triumph for Nancy Kress and her publisher, Tachyon Books. This is a short novel, but it is tightly written and engaging throughout. I highly recommend it.

The Galactic Center Companion
by Gregory Benford
Lucky Bat Books - 2014
Amazon Digital Services (E-book)

Gregory Benford's Galactic Center novels appeared over a number of years. While they did not suggest a series when he started out (as the author freely admits), time and his own scientific research (and the enthusiasm of his publisher) allowed the books to evolve into one of the most rewarding series in science fiction. Collectively, the Galactic Center series tells the tale of humanity's expansion into the galaxy and what they find at the galaxy's center.

The novels in the series are: *In the Ocean of Night* (1977), *Across the Sea of Suns* (1984), *Great Sky River* (1987), *Tides of Light* (1989), *Furious Gulf* (1994), *Sailing Bright Eternity* (1995), and a novella, "A Hunger for the Infinite" (1999) which originally appeared in *Far Horizons*. The novella appears here in *The Galactic Center Companion* and is reason enough to get this book.

Gregory Benford is an accomplished astrophysicist who teaches at the University of California at Irvine, and the entire Galactic Center series springs from his actual scientific research. As mentioned above, the collection begins with the harrowing novella, "A Hunger for the Infinite." It is followed by various essays about the writing of the series, including one of Benford's early scientific publications, "An Electrodynamic Model of the Galactic Center." It was published in *The Astrophysical Journal* in 1988 and the novels in the series that came after its publication reflect some of Benford's findings. It certainly shows Benford's interest in stellar dynamics at the center of the Milky Way, which, by the way, we can't "see" directly because of where the sun is located (along the galactic plane) and because of all the stars and gas in between. Everything we know about the galaxy's actual center comes through radio astronomy and what we can discern through the physics of electrodynamics.

No other series in science fiction is based on actual scientific research. Benford, of course, injects into the series all kinds of fantastic speculation of what humanity might find there, including a mechanized life-form that, in its mercilessness and indifference, is unparalleled in the field. This is what makes these novels so exciting to read–at least for those of us who love "hard science" science fiction. I have to admit that the major essay here is quite technical–as befitting a publication appearing in a refereed journal–but everything else Benford provides is clear and to the point. Most informative is the chapter on the Galactic Series and how it evolved. Also included is an interview with Gregory Benford, as well as several reviews of the novels that appeared in the series.

Benford has gone out of his way to make this collection an exciting, informative read. Don't let the inclusion of the one scientific article prevent you from getting this inexpensive e-book. It's a must for anyone who's read the Galactic Center series and wants to know more about how it evolved and how the individual novels fall in place. It certainly came as a revelation to me. I've read all of the books, but it wasn't until this collection that I fully understood all that went into the writing of them. I think you'll enjoy this book. I certainly did.

FROM THE VAULT:
Reprints, Reissues and Re-releases of Note
Secret of the Stars
by Andre Norton
Baen Books - 2014 (Reprint)
ISBN: 978-1476736747 (Trade paperback)

Over the last decade or so, Baen Books has been re-issuing the novels of Andre Norton, an author most of us of a certain age grew up reading. She more or less established the YA sub-genre of science fiction (and fantasy) and today we have an award honoring her. The Best Young Adult Science Fiction and Fantasy novel award is a highly sought-after, very prestigious award, and each year more and more novels appear to vie for it. (This year's winner is Nalo Hopkinson's *Sister Mine*, which I haven't read. Last year's award went to E.C. Meyers' *Fair Coin*, which I have read and thoroughly enjoyed.)

Secret of the Stars collects two of Norton's absolute best early novels, *Secret of the Lost Race* (1959) and *Star Hunter* (1961). What struck me about rereading these short novels was how un-Young Adult they are—at least compared to today's YA science fiction, which seems rather benign. In both novels, the main characters respond to their situations much in the same manner as any adult would. Moreover, the situations are particularly dire, especially in *Secret of the Lost Race*. There is nothing YA about them and if you haven't read any of Andre Norton's books, track these down. As I said earlier, these are among her best and I think you'd enjoy them. I certainly did.

Copyright © 2014 by Paul Cook

Greg Benford is a Nebula winner and a former Worldcon Guest of Honor. He is the author of more than 30 novels and 6 books of non-fiction, and has edited 10 anthologies.

WAITING FOR SHAKESPEARE?

by Gregory Benford

When I began writing science fiction, as a graduate student in 1964, it was commonplace to regard the sf field as just entering its great phase. Of course there had been the Golden Age of 1939-45, and arguably a Silver Age of the early 1950s … but 1964 was rife with the hubbub of the early New Wave, remember, and promise seemed to brim everywhere.

An academic then referred to the field as "waiting for its Shakespeare"—that is, for a towering figure who could take the form to its heights, never to be equaled. The Bard came upon the Elizabethan stage and drama has never been the same since. Strikingly, he came early in the history of modern drama, though the Greeks had been staging great plays nearly two millennia before, and wrenched the form around until it accommodated the sensibilities of a quite different culture.

Other critics such as Brian Aldiss, particularly in his *Billion Year Spree* (later updated to *Trillion*), argued that H.G. Wells may have been the founder of modern sf and its Shakespeare all in one. Jules Verne came before, and in his attention to detail and plausibility may be said to be the founder of hard sf, but Verne mostly stuck to adventure stories, not heart-strumming dramas, "real novels." Verne was not broad enough.

Wells indeed did lay down many of the great idea-novels of the genre (though it wasn't a genre then), principally in his first decade: *The Time Machine, War of the Worlds, The Island of Dr. Moreau, The Invisible Man.* When has any writer had such a run, such a gusher of creation? Of course there were antecedents to many of his ideas. But he brought them to full, heartfelt dimension with true dramatic clout—and often, in novels that we would term novellas today, marvels of compression.

This he had in common with Shakespeare, who came to the young English stage and made it grow up.

But the New Wave advocates felt that truly adult sf would come only after the methods and crafts of mainstream literary styles were imported to bring to fruition sf's themes. And Tom Disch did produce *Camp Concentration*, Joanna Russ *And Chaos Died*, Samuel Delany both *Nova* and *Dhalgren*, Roger Zelazny *This Immortal*, Harlan Ellison kept a high standard in groundbreaking short stories, while Brian Aldiss, Michael Moorcock and J.G. Ballard had their peaks as well. Sadly, most of these works are long out of print, perhaps to be revived in a zombie-like way by on-demand publishing—which will cater to small audiences wishing to catch up on some of the fine works of the last half century.

But Shakespeare? None of these authors became the commanding figure Wm. S. was in his age. (Or may have been. There is curiously little documentation of Shakespeare the man—no letters, occasional pieces, not a single original manuscript. This has led some to suppose that Edward de Vere in fact wrote the works, with the actor Shakespeare as a useful front. This leads to a wholly different reading of the plays and sonnets—an intriguing possibility, reminding us that even great figures can carry with them an artful ambiguity, to this day.)

How come? Perhaps because no one can command the range of science, fiction and worldly knowledge demanded of a great novelist now. That may be why we have no looming figures of Tolstoy's scale. Science fiction, which takes on the largest issues confronting the human heart and head, demands much more than a conventional novelist needs to muster.

Maybe it's *impossible* to become the Shakespeare of sf any longer?

Or … could we somehow have missed him? (Or her?!)

I've seen a heady rush sweep through the field as new, powerful writers arrived, at times greeted with hosannas that suggested the arrival of The Master. Ursula Le Guin's early Ace novels led to a remarkable string: *The Left Hand of Darkness, The Lathe of Heaven, The Dispossessed*, and on into some fine work.

The first edition of the Nicholls & Clute *Encyclopedia of Science Fiction* pronounced her the best living sf writer. But while her acceptance by the mainstream is unparalleled in sf by any other than Clarke, her highly successful career since has not been of Shakespearean dimension. Perhaps this will later seem just a change in fashion, for Le Guin wrote primarily "social sf" that resonated with the questioning of fundamentals going on in the advanced nations in the 1960s and 1970s. When society reinspects itself again, her repute may benefit. To me, *The Dispossessed* is the best consideration of the nature of utopia literature has yet produced—and it has a scientist as its central figure.

The second edition of the *Encyclopedia of Science Fiction* made a case for Gene Wolfe as the greatest living sf author. Admittedly, their case seemed a bit half-hearted, and they made no such case for Le Guin (fickle critics!). I like his work, he may be our best stylist—but I doubt he's our Bard, for reaching a large audience is surely a signature, and Gene is a cultivated taste.

Based on his postmortem fame, Phil Dick seems a plausible candidate. He's widely read and has inspired half a dozen films. He has enjoyed the greatest rise to prominence of any writer I know.

Similarly, we saw Dan Simmons heralded by some as a writer who knew his science (not from experience; he got it from reading, just as the Bard apparently got his knowledge of, say, Italy) and had a flair for novels. He found a large audience, too. Greg Bear fit that description as well, and has produced fine work. Joe Haldeman we greeted in the mid-1970s in the backwash of the New Wave, and for a while held the record for the highest advance paid for an sf novel ($50,000—it seemed huge, then). Joe probably never thought of Shakespeare; Hemingway is his literary idol. William Gibson made a big splash in 1984 with a polished, insightful style that unhinged an aspect of techno-culture we had little glimpsed before. Further, he rode the wave created by the films *Blade Runner* (noir future) and *Tron* (virtual reality dramas, jacking in). But cyberpunk was, like social sf, a passing taste—still powerful, but not a revolution in the sense that John Campbell's first team wrought one in that distant first Golden Age.

So it seems no recent arrival is the Bard in disguise.

Consider a smaller question, then: who is the reigning figure, still alive, in modern sf? My money until the year 2000 would have been on two old favorites, Arthur Clarke and Ray Bradbury. Clarke gave us *2001* and Bradbury *The Martian Chronicles*, works that will live a very long while indeed. Bradbury said he wasn't an sf writer, but he clearly came out of the magazines that termed themselves that.

But was either our Shakespeare? Somehow I doubt that either has the range to deserve the label. Of the two, Clarke comes closest, for my money. His amusing essays and *Tales from the White Hart* show his comic side, while many stories and novels display his grasp of the largest scales available to the modern intellect. But Bradbury plainly had the larger audience, winning the National Medal of Arts in 2004. He may become the best remembered sf writer of the 20th century.

It is worth pondering who we will have to fill their shoes. Among living American sf writers, Gene Wolfe, Ursula Le Guin and Robert Silverberg probably have spanned the greatest range, summoned up deep emotions and plumbed the reaches of many ideas. Right now, 2014, I think our most prominent writer is Ursula Le Guin, who just won the Medal for Distinguished Contribution to American Letters by the National Book Foundation, a lifetime achievement award. But none of these fine writers would pretend to be a Shakespeare comparable to Wells.

And maybe there's a reason for that.

Sf has become the preeminent genre, emerging from lowly pulp origins to rule the visual media. Alas, it is still a stepped-upon subsection of the lit'ry world, excluded from serious consideration, relegated to a box in the back at the *New York Times Book Review*.

But the written forms feed the visual ones, as many authors (like me) who have had their work purloined by screenwriters have woefully found. So we are influential, if not rich or famous. So here's an audacious thought: maybe our Shakespeare was Stanley Kubrick.

After all, in a stunning series he gave us in a mere few years *Dr. Strangelove*, *2001*, *A Clockwork Orange*—all near-future works of genius, derived from novels, two of them acknowledged as sf. They showed us worlds nobody had yet visited, and made his name. When Kubrick died, he was going to resume work on a film about artificial intelligence, on which he had already lavished years of script labor, working in turn with Brian Aldiss, Bob Shaw and Ian Watson. Stephen Spielberg took up the project, with good results, using footage Kubrick had shot as well.

It's startling to entertain the notion of Kubrick as our Shakespeare—but remember, the Bard primarily wrote for a visual medium, too. And in keeping with our station in life, nobody in the general culture thinks of Kubrick as a science fiction person at all …

Still … there is a deeper problem here, rummaging around for a science fictional Shakespeare. We are *the* genre, the inventor of fandom itself, fanzines, big fan conventions, a fount of cultural innovation. But rather than see ourselves as a partitioned piece of literature, better to say that we are a *continuing conversation*.

No other genre refers back so far and so often to its Golden Age(s), citing works and comparing writers—just as this column has done. In weeding out the new but derivative, by holding it up to the light of other days, we confer Grand Master status only upon those who truly extend our mental frontiers, and relegate those who merely rearrange conceptual deck chairs to the lesser ranks (where, these days, they get stuck writing franchise fiction and work-for-hire media tie-ins, just to make ends meet.)

We inspect ideas anew in ways other genres do not. Where in mysteries, say, does one see a gang of young Turks write a three-novel sequence to reimagine a classic work? Yet that's what I did with Greg Bear and David Brin, when we wrote the Second Foundation Trilogy. Isaac Asimov's grand ideas rewarded revisiting, we thought, seen through the eyes of another generation. Of course, some Asimov fans thought this was overtly a bad idea. We expected that, along with the hard core of fans who do not want their view of the sacred texts challenged. All this is part of the debate, too.

Most generally, our field comprises a way for the general culture to see itself in a fresh light. Science particularly has always used sf to think about the implications of its own work. That's why so many scientists have written sf (again, like me—a phenomenon you can study further in some essays at my website, available through gregorybenford.com).

Rather than look upon our great works as resembling classical symphonies, to be played in grand halls to a passive audience, think of us as a jazz band—swinging down Basin Street in full voice, blaring our messages, running new riffs on old standards, fresh melodic lines, improvisation as the blood and rhythm of the enterprise itself. Our band's sign might well read,

JAZZ, THAT'S WHAT WE ARE.

—because it's what we truly do well.

And New Orleans never needed a Shakespeare.

Copyright © 2001, revised 2014 by Gregory Benford

Views expressed by guest or resident columnists are entirely their own.

Barry N. Malzberg is the winner of the very first Campbell Memorial Award, a multiple Hugo and Nebula winner, and the author of more than 90 books.

FROM THE HEART'S BASEMENT

by Barry N. Malzberg

AS YOUNG AS YOU FEEL

Watching Marilyn Monroe in this 1951 film, her first "major" role, hardly so major, a bustling preoccupied office secretary with maybe ten minutes of screen time, 50 words of dialogue, I was overcome by the young actress's panic barely held in place by minimum professionalism and the skill of the experienced actors surrounding her. (It is a species of the so-called Little Guy narrative on which Preston Sturges and Frank Capra made their reputation, the wisdom and grit of the common working man toppling, or at least shaking, the monolithic corporation or government bigwigs.) I felt myself like the great film critic David Thomson identifying with the actress, almost merging emotionally with her: she is on a precipice and knows it. Twenty-five years old already, facing another decade of the casting couch and the abyss which will then await her, Monroe seems to be held in place by her vision of this empty future. Her body will sink, her heart will shatter: how much more of this can she take unless she is successful, unless she breaks through? She came like almost everyone she knows from nowhere, wore tight sweaters attracting sudden attention in high school, married a cop in her teens, then bolted to the fringes of Hollywood. If she does not make it where will she go? What will happen to her? Will the failed actress she feels she is on the verge of becoming be a suicide at 36, lying alone on a Saturday night, surrounded by half-empty pill bottles? Will anyone even notice that she has disappeared?

That knowledge seems to creep into her gestures in this mindless, plucky little film, seems to inform her motions. She is too quick, too desperate even for a secretary. She slams drawers, flutters in anticipation of a blow, merges deference with obsequity. It is a performance manufactured on what she fears to be the cusp of oblivion. And yet, as audiences like to say, she steals the three or four scenes in which she plays. That old pro Monty Woolley is acting skillfully, Thelma Ritter is as always satisfyingly cynical. But these are performances. Monroe is in the thrall of something either much larger or smaller. She is fighting for her life in this forgotten film, in the heap of desperate lies which are the postwar legacy given Hollywood along with the specter of television, she has a true and real vision of American life as it is lived and will continue to be lived by most of us and that alertness has taken her past desperation. Past optimism, even past technique. She has never been more faithful to herself, not even in *The Misfits*, which in the consensus is her most transparent project. Arthur Miller wrote her a script which sentimentalized and sexualized her desperation. Then as his last gift to that untruth, he left her. She had less than three years more.

Monroe, never a great actress, barely a good one, became something greater yet through her projection and parallel of a condition which was to become the culture ever more explicitly in the half century after her death. (Which was ruled a suicide, thus acquitting all of us including certain Heads of State.) Marilyn can in this film be understood to have comprehended the future in full expanse … what was terrorizing her in this film was not her own life (a version of which was appalling enough) but the country, the system, the engineering and the outcome. What Sturges and Capra, themselves crumbling figures of the prewar Hollywood, were selling in their plucky films was a profound lie and Marilyn knew it. Capra and Sturges by then must have known it too (consider their own fate) but they deemed themselves insulated by reputation, by accomplishment, by knowing that their calls would be returned. Marilyn in 1951 knew that when she was their age no one was likely to be returning her calls. Her letter to the world was on the verge of being returned postage due.

✦

This has past your first reaction *everything* to do with science fiction.

By 1951 science fiction had its own clear view of where it was all going, and almost everything which happened after the spate of post-apocalyptic stories overwhelming *Astounding* in the first post-Hiroshima reaction can be seen as a symptom of that general awareness and the terror it induced. Dianetics, of course—manage through Better Engineering societal collapse, societal insanity as one kind of coping mechanism. But not just Dianetics (although that river runs still turbulent through the abandoned cities today). The dystopias and satire of the *Galaxy* school, the exhaustion of *A Canticle for Leibowitz*, the wish fulfillments of Heinlein disguised as cultural extrapolation … all were versions of Marilyn slamming drawers and shaking with fear before her boss. They are not only symptoms, they are the medium itself, and then of course when fantasy, always science fiction's commercial bedmate, began to outgrow the furniture the fix was in. Science fiction was implicitly giving it up. Tolkien marks for most critics the great or greater divide, but the Hobbits would never have come to dine if the house had not already become a tourist trap with signs posted in all locales.

Fantasy was on the way to eating science fiction alive even before *Star Wars* came to the banquet and carried off the furniture. Born, no coincidence here, the same year as Norma Jean Baker (first issue of *Amazing* was dated 4/26) science fiction was in 1951 chronologically where Marilyn dwelt, and had the same shaking clarity on the future which impels Marilyn's performance. Hence the desperate mid-fifties obsession of Merril and Milford to "join the mainstream", to get out while it was still possible. Hence the New Wave and the faltering or less faltering attempts to relive Dada, surrealism, the New Criticism. To imagine what or how Marilyn might have been in the mid-nineties, it is only necessary to look at science fiction in that period.

Not only the Towers but the flesh had fallen. A journey to the center of the Earth headed a constant South.

✦

And that is how I felt in 1965, in flight from a mainstream which would not have me anyway, holding myself upright, barely, by the handhold of the Scott Meredith Fee Department. I was 25, just as Marilyn had been in that film. I had a clear vision of what my life would be unless I was able, impossibly, to make a career as a science fiction writer. Oblivion would be home.

I had Marilyn's desperation and even a shred of her cunning. I was able to make it out of the Fee Department and into science fiction. And then in the continuing event – oh boy, like Monty Woolley in that film, I found myself out of a job. With Preston Sturges and Frank Capra long gone.

September 2014: New Jersey

SERIALIZATION
Lest Darkness Fall

Part 5

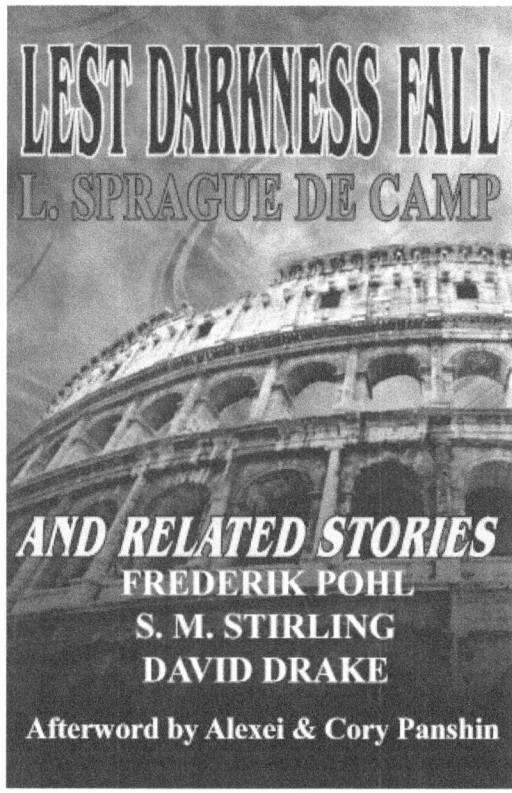

LEST DARKNESS FALL &
RELATED STORIES

(only Lest Darkness Fall is being serialized)
by L. Sprague de Camp
Phoenix Pick, 2011
Trade Paperback: 290 pages.
ISBN: 978-1-61242-015-8

L. Sprague de Camp came pretty close to being the compleat science fiction writer. His work included novels, short stories, science fiction, fantasy, poetry, criticism, history, you name it. He won the Hugo and the International Fantasy Award, was the Guest of Honor at the 1966 Worldcon, won the World Fantasy Lifetime Achievement Award in 1984, became a Nebula Grand Master (the fourth ever) in 1979, and was given a Special Achievement Sidewise Award for Alternate History in 1996. He also edited and continued Robert E. Howard's Conan saga.

De Camp's career lasted for more than 60 years, and he authored more than 100 books, alone and in collaboration with his wife Catherine, and also with Fletcher Pratt (the Incomplete Enchanter and Gavagan's Bar series) and Lin Carter (the Conan series). His other series include the Viagens Interplanetarias, Reginald Rivers, Pusadian, Novaria, Marko Prokopiu, and The Incorporated Knight.

LEST DARKNESS FALL
L. Sprague de Camp
(continued from issue 10)

CHAPTER XV

The members of the Gothic Royal Council appeared at Padway's office with a variety of scowls. They were men of substance and leisure, and did not like being dragged practically away from their breakfast tables, especially by a mere civil functionary.

Padway acquainted them with the circumstances. His news shocked them to temporary silence. He continued: "As you know, my lords, under the unwritten constitution of the Gothic nation, an insane king must be replaced as soon as possible. Permit me to suggest that present circumstances make the replacement of the unfortunate Thiudahad an urgent matter."

Wakkis growled: "That's partly *your* doing, young man. We could have bought off the Franks—"

"Yes, my lord. I know all that. The trouble is that the Franks won't stay bought, as you very well know. In any event, what's done is done. Neither the Franks nor Justinian have moved against us yet. If we can run the election of a new king off quickly, we shall not be any worse off than we are."

Wakkis replied: "We shall have to call another convention of the electors, I suppose."

Another councilor, Mannfrith, spoke up: "Apparently our young friend is right, much as I hate to take advice from outsiders. When and where shall the convention be?"

There were a lot of uncertain throaty noises from the Goths. Padway said: "If my lords please, I have a suggestion. Our new civil capital is to be at Florence, and what more fitting way of inaugurating it is there than holding our election there?"

There was more growling, but nobody produced a better idea. Padway knew perfectly well that they didn't like following his directions, but that, on the other hand, they were glad to shirk thought and responsibility themselves.

Wakkis said: "We shall have to give time for the messages to go out, and for the electors to reach Florence—"

Just then Urias came in. Padway took him aside and whispered: "What did she say?"

"She says she will."

"When?"

"Oh, in about ten days, I think. It don't look very nice so soon after my uncle's death."

"Never mind that. It's now or never."

Mannfrith asked. "Who shall the candidates be? I'd like to run myself, only my rheumatism has been bothering me so."

Somebody said: "Thiudegiskel will be one. He's Thiudahad's logical successor."

Padway said: "I think you'll be pleased to hear that our esteemed General Urias will be a candidate."

"What?" cried Wakkis. "He's a fine young man, I admit, but he's ineligible. He's not an Amaling."

Padway broke into a triumphant gran. "Not now, my lords, but he will be by the time the election is called." The Goths looked startled. "And, my lords, I hope you'll all give us the pleasure of your company at the wedding."

During the wedding rehearsal, Mathaswentha got Padway aside. She said: "Really, Martinus, you've been most noble about this. I hope you won't grieve too much."

Padway tried his best to look noble. "My dear, your happiness is mine. And if you love this young man, I think you're doing just the right thing."

"I *do* love him," replied Mathaswentha. "Promise me you won't sit around and mope, but will go out and find some nice girl who is suited to you."

Padway sighed convincingly. "It'll be hard to forget, my dear. But since you ask it, I'll promise. Now, now, don't cry. What will Urias think? You want to make *him* happy, don't you? There, that's a sensible girl."

The wedding itself was quite a gorgeous affair in a semi-barbaric way. Padway discovered an unsuspected taste for stage management, and introduced a wrinkle he'd seen in pictures of United States Military Academy weddings: that of having Urias' friends make an arch of swords under which the bride and groom walked on their way down the church steps. Padway himself looked as dignified as his moderate stature and nondescript features permitted. Inwardly he was holding on tight to repress a snicker. It had just occurred to him that Urias' long robe looked amazingly like a bathrobe he, Padway, had once owned, except that Padway's robe hadn't had pictures of saints embroidered on it in gold thread.

As the happy couple departed, Padway ducked out of sight around a pillar. Mathaswentha, if she saw him out of the tail of her eye, may have thought that he was shedding a final tear. But actually he was allowing himself the luxury of a longdrawn "*Whew!*" of relief.

Before he reappeared, he heard a couple of Goths talking on the other side of the pillar:

"He'd made a good king, eh, Albehrts?"

"Maybe. *He* would, by himself. But I fear he'll be under the influence of this Martinus person. Not that I have anything specifically against Mysterious Martin, you understand. But—you know how it is."

"*Ja, ja.* Oh, well, one can always flip a sesterce to decide which to vote for."

Padway had every intention of keeping Urias under his influence. It seemed possible. Urias disliked and was impatient with matters of civil administration. He was a competent soldier, and at the same time was receptive to Padway's ideas. Padway thought somberly that if anything happened to *this* king he'd hunt a long time before finding another as satisfactory.

Padway had the news of the impending election sent out over the telegraph, thereby saving the week that would normally be necessary for messengers to travel the length and breadth of Italy, and incidentally convincing some of the Goths of the value of his contraptions. Padway also sent our another message, ordering all the higher military commanders to remain at their posts. He sold Urias the idea by arguing military necessity. His real reason was a determination to keep Thiudegiskel in Calabria during the election. Knowing Urias, he didn't dare explain this plan to him, for fear Urias would have an attack of knightly honor and, as ranking general, countermand the order.

The Goths had never seen an election conducted on time-honored American principles. Padway showed them. The electors arrived in Florence to find the town covered with enormous banners and posters reading:

VOTE FOR URIAS
THE PEOPLE'S CHOICE!
Lower taxes! Bigger public works!
Security for the aged! Efficient government!

And so forth. They also found a complete system of ward-heelers to take them in tow, show them the town—not that Florence was much to see in those days—and butter them up generally.

Three days before the election was due, Padway held a barbecue. He threw himself into debt for the fixings. Well, not exactly; he threw poor Urias into debt, being much too prudent to acquire any more liabilities in his own name than he could help.

While he kept modestly in the background, Urias made a speech. Padway later heard comments to the effect that nobody had known Urias could make such good speeches. He grinned to himself. He had written the speech and had spent all his evenings for a week teaching Urias to deliver it. Privately Padway

thought that his candidate's delivery still stank. But if the electors didn't mind, there was no reason why he should.

Padway and Urias relaxed afterward over a bottle of brandy. Padway said that the election looked like a pushover, and then had to explain what a pushover was. Of the two opposing candidates, one had withdrawn, and the other, Harjis Austrowald's son, was an elderly man with only the remotest connection with the Amal family.

Then one of the ward-heelers came in breathless. It seemed to Padway that people were always coming to see him breathless.

The man barked: "Thiudegiskel's here."

Padway wasted no time. He found where Thiudegiskel was staying, rounded up a few Gothic soldiers, and set out to arrest the young man. He found that Thiudegiskel had, with a gang of his own friends, taken over one of the better inns in town, pitching the previous guests and their belongings out in the street.

The gang were gorging themselves downstairs in plain sight. They hadn't yet changed their traveling clothes, and they looked tired but tough. Padway marched in. Thiudegiskel looked up. "Oh, it's *you* again. What do you want?"

Padway announced: "I have a warrant for your arrest on grounds of insubordination and deserting your post, signed by Ur—"

The high-pitched voice interrupted: "*Ja, ja,* I know all about that, my dear *Sineigs.* Maybe you thought I'd stay away from Florence while you ran off an election without me, eh? *But* I'm not like that, Martinus. Not one little bit. I'm here, I'm a candidate, and anything you try now I'll remember when I'm king. That's one thing about me; I've got an infernally long memory."

Padway turned to his soldiers: "Arrest him!"

There was a great scraping of chairs as the gang rose to its feet and grasped its collective sword hilts. Padway looked for his soldiers; they hadn't moved.

"Well?" he snapped.

The oldest of them, a kind of sergeant, cleared his throat. "Well, sir, it's this way. Now we know you're our superior and all that. But things are kind of uncertain, with this election and all, and we don't know whom we'll be taking orders from in a couple of days. Suppose we arrest this young man, and then he gets elected king? That wouldn't be so good for us, now would it, sir?"

"Why—you—" raged Padway.

But the only effect was that the soldiers began to slide out the door. The young Gothic noble named Willimer was whispering to Thiudegiskel, sliding his sword a few inches out of the scabbard and back.

Thiudegiskel shook his head and said to Padway: "My friend here doesn't seem to like you, Martinus. He swears he'll pay you a visit as soon as the election is over. So it might be healthier if you left Italy for a little trip. In fact, it's all I can do to keep him from paying his visit right now."

The soldiers were mostly gone now. Padway realized that he'd better go too, if he didn't want these well-born thugs to make hamburger of him.

He mustered what dignity he could. "You know the law against duelling."

Thiudegiskel's invincibly good-natured arrogance wasn't even dented. "Sure, I know it. But remember. *I'll* be the one enforcing it. I'm just giving you fair warning, Martinus. That's one thing about—"

But Padway didn't wait to hear Thiudegiskel's next contribution to the inexhaustible subject of himself. He went, full of rage and humiliation. By the time he finished cursing his own stupidity and thought to round up his eastern troops—the few who weren't up north with Belisarius—and make a second attempt, it was too late. Thiudegiskel had collected a large crowd of partisans in and around the hotel, and it would take a battle to dislodge them. The ex-Imperialists seemed far from enthusiastic over the prospect, and Urias muttered something about its being only honorable to let the late king's son have a fair try for the crown.

The next day Thomasus the Syrian arrived. He came in wheezing. "How are you, Martinus? I didn't want to miss all the excitement, so I came up from Rome. Brought my family along."

That meant something, Padway knew, for Thomasus' family consisted not only of his wife and four children, but an aged uncle, a nephew, two nieces, and his black house slave Ajax and *his* wife and children.

He answered: "I'm fine, thanks. Or I shall be when I catch up on my sleep. How are you?"

"Fine, thanks. Business has been good for a change."

"And how is your friend God?" Padway asked with a straight face.

"He's fine too—why, you blasphemous young scoundrel! That will cost you an extra interest on your next loan. How's the election?"

Padway told him. "It won't be as easy as I thought. Thiudegiskel has developed a lot of support among the conservative Goths, who don't care for self-made men like Wittigis and Urias. The upper crust prefer an Amaling by birth—"

"Upper crust? Oh, I see! Ha, ha, ha! I hope God listens to you. It might put Him in a good humor the next time He considers sending a plague or a quake."

Padway continued: "And Thiudegiskel is not as stupid as one might expect. He'd hardly arrived before he'd sent out friends to tear down my posters and put up some of his own. His weren't much to look at, but I was surprised that he thought of using any. There were fist-fights and one stabbing, not fatal, fortunately. So—you know Dagalaif Nevitta's son?"

"The marshal? By name only."

"He's not eligible to vote. Well, the town watch is too scared of the Goths to keep order, and I don't dare use my own guards for fear of rousing all the Goths against the 'foreigners.' I blackmailed the city fathers into hiring Dagalaif to deputize the other marshals who are not electors as election police. As Nevitta is on our side, I don't know how impartial my friend Dagalaif will be. But it'll save us from a pitched battle, I hope."

"Wonderful, wonderful, Martinus. Don't over-reach yourself; some of the Goths call your electioneering methods newfangled and undignified. I'll ask God to keep a special watch over you and your candidate."

☼

The day before the election, Thiudegiskel showed his political astuteness by throwing a barbecue even bigger than Padway's. Padway, having some mercy on Urias' modest purse, had limited his party to the electors. Thiudegiskel, with the wealth of Thiuda-had's immense Tuscan estates to draw upon, shot the works. He invited all the electors and their families and friends also.

Padway and Urias and Thomasus, with the former's ward-heelers, the latter's family, and a sizable guard, arrived at the field outside Florence after the festivities had begun. The field was covered with thousands of Goths of all ages, sizes, and sexes, and was noisy with East-German gutturals, the clank of scabbards, and the *flop-flop* of leather pants.

A Goth bustled up to them with beer suds in his whiskers. "Here, here, what are you people doing? You weren't invited."

"*Ni ogs, frijond*," said Padway.

"What? You're telling *me* not to be afraid?" The Goth bristled.

"We aren't even trying to come to your party. We're just having a little picnic of our own. There's no law against picnics, is there?"

"Well—then why all the armament? Looks to me as though you were planning a kidnapping."

"There, there," soothed Padway. "You're wearing a sword, aren't you?"

"But I'm official. I'm one of Willimer's men."

"So are these people our men. Don't worry about us. We'll stay on the other side of the road, if it'll make you happy. Now run along and enjoy your beer."

"Well, don't try anything. We'll be ready for you if you do." The Goth departed, muttering over Padway's logic.

Padway's party made themselves comfortable across the road, ignoring the hostile glares from Thiudegiskel's partisans. Padway himself sprawled on the grass, eating little and watching the barbecue through narrowed eyes.

Thomasus said: "Most excellent General Urias, that look tells me our friend Martinus is planning something particularly hellish."

Thiudegiskel and some of his gang mounted the speakers' stand. Willimer introduced the candidate with commendable brevity. Then Thiudegiskel began to speak. Padway hushed his own party and strained his ears. Even so, with so many people, few of them completely silent, between him and the speaker, he missed a lot of Thiudegiskel's shrill Gothic. Thiudegiskel appeared to be bragging as usual about his own wonderful character. But, to Padway's consternation, his audience ate it up. And they howled with laughter at the speaker's rough and ready humor.

"—and did you know, friends, that General Urias was twelve years old before his poor mother could train him not to wet his bed? It's a fact. That's one thing about me; I never exaggerate. Of course you *couldn't* exaggerate Urias' peculiarities. For instance, the first time he called on a girl—"

Urias was seldom angry, but Padway could see the young general was rapidly approaching incandescence. He'd have to think of something quickly, or there *would* be a battle.

His eye fell on Ajax and Ajax's family. The slave's eldest child was a chocolate-colored, frizzy-haired boy of ten.

Padway asked: "Does anybody know whether Thiudegiskel's married?"

"Yes," replied Urias. "The swine was married just before he left for Calabria. Nice girl, too; a cousin of Willimer."

"*Hm-m-m.* Say, Ajax, does that oldest boy of yours speak any Gothic?"

"Why no, my lord, why should he?"

"What's his name?"

"Priam."

"Priam, would you like to earn a couple of sesterces, all your own?"

The boy jumped up and bowed. Padway found such a servile gesture in a child vaguely repulsive. Must do something about slavery some day, he thought. "Yes, my lord," squeaked the boy.

"Can you say the word '*atta*'? That's Gothic for 'father.'"

Priam dutifully said: "*Atta.* Now where are my sesterces, my lord?"

"Not so fast, Priam. That's just the beginning of the job. You practice saying '*atta*' for a while."

Padway stood up and peered at the field. He called softly: "*Hai*, Dagalaif!"

The marshal detached himself from the crowd and came over. "*Hails*, Martinus! What can I do for you?"

Padway whispered his instructions.

Then he said to Priam: "You see the man in the red cloak on the stand, the one who is talking? Well, you're to go over there and climb up on the stand, and say '*atta*' to him. Loudly, so everybody can hear. Say it a lot of times, until something happens. Then you run back here."

Priam frowned in concentration. "But the man isn't my father! This is my father!" He pointed to Ajax.

"I know. But you do as I say if you want your money. Can you remember your instructions?"

So Priam trailed off through the crowd of Goths with Dagalaif at his heels. They were lost to Padway's sight for a few minutes, while Thiudegiskel shrilled on. Then the little Negro's form appeared on the stand, boosted up by Dagalaif's strong arms. Padway clearly heard the childish cry of "*Atta!*"

Thiudegiskel stopped in the middle of a sentence. Priam repeated: "*Atta! Atta!*"

"He seems to know you!" shouted a voice down front.

Thiudegiskel stood silent, scowling and turning red. A low mutter of laughter ran through the Goths and swelled to a roar.

Priam called "*Atta!*" once more, louder.

Thiudegiskel grabbed his sword hilt and started for the boy. Padway's heart missed a beat.

But Priam leaped off the stand into Dagalaif's arms, leaving Thiudegiskel to shout and wave his sword. He was apparently yelling, "It's a lie!" over and over. Padway could see his mouth move, but his words were lost in the thunder of the Gothic nation's Wagnerian laughter.

Dagalaif and Priam appeared, running toward them. The Goth was staggering slightly and holding his midriff. Padway was alarmed until he saw Dagalaif was suffering from a laughing and coughing spell.

He slapped him on the back until the coughs and gasps moderated. Then he said: "If we hang around here, Thiudegiskel will recover his wits, and he'll be angry enough to set his partisans on us with cold steel. In my country we had a word 'scram' that is, I think, applicable. Let's go."

"Hey, my lord," squealed Priam, "where's my two sesterces? Oh, thank you, my lord. Do you want me to call anybody else 'father,' my lord?"

CHAPTER XVI

Padway told Urias: "It looks like a sure thing now. Thiudegiskel will never live this afternoon's episode down. We Americans have some methods for making elections come out the right way, such as stuffing ballot boxes, and the use of floaters. But I don't think it'll be necessary to use any of them."

"What on earth is a floater, Martinus? You mean a float such as one uses in fishing?"

"No; I'll explain sometime. I don't want to corrupt the Gothic electoral system more than is absolutely necessary."

"Look here, if anybody investigates, they'll learn that Thiudegiskel was the innocent victim of a joke this afternoon. Then won't the effect be lost?"

"No, my dear Urias, that's not how the minds of electors work. Even if he's proved innocent, he's been made such an utter fool of that nobody will take him seriously, regardless of his personal merits, if any."

Just then a ward-heeler came in breathless. He gasped: "Thiu-Thiudegiskel—"

Padway complained: "I am going to make it a rule that people who want to see me have to wait outside until they get their breath. What is it, Roderik?"

Roderik finally got it out. "Thiudegiskel has left Florence, distinguished Martinus. Nobody knows whither. Willimer and some of his other friends went with him."

Padway immediately sent out over the telegraph Urias' order depriving Thiudegiskel of his colonel's rank—or its rough equivalent in the vague and amorphous Gothic system of command. Then he sat and stewed and waited for news.

It came the next morning during the voting. But it did not concern Thiudegiskel. It was that a large Imperialist army had crossed over from Sicily and landed, not at Scylla on the toe of the Italian boot where one would expect, but up the coast of Bruttium at Vibo.

Padway told Urias immediately, and urged: "Don't say anything for a few hours. This election is in the bag—I mean it's certain—and we don't want to disturb it."

But rumors began to circulate. Telegraph systems are run by human beings, and few groups of more than a dozen human beings have kept a secret for long. By the time Urias' election by a two-to-one majority was announced, the Goths were staging an impromptu demonstration in the streets of Florence, demanding to be led against the invader.

Then more details came in. The Imperialists' army was commanded by Bloody John, and numbered a good fifty thousand men. Evidently Justinian, furious about Padway's letter, had been shipping adequate force into Sicily in relays.

Padway and Urias figured that they could, without recalling troops from Provence and Dalmatia, assemble perhaps half again as many troops as Bloody John had. But further news soon reduced this estimate. That able, ferocious, and unprincipled soldier sent a detachment across the Sila Mountains by a secondary road from Vibo to Scyllacium, while he advanced with his main body down the Popilian Way to Reggio. The Reggio garrison of fifteen thousand men, trapped at the end of the toe of the boot, struck a few blows for the sake of their honor and surrendered. Bloody John reunited his forces and started north toward the ankle.

Padway saw Urias off in Rome with many misgivings. The army looked impressive, surely, with its new corps of horse archers and its batteries of mobile catapults. But Padway knew that the new units were inexperienced in their novel ways of fighting, and that the organization was likely to prove brittle in practice.

Once Urias and the army had left, there was no more point in worrying. Padway resumed his experiments with gunpowder. Perhaps he should try charcoal from different woods. But this meant time, a commodity of which Padway had precious little. He soon learned that he had none at all.

By piecing together the contradictory information that came in by telegraph, Padway figured out that this had happened: Thiudegiskel had reached his force in Calabria without interference. He had refused to recognize the telegraphic order depriving him of his command, and had talked his men into doing likewise. Padway guessed that the words of an able and self-confident speaker like Thiudegiskel would carry more weight with the mostly illiterate Goths than a brief, cold message arriving over the mysterious contraption.

Bloody John had moved cautiously; he had only reached Consentia when Urias arrived to face him. That might have been arranged beforehand with

Thiudegiskel, to draw Urias far enough south to trap him.

But, while Urias and Bloody John sparred for openings along the river Crathis, Thiudegiskel arrived in Urias' rear—on the Imperialist side. Though he had only five thousand lancers, their unexpected charge broke the main Gothic army's morale. In fifteen minutes the Crathis Valley was full of thousands of Goths—lancers, horse archers, foot archers, and pikemen—streaming off in every direction. Thousands were ridden down by Bloody John's cuirassiers and the large force of Gepid and Lombard horse he had with him. Other thousands surrendered. The rest ran off into the hills, where the rapidly gathering dusk hid them.

Urias managed to hold his lifeguard regiment together, and attacked Thiudegiskel's force of deserters. The story was that Urias had personally killed Thiudegiskel. Padway, knowing the fondness of soldiers for myths of this sort, had his doubts. But it was agreed that Thiudegiskel had been killed, and that Urias and his men had disappeared into the Imperial host in one final, desperate charge, and had been seen no more by those on the Gothic side who escaped from the field.

For hours Padway sat at his desk, staring at the pile of telegraph messages and at a large and painfully inaccurate map of Italy.

"Can I get you anything, excellent boss?" asked Fritharik.

Padway shook his head.

Junianus shook his head. "I fear that our Martinus' mind has become unhinged by disaster."

Fritharik snorted. "That just shows you don't know him. He gets that way when he's planning something. Just wait. He'll have a devilish clever scheme for upsetting the Greeks yet."

Junianus put his head in the door. "Some more messages, my lord."

"What are they?"

"Bloody John is halfway to Salerno. The natives are welcoming him. Belisarius reports he has defeated a large force of Franks."

"Come here, Junianus. Would you two boys mind stepping out for a minute? Now, Junianus, you're a native of Lucania, aren't you?"

"Yes, my lord."

"You were a serf, weren't you?"

"Well … uh … my lord … you see—" The husky young man suddenly looked fearful.

"Don't worry; I wouldn't let you be dragged back to your landlord's estate for anything."

"Well—yes, my lord."

"When the messages speak of the 'natives' welcoming the Imperialists, doesn't that mean the Italian landlords more than anybody else?"

"Yes, my lord. The serfs don't care one way or the other. One landlord is as oppressive as the next, so why should they get themselves killed fighting for any set of masters, Greek or Italian or Gothic as the case may be?"

"If they were offered their holdings as free proprietors, with no landlords to worry about, do you think they'd fight for that?"

"Why"—Junianus took a deep breath—"I think they would. Yes. Only it's such an extraordinary idea, if you don't mind my saying so."

"Even on the side of Arian heretics?"

"I don't think that would matter. The curials and the city folk may take their Orthodoxy seriously. But a lot of the peasants are half pagan anyway. And they worship their land more than any alleged heavenly powers."

"That's about what I thought," said Padway. "Here are some messages to send out. The first is an edict, issued by me in Urias' name, emancipating the serfs of Bruttium, Lucania, Calabria, Apulia, Campania, and Samnium. The second is an order to General Belisarius to leave screening force in Provence to fight a delaying action in case the Franks attack again and return south with his main body at once. Oh, Fritharik! Will you get Gudareths for me? And I want to see the foreman of the printshop."

When Gudareths arrived, Padway explained his plans to him. The little Gothic officer whistled. "My, my, that *is* a desperate measure, respectable Martinus. I'm not sure the Royal Council will approve. If you free all these low-born peasants, how shall we get them back into serfdom again?"

"We won't," snapped Padway. "As for the Royal Council, most of them were with Urias."

"But, Martinus, you can't make a fighting force out of them in a week or two. Take the word of an old

soldier who has killed hundreds of foes with his own right arm. Yes, thousands, by God!"

"I know all that," said Padway wearily.

"What then? These Italians are no good for fighting. No spirit. You'd better rely on what Gothic forces we can scrape together. Real fighters, like me."

Padway said: "I don't expect to lick Bloody John with raw recruits. But we can give him a hostile country to advance through. You tend to those pikes, and dig up some more retired officers."

Padway got his army together and set out from Rome on a bright spring morning. It was not much of an army to look at: elderly Goths who had supposed themselves retired from active service, and young sprigs whose voices had not finished changing.

As they cluttered down Patrician Street from the Pretorian Camp, Padway had an idea. He told his staff to keep on; he'd catch up with them. And off he cantered, *poddle-op, poddle-op,* up the Suburban Slope toward the Esquiline.

Dorothea came out of Anicius' house. "Martinus!" she cried. "Are you off somewhere again?"

"That's right."

"You haven't paid us a real call in months! Every time I see you, you have only a minute before you must jump on your horse and gallop off somewhere."

Padway made a helpless gesture. "It'll be different when I've retired from all this damned war and politics. Is your excellent father in?"

"No; he's at the library. He'll be disappointed not to have seen you."

"Give him my best."

"Is there going to be more war? I've heard Bloody John is in Italy."

"It looks that way."

"Will you be in the fighting?"

"Probably."

"Oh, Martinus. Wait just a moment." She ran into the house.

She returned with a little leather bag on a loop of string. "This will keep you safe if anything will."

"What is it?"

"A fragment of St. Polycarp's skull."

Padway's eyebrows went up. "Do you believe in its effectiveness?"

"Oh, certainly. My mother paid enough for it, there's no doubt that it's genuine." She slipped the loop over his head and tucked the bag through the neck opening in his cloak.

It had not occurred to Padway that a well-educated girl would accept the superstitions of her age. At the same time he was touched. He said: "Thank you, Dorothea, from the bottom of my heart. But there's something that I think will be a more effective charm yet."

"What?"

"This." He kissed her mouth lightly, and threw himself aboard his horse. Dorothea stood with a surprised but not displeased look. Padway swung the animal around and sent it back down the avenue, *poddle-op*, *poddle-op*. He turned in the saddle to wave back—and was almost pitched off. The horse plunged and skidded into the nigh ox of a team that had just pulled a wagon out of a side street.

The driver shouted: "Carus-dominus, Jesus-Christus, Maria-mater-Dei, why don't you look where you're going? San'tus-Petrus-Paulusque-Joannesque-Lucasque ..."

By the time the driver had run out of apostles Padway had ascertained that there was no damage. Dorothea was not in sight. He hoped that she had not witnessed the ruin of his pretty gesture.

CHAPTER XVII

It was the latter part of May, 537, when Padway entered Benevento with his army. Little by little the force had grown as the remnants of Urias' army trickled north. Only that morning a forage-cutting party had found three of these Goths who had settled down comfortably in a local farmhouse over the owner's protests, and prepared to sit out the rest of the war in comfort. These joined up, too, though not willingly.

Instead of coming straight down the Tyrrhenian or western coast to Naples, Padway had marched across Italy to the Adriatic, and had come down that coast to Teate. Then he had cut inland to Lucera and Benevento. As there was no telegraph line yet on the east coast, Padway kept in touch with Bloody John's movements by sending messengers across the Apennines to the telegraph stations that were still out of the enemy's hands. He timed his movements to reach Benevento after John had captured Salerno on the other side of the peninsula, had left a detachment masking Naples, and had started for Rome by the Latin Way.

Padway hoped to come down on his rear in the neighborhood of Capua, while Belisarius, if he got his orders straight, would come directly from Rome and attack the Imperialists in front.

Somewhere between Padway and the Adriatic was Gudareths, profanely shepherding a train of wagons full of pikes and of handbills bearing Padway's emancipation proclamation. The pikes had been dug out of attics and improvised out of fence palings and such things. The Gothic arsenals at Pavia, Verona, and other northern cities had been too far away to be of help in time.

The news of the emancipation had spread like a gasoline fire. The peasants had risen all over southern Italy. But they seemed more interested in sacking and burning their landlords' villas than in joining the army.

A small fraction of them had joined up; this meant several thousand men. Padway, when he rode back to the rear of his column and watched this great disorderly rabble swarming along the road, chattering like magpies and taking time out to snooze when they felt like it, wondered how much of an asset they would be. Here and there one wore great-grandfather's legionary helmet and loricated cuirass, which had been hanging on the wall of his cottage for most of a century.

Benevento is on a small hill at the confluence of the Calore and Sabbato Rivers. As they plodded into the town, Padway saw several Goths sitting against one of the houses. One of these looked familiar. Padway rode up to him, and cried: "Dagalaif!"

The marshal looked up. "*Hails*," he said in a toneless, weary voice. There was a bandage around his head, stained with black blood where his left ear should have been. "We heard you were coming this way, so we waited."

"Where's Nevitta?"

"My father is dead."

"What? Oh." Padway was silent for seconds. Then he said: "Oh, hell. He was one of the few real friends I had."

"I know. He died like a true Goth."

Padway sighed and went about his business of getting his force settled. Dagalaif continued sitting against the wall, looking at nothing in particular.

They lay in Benevento for a day. Padway learned that Bloody John had almost passed the road junction at Calatia on his way north. There was no news from Belisarius, so that the best Padway could hope for was to fight a delaying action, and hold John in southern Italy until more forces arrived.

Padway left his infantry in Benevento and rode down to Calatia with his cavalry. But this time he had a fairly respectable force of mounted archers. They were not as good as the Imperialist cuirassiers, but they would have to do.

Fritharik, riding beside him, said: "Aren't the flowers pretty, excellent boss? They remind me of the gardens in my beautiful estate in Carthage. Ah, that was something to see—"

Padway turned a haggard face. He could still grin, though it hurt. "Getting poetical, Fritharik?"

"*Me* a poet? *Honh!* Just because I like to have some pleasant memories for my last earthly ride—"

"What do you mean, your last?"

"I mean my last, and you can't tell me anything different. Bloody John outnumbers us three to one, they say. It won't be a nameless grave for us, because they won't bother to bury us. Last night I had a prophetic dream ..."

As they approached Calatia, where Trajan's Way athwart Italy joined the Latin Way from Salerno to Rome, their scouts reported that the tail of Bloody John's army had just pulled out of town. Padway snapped his orders. A squadron of lancers trotted out in front, and a force of mounted archers followed them. They disappeared down the road. Padway rode up to the top of a knoll to watch them. They got smaller and smaller, disappearing and reappearing over humps in the road. He could hear the faint murmur of John's army, out of sight over the olive groves.

Then there was shouting and clattering, tiny with distance, like a battle between gnats and mosquitoes. Padway fretted with impatience. His telescope was no help, not being able to see around corners. The little sounds went on, and on, and on. Faint columns of smoke began to rise over the olive trees. Good; that meant that his men had set fire to Bloody John's

wagon train. His first worry had been that they'd insist on plundering it in spite of orders.

Then a little dark cluster, toppled by rested lances that looked as thin as hairs, appeared on the road. Padway squinted through his telescope to make sure they were his men. He trotted down the knoll and gave some more orders. Half his horse archers spread themselves out in a long crescent on either side of the road, and a body of lancers grouped themselves behind it.

Time passed, and the men sweated in their scale-mail shirts. Then the advance guard appeared, riding hard. They were grinning, and some waved bits of forbidden plunder. They clattered down the road between the waiting bowmen.

Their commander rode up to Padway. "Worked like a charm!" he shouted. "We came down on their wagons, chased off the wagon guards, and set them on fire. Then they came back at us. We did like you said; spread the bowmen out and filled them full of quills as they charged; then hit them with the lance when they were all nice and confused. They came back for more, twice. Then John himself came down on us with his whole damned army. So we cleared out. They'll be along any minute."

"Fine," replied Padway. "You know your orders. Wait for us at Mt. Tifata pass."

So they departed, and Padway waited. But not for long. A column of Imperial cuirassiers appeared, riding hell-for-leather. Padway knew this meant Bloody John was sacrificing order to speed in his pursuit, as troops couldn't travel through the fields and groves alongside the road at any such rate. Even if he'd deployed it would take his wings some time to come up.

The Imperialists grew bigger and bigger, and their hoofs made a great pounding on the stone-paved road. They looked very splendid, with their cloaks and plumes on their officers' helmets streaming out behind. Their commander, in gilded armor, saw what he was coming to and gave an order. Lances were slung over shoulders and bows were strung. By that time they were well within range of the crescent, and the Goths opened fire. The quick, flat snap of the bowstrings and the whiz of the arrows added themselves to the clamor of the Byzantines' approach. The commander's horse, a splendid white animal, reared up and was bowled over by another horse that charged into it. The head of the Imperialist column crumpled up into a mass of milling horses and men.

Padway looked at the commander of his body of lancers; swung his arm around his head twice and pointed at the Imperialists. The line of horse archers opened up, and the Gothic knights charged through. As usual they went slowly at first, but by the time they reached the Imperialists their heavy horses had picked up irresistible momentum. Back went the cuirassiers with a great clatter, defending themselves desperately at close quarters, but pulling out and getting their bows into action as soon as they could.

Out of the corner of his eye, Padway saw a group of horsemen ride over a nearby hilltop. That meant that Bloody John's wings were coming up. He had his trumpeter signal the retreat. But the knights kept on pressing the Imperialist column back. They had the advantage in weight of men and horses, and they knew it. Padway kicked his horse into a gallop down the road after them. If he didn't stop the damned fools they'd be swallowed up by the Imperialist army.

An arrow went by Padway uncomfortably close. He found the peculiar screech that it made much harder on the nerves than he'd expected. He caught up with his Goths, dragged their commander out of the press by main force, and shouted in his ear that it was time to withdraw.

The men yelled back at him: "*Ni!-Nist!* Good fighting!" and tore out of Padway's grip to plunge back in.

While Padway wondered what to do, an Imperialist broke through the Goths and rode straight at him. Padway had not thought to get his sword out. He drew it now, then had to throw himself to one side to avoid the other's lance point. He lost a stirrup, lost his reins, and almost lost his sword and his horse. By the time he had pulled himself back upright, the Imperialist was out of sight. Padway in his haste had nicked his own horse with his sword. The animal began to dance around angrily. Padway dug his left fingers into its mane and hung on.

The Goths now began to stream back down the road. In a few seconds they were all galloping off except a few surrounded by the Imperialists. Padway wondered miserably if he'd be left on this uncon-

trollable nag to face the Byzantines alone, when the horse of its own accord set off after its fellows.

In theory it was a strategic retreat. But from the look of the Gothic knights, Padway wondered if it would be possible to stop them this side of the Alps.

Padway's horse tossed its reins up to where Padway could grab them. Padway had just begun to get the animal under control when he sighted a man on foot, bareheaded but gaudy in gilded armor. It was the commander of the Imperialist column. Padway rode at him. The man started to run. Padway started to swing his sword, then realized that he had no sword to swing. He had no recollection of dropping it, but he must have done so when he grabbed the reins. He leaned over and grabbed a fistful of hair. The man yelled, and came along in great bucking jumps.

A glance back showed that the Imperialists had disposed of the Goths who had not been able to extricate themselves, and were getting their pursuit under way.

Padway handed his prisoner over to a Goth. The Goth leaned and pulled the Imperialist officer up over his pommel, face down, so that half of him hung on each side. Padway saw him ride off, happily spanking the unfortunate Easterner with the flat of his sword.

According to plan, the horse archers fell in behind the lancers and galloped after them, the rearmost ones shooting backward.

It was nine miles to the pass, most of it uphill. Padway hoped never to have such a ride again. He was sure that at the next jounce his guts would burst from his abdomen and spill abroad. By the time they were within sight of the pass, the horses of both the pursued and the pursuers were so blown that both were walking. Some men had even dismounted to lead their horses. Padway remembered the story of the day in Texas that was so hot that a coyote was seen chasing a jackrabbit with both walking. He translated the story into Gothic, making a coyote a fox, and told it to the nearest soldier. It ran slowly down the line.

The bluffs were yellow in a late afternoon sun when the Gothic column finally stumbled through the pass. They had lost few men, but any really vigorous pursuer could have ridden them down and rolled them out of their saddles with ease. Fortunately the Imperialists were just about as tired. But they came on nevertheless.

Padway heard one officer's shout, echoing up the walls of the pass: "You'll rest when I tell you to, you lazy swine!"

Padway looked around, and saw with satisfaction that the force he had sent up ahead were waiting quietly in their places. These were the men who had not been used at all yet. The gang who had burned the wagons were drawn up behind them, and those who had just fled sprawled on the ground still farther up the pass.

On came the Imperialists. Padway could see men's heads turn as they looked nervously up the slopes. But Bloody John had apparently not yet admitted that his foe might be conducting an intelligent campaign. The Imperialist column clattered echoing into the narrowest part of the pass, the slanting rays of the sun shooting after them.

Then there was a great thumping roar as boulders and tree trunks came bounding down the slopes. A horse shrieked quite horribly, and the Imperialists scuttled around like ants whose nest had been disturbed. Padway signaled a squadron of lancers to charge.

There was room for only six horses abreast, and even so it was a tight fit. The rocks and logs hadn't done much damage to the Imperialists, except to form a heap cutting their leading column in two. And now the Gothic knights struck the fragment that had passed the point of the break. The cuirassiers, unable to maneuver or even to use their bows, were jammed back against the barrier by their heavier opponents. The fight ended when the surviving Imperialists slid off their horses and scrambled back to safety on foot. The Goths rounded up the abandoned horses and led them back whooping.

Bloody John withdrew a couple of bowshots. Then he sent a small group of cuirassiers forward to lay down a barrage of arrows. Padway moved some dismounted Gothic archers into the pass. These, shooting from behind the barrier, caused the Imperialists so much trouble that the cuirassiers were soon withdrawn.

Bloody John now sent some Lombard lancers forward to sweep the archers out of the way. But the barrier stopped their charge dead. While they were picking their way, a step at a time, among the boulders, the Goths filled them full of arrows at close range. By the time the bodies of a dozen horses and an equal number of Lombards had been added to the barrier, the Lombards had had enough.

By this time it would have been obvious to a much stupider general than Bloody John that in those confined quarters horses were about as useful as green parrots. The fact that the Imperialists could hold their end of the pass as easily as Padway held his could not have been much comfort, because they were trying to get through it and Padway was not. Bloody John dismounted some Lombards and Gepids and sent them forward on foot. Padway meanwhile had moved some dismounted lancers up behind the barrier, so that their spears made a thick cluster. The archers moved back and up the walls to shoot over the knights' heads.

The Lombards and Gepids came on at a slow dog-trot. They were equipped with regular Imperialist mail shirts, but they were still strange-looking men, with the backs of their heads shaven and their front hair hanging down on each side of their faces in two long, butter-greased braids. They carried swords, and some had immense two-handed battleaxes. As they got closer they began to scream insults at the Goths, who understood their East-German dialects well enough and yelled back.

The attackers poured howling over the barrier and began hacking at the edge of spears which were too close together to slip between easily. More attackers, coming from behind, pushed the leaders into the spear points. Some were stuck. Others wedged their bodies in between the spear shafts and got at spearmen. Presently the front ranks were a tangle of grunting, snarling men packed too closely to use their weapons, while those behind them tried to reach over their heads.

The archers shot and shot. Arrows bounced off helmets and stuck quivering in big wooden shields. Men who were pierced could neither fall nor withdraw.

An archer skipped back among the rocks to get more arrows. Gothic heads turned to look at him. A couple more archers followed, though the quivers of these had not been emptied. Some of the rearmost knights started to follow them.

Padway saw a rout in the making. He grabbed one man and took his sword away from him. Then he climbed up to the rock vacated by the first archer, yelling something unclear even to himself. The men turned their eyes on him.

The sword was a huge one. Padway gripped it in both hands, hoisted it over his head, and swung at the nearest enemy, whose head was on a level with his waist. The sword came down on the man's helmet with a clang, squashing it over his eyes. Padway struck again and again. That Imperialist disappeared; Padway hit at another. He hit at helmets and shields and bare heads and arms and shoulders. He never could tell when his blows were effective, because by the time he recovered from each whack the picture had changed.

Then there were no heads but Gothic ones within reach. The Imperialists were crawling back over the barrier, lugging wounded men with blood-soaked clothes and arrows sticking in them.

At a glance there seemed to be about a dozen Goths down. Padway for a moment wondered angrily why the enemy had left fewer bodies than that. It occurred to him that some of these dozen were only moderately wounded, and that the enemy had carried off most of their casualties.

Fritharik and his orderly Tirdat and others were clustering around Padway, telling him what a demon fighter he was. He couldn't see it; all he had done was climb up on a rock, reach over the heads of a couple of his own men, and take a few swipes at an enemy who was having troubles of his own and could not hit back. There had been no more science to it than to using a pickax.

✿

The sun had set, and Bloody John's army retired down the valley to set up its tents and cook its supper. Padway's Goths did likewise. The smell of cooking-fires drifted up and down pleasantly. Anybody would have thought that here were two gangs of pleasure-seeking campers, but for the pile of dead men and horses at the barrier.

Padway had no time for introspection. There were injured men, and he had no confidence in their abil-

ity to give themselves first aid. He raised no objections to their prayers and charms and potations of dust from a saint's tomb stirred in water. But he saw to it that bandages were boiled—which of course was a bit of the magic of Mysterious Martinus—and applied rationally.

One man had lost an eye, but was still full of fight Another had three fingers gone, and was weeping about it. A third was cheerful with a stab in the abdomen. Padway knew this one would die of peritonitis before long, and that nothing could be done about it.

Padway, not underestimating his opponent, threw out a very wide and close-meshed system of outposts. He was justified; an hour before dawn his sentries began to drift in. Bloody John, it transpired, was working two large bodies of Anatolian foot archers over the hills on either side of them. Padway saw that his position would soon be untenable. So his Goths, yawning and grumbling, were routed out of their blankets and started for Benevento.

When the sun came up and he had a good look at his men, Padway became seriously concerned for their morale. They grumbled and looked almost as discouraged as Fritharik did regularly. They did not understand strategic retreats. Padway wondered how long it would be before they began to run away in real earnest.

At Benevento there was only one bridge over the Sabbato, a fairly swift stream. Padway thought he could hold this bridge for some time, and that Bloody John would be forced to attack him because of the loss of his provisions and the hostility of the peasantry.

When they came out on the plain around the confluence of the two little rivers, Padway found a horrifying surprise. A swarm of his peasant recruits was crossing the bridge toward him. Several thousand had already crossed. He had to be able to get his own force over the bridge quickly, and he knew what would happen if that bottleneck became jammed with retreating troops.

Gudareths rode out to meet him. "I followed your orders!" he shouted. "I tried to hold them back. But they got the idea they could lick the Greeks themselves, and started out regardless. I told you they were no good!"

Padway looked back. The Imperialists were in plain sight, and as he watched they began to deploy. It looked like the end of the adventure. He heard Fritharik make a remark about graves, and Tirdat ask if there wasn't a message he could take—preferably to a far-off place.

The Italian serfs had meanwhile seen the Gothic cavalry galloping up with the Imperialists in pursuit, and had formed their own idea that the battle was lost. Ripples of movement ran through their disorderly array, and its motion was presently reversed. Soon the road up to the town was white with running Italians. Those who had crossed the bridge were jammed together in a clawing mob trying to get back over.

Padway yelled in a cracked voice, to Gudareths: "Get back over the river somehow! Send mounted men out on the roads to stop the runaways! Let those on this side get back over. I'll try to hold the Greeks here."

He dismounted most of his troops. He arranged the lancers six deep in a semicircle in front of the bridgehead, around the caterwauling peasants, with lances outward. Along the river bank he posted the archers in two bodies, one on each flank, and beyond them his remaining lancers, mounted. If anything would hold Bloody John, that would.

The Imperialists stood for perhaps ten minutes. Then a big body of Lombards and Gepids trotted out, cantered, galloped straight at his line of spears. Padway, standing afoot behind the line, watched them grow larger and larger. The sound of their hoofs was like that of a huge orchestra of kettledrums, louder and louder. Watching these big, longhaired barbarians loom up out of the dust their horses raised, Padway sympathized with the peasant recruits. If he hadn't had his pride and his responsibility, he'd have run himself until his legs gave out.

On came the Imperialists. They looked as though they could ride over any body of men on earth. Then the bowstrings began to snap. Here a horse reared or buckled; there a man fell off with a musical clash of scale-mail. The charge slowed perceptibly. But they came on. To Padway they looked twenty feet tall. And then they were right on the line of spears. Padway could see the spearmen's tight lips and white faces. If they held—They did. The Imperialist horses

reared, screaming, when the lancers pricked them. Some of them stopped so suddenly that their riders were pitched out of the saddle. And then the whole mass was streaming off to right and left, and back to the main army. It wasn't the horses' war, and they had no intention of spitting themselves on the unpleasant-looking lances.

Padway drew his first real breath in almost a minute. He'd been lecturing his men to the effect that no cavalry could break a really solid line of spearmen, but he hadn't believed it himself until now.

Then an awful thing happened. A lot of his lancers, seeing the Imperialists in flight, broke away from the line and started after their foes on foot. Padway screeched at them to come back, but they kept on running, or rather trotting heavily in their armor. Like at Senlac, thought Padway. With similar results. The alert John sent a regiment of cuirassiers out after the clumsily running mob of Goths, and in a twinkling the Goths were scattering all over the field and being speared like so many boars. Padway raved with fury and chagrin; this was his first serious loss. He grabbed Tirdat by the collar, almost strangling him.

He shouted: "Find Gudareths! Tell him to round up a few hundred of those Italians! I'm going to put them in the line!"

Padway's line was now perilously thin, and he couldn't contract it without isolating his archers and horsemen. But this time John hurled his cavalry against the flanking archers. The archers dropped back down the river bank, where the horses couldn't get at them, and Padway's own cavalry charged the Imperialists, driving them off in a dusty chaos of whirling blades.

Presently the desired peasantry appeared, shepherded along by dirty and profane Gothic officers. The bridge was carpeted with pikes dropped in flight; the recruits were armed with these and put in the front line. They filled the gap nicely. Just to encourage them, Padway posted Goths behind them, holding sword points against their kidneys.

Now, if Bloody John would let him alone for a while, he could set about the delicate operation of getting his whole force back across the bridge without exposing any part of it to slaughter.

But Bloody John had no such intention. On came two big bodies of horse, aimed at the flanking Gothic cavalry.

Padway couldn't see what was happening, exactly, between the dust and the ranks of heads and shoulders in the way. But by the diminishing clatter he judged his men were being drawn off. Then came some cuirassiers galloping at the archers, forcing them off the top of the bank again. The cuirassiers strung their bows, and for a few seconds Goths and Imperialists twanged arrows at each other. Then the Goths began slipping off up and down the river, and swimming across.

Finally, on came the Gepids and Lombards, roaring like lions. This time there wouldn't be any arrow fire to slow them up. Bigger and bigger loomed the onrushing mass of longhaired giants on their huge horses, waving their huge axes.

Padway felt the way a violin string must the moment before it snaps.

There was a violent commotion in his own ranks right in front of him. The backs of the Goths were replaced by the brown faces of the peasants. These had dropped their pikes and clawed their way back through the ranks, sword points or no sword points. Padway had a glimpse of their popping eyes, their mouths gaping in screams of terror, and he was bowled over by the wave. They stepped all over him. He squirmed and kicked like a newt on a hook, wondering when the bare feet of the Italians would be succeeded by the hoofs of the hostile cavalry. The Italo-Gothic kingdom was done for, and all his work for nothing …

The pressure and the pounding let up. A battered Padway untangled himself from those who had tripped over him. His whole line had begun to give way, but then had been frozen in the act, staring— all but a Goth in front of him who was killing an Italian.

The Imperialist heavy cavalry was not to be seen. The dust was so thick that nothing much could be seen. From beyond the pall in front of Padway's position came tramplings and shoutings and clatterings.

"What's happened?" yelled Padway. Nobody answered. There was nothing to be seen in front of

them but dust, dust, dust. A couple of riderless horses ran dimly past them through it, seeming to drift by like fish in a muddy aquarium tank.

Then a man appeared, running on foot. As he slowed down and walked up to the line of spears, Padway saw that he was a Lombard.

While Padway was wondering if this was some lunatic out to tackle his army single-handed, the man shouted: "*Armaio! Mercy!*" The Goths exchanged startled glances.

Then a couple of more barbarians appeared, one of them leading a horse. They yelled: "*Armaio, timrja!* Mercy, comrade! *Armaio, frijond!* Mercy, friend!"

A plumed Imperial cuirassier rode up behind them, shouting in Latin: "*Amicus!*" Then appeared whole companies of Imperialists, horse and foot, German, Slav, Hun, and Anatolian mixed, bawling, "Mercy, friend!" in a score of languages.

A solid group of horsemen with a Gothic standard in their midst rode through the Imperialists. Padway recognized a tall, brown-bearded figure in their midst. He croaked: "Belisarius!"

The Thracian came up, leaned over, and shook hands. "Martinus! I didn't know you with all that dust on your face. I was afraid I'd be too late. We've been riding hard since dawn. We hit them in the rear, and that was all there was to it. We've got Bloody John, and your King Urias is safe. What shall we do with all these prisoners? There must be twenty or thirty thousand of them at least."

Padway rocked a little on his feet. "Oh, round them up and put them in a camp or something. I don't really care. I'm going to sleep on my feet in another minute."

CHAPTER XVIII

Back in Rome, Urias said slowly: "Yes, I see your point. Men won't fight for a government they have no stake in. But do you think we can afford to compensate all the loyal landlords whose serfs you propose to free?"

"We'll manage," said Padway. "It'll be over a period of years. And this new tax on slaves will help." Padway did not explain that he hoped, by gradually boosting the tax on slaves, to make slavery an altogether unprofitable institution. Such an idea would have been too bewilderingly radical for even Urias' flexible mind.

Urias continued: "I don't mind the limitations on the king's power in this new constitution of yours. For myself, that is. I'm a soldier, and I'm just as glad to leave the conduct of civil affairs to others. But I don't know about the Royal Council."

"They'll agree. I have them more or less eating out of my hand right now. I've shown them how without the telegraph we could never have kept such good track of Bloody John's movements, and without the printing press we could never have roused the serfs so effectively."

"What else is there?"

"We've got to write the kings of the Franks, explaining politely that it's not our fault if the Burgunds prefer our rule to theirs, but that we certainly don't propose to give them back to their Meroving majesties.

"We've also got to make arrangements with the king of Visigoths for fitting out our ships at Lisbon for their trip to the lands across the Atlantic. He's named you his successor, by the way, so when he dies the east and west Goths will be united again. Reminds me, I have to make a trip to Naples. The shipbuilder down there says he never saw such a crazy design as mine, which is for what we Americans would call a Grand Banks schooner. Procopius'll have to go with me, to discuss details of his history course at our new university."

"Why are you so set on this Atlantic expedition, Martinus?"

"I'll tell you. In my country we amused ourself by sucking the smoke of a weed called tobacco. It's a fairly harmless little vice if you don't overdo it. Ever since I arrived here I've been wishing for some tobacco, and the land across the Atlantic is the nearest place you can get any."

Urias laughed his big, booming laugh. "I've got to be off. I'd like to see the draft of your letter to Justinian before you send it."

"Okay, as we say in America. I'll have it for you tomorrow, and also the appointment of Thomasus the Syrian as minister of finance for you to sign. He arranged to get those skilled ironworkers from Da-

mascus through his private business connections, so I shan't have to ask Justinian for them."

Urias asked: "Are you sure your friend Thomasus is honest?"

"Sure he's honest. You just have to watch him. Give my regards to Mathaswentha. How is she?"

"She's fine. She's calmed down a lot since all the people she most feared have died or gone mad. We're expecting a little Amaling, you know."

"I didn't know! Congratulations."

"Thanks. When are you going to find a girl, Martinus?"

Padway stretched and grinned. "Oh, just as soon as I catch up on my sleep."

Padway watched Urias go with a twinge of envy. He was at the age when bachelors get wistful about their friends' family life. Not that he wanted a repetition of his fiasco with Betty, or a stick of female dynamite like Mathaswentha. He hoped Urias would keep his queen pregnant practically from now on. It might keep her out of mischief.

Padway wrote:

☼

Urias, King of the Goths and Italians, to his Radiant Clemency Flavius Anicius Justinian, Emperor of the Romans, Greetings.

Now that the army sent by your Serene Highness to Italy, under John, the nephew of Vitalianus, better known as Bloody John, is no longer an obstacle to our reconciliation, we resume discussion for terms for the honorable termination of the cruel and unprofitable war between us.

The terms proposed in our previous letter stand, with this exception: Our previously asked indemnity of a hundred thousand solidi is doubled, to compensate our citizens for damages caused by Bloody John's invasion.

There remains the question of the disposal of your general, Bloody John. Though we have never seriously contemplated the collection of Imperial generals as a hobby, your Serenity's actions have forced us into a policy that looks much like it. As we do not wish to cause the Empire a serious loss, we shall release the said John on payment of a modest ransom of fifty thousand solidi.

We earnestly urge your Serenity to consider this course favorably. As you know, the Kingdom of Persia is ruled by King Khusrau, a young man of great force and ability. We have reason to believe that Khusrau will soon attempt another invasion of Syria. You will then need the ablest generals you can find.

Further, our slight ability to foresee the future informs us that in about thirty years there will be born in Arabia a man named Mohammed, who, preaching a heretical religion, will, unless stopped, instigate a great wave of barbarian conquest, subverting the rule both of the Persian Kingdom and the East Roman Empire. We respectfully urge the desirability of securing control of the Arabian Peninsula forthwith, that this calamity shall be stopped at the source.

Please accept this warning as evidence of our friendliest sentiments. We await the gracious favor of an early reply.

by

Martinus Paduei, Quaestor.

✿

Padway leaned back and looked at the letter. There were other things to attend to: the threat of invasion of Noricum by the Bavarians, and the offer by the Khan of the Avars of an alliance to exterminate the Bulgarian Huns. The alliance would be courteously refused. The Avars would make no pleasanter neighbors than the Bulgars.

Let's see: There was a wandering fanatical monk who was kicking up another row about sorcery. Should he try to smother the man in cream, as by giving him a job? Better see the Bishop of Bologna first; if he had influence in that direction, Padway knew how to make use of it. And it was time he cottoned up to that old rascal Silverius …

And should he go on with his gunpowder experiments? Padway was not sure that this was desirable. The world had enough means of inflicting death and destruction already. On the other hand his own interests were tied up with those on the Italo-Gothic State, which must therefore be saved at all costs …

To hell with it, thought Padway. He swept all the papers into a drawer in his desk, took his hat off the peg, and got his horse. He set out for Anicius' house. How could he expect to cut any ice with Dorothea if he didn't even look her up for days after his return to Rome?

Dorothea came out to meet him. He thought how pretty she was.

But there was nothing of hail-the-conquering-hero about her manner. Before he could get a word out, she began: "You beast! You slimy thing! We befriended you, and you ruin us! My poor old father's heart is broken! And now you've come around to gloat, I suppose!"

"What?"

"Don't pretend you don't know! I know all about that illegal order you issued, freeing the serfs on our estates in Campania. They burned our house, and stole the things I've kept since I was a little girl—" She began to weep.

Padway tried to say something sympathetic, but she flared up again. "Get out! I never want to see you again! It'll take a squad of your barbarian soldiers to get you into our house. *Get out!*"

Padway got, slowly and dispiritedly. It was a complex world. Almost anything big you did was bound to hurt somebody.

Then his back straightened. It was nothing to feel sorry for oneself about. Dorothea was a nice girl, yes, pretty, and reasonably bright. But she was not extraordinary in these respects; there were plenty of others equally attractive. To be frank, Dorothea was a pretty average young woman. And being Italian, she'd probably be fat at thirty-five.

Government compensation for their losses would do a lot to mend the broken hearts of the Anicii. If they tried to apologize for treating him roughly, he'd be polite and all, but he didn't think he'd go back.

Girls were okay, and he'd probably fall one of these days. But he had more important things to worry over. His success so far in the business of civilization outweighed any little failures in personal relationships.

His job wasn't over. It never would be—until disease or old age or the dagger of some local enemy ended it. There was so much to do, and only a few decades to do it in; compasses and steam engines and microscopes and the writ of habeas corpus.

He'd teetered along for over a year and a half, grabbing a little power here, placating a possible enemy there, keeping far enough out of the bad graces of the various churches, starting some little art such as spinning of sheet copper. Not bad for Mouse Padway! Maybe he could keep it up for years.

And if he couldn't—if enough people finally got fed up with the innovations of Mysterious Martinus—well, there was a semaphore telegraph system running the length and breadth of Italy, some day to be replaced by a true electric telegraph, if he could find time for the necessary experiments. There was a public letter post about to be set up. There were presses in Florence and Rome and Naples pouring out books and pamphlets and newspapers. Whatever happened to him, these things would go on. They'd become too well rooted to be destroyed by accident.

History had, without question, been changed.

Darkness would not fall.

✻THE END✾

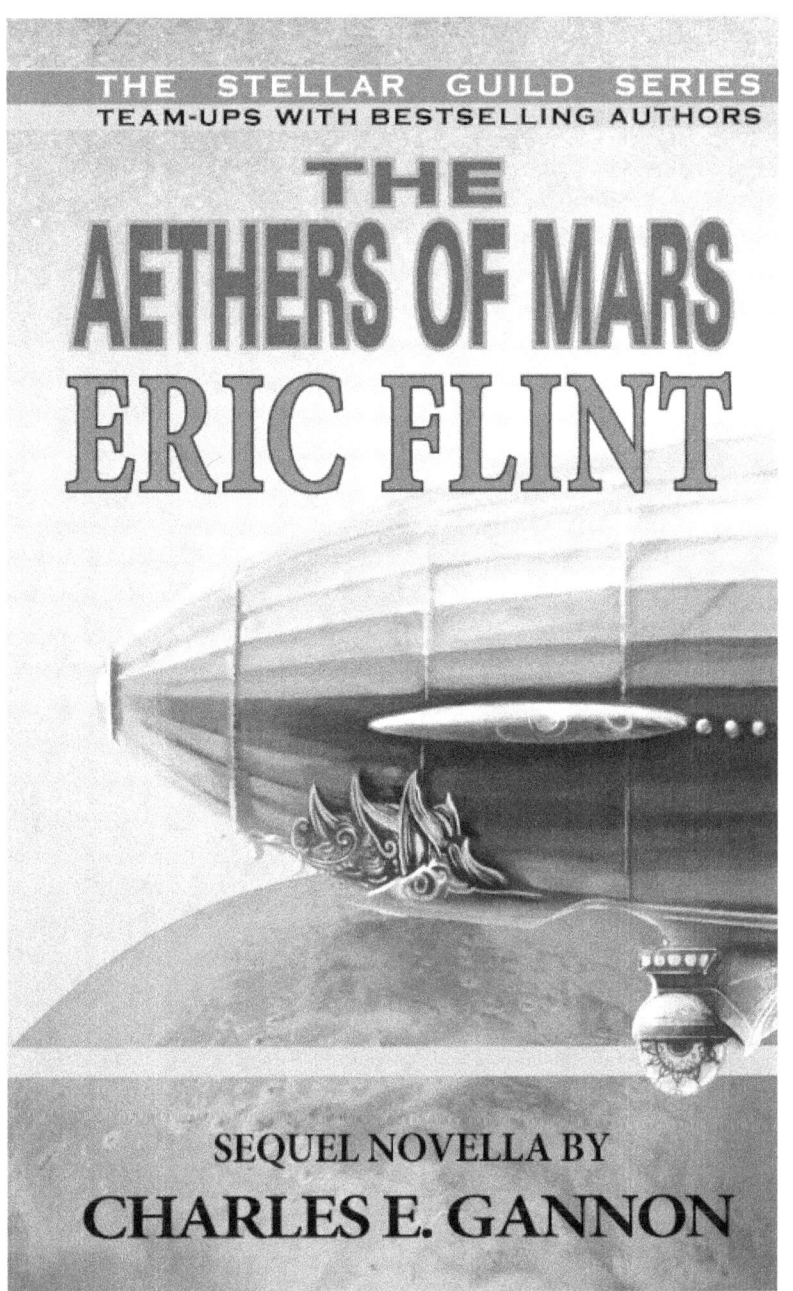

THE STELLAR GUILD SERIES
TEAM-UPS WITH BESTSELLING AUTHORS

THE
AETHERS OF MARS
ERIC FLINT

SEQUEL NOVELLA BY

CHARLES E. GANNON

Welcome to Mars…circa 1900. Cecil Rhodes rules Mars and is on his way to transforming the British Empire into his vision of a powerful force, managed by the "right" type of people.

But what of Savinkov…presumably on board the British aethership Agincourt, travelling from Earth to Mars? Savinkov is a legendary revolutionary and as-sassin and, with Russian secret agents hot on his heels, is reputedly planning something truly dramatic and Mars-shattering.

www.ingramcontent.com/pod-product-compliance
Lightning Source LLC
Chambersburg PA
CBHW080822120626
46556CB00010B/3362